The little girl was only three. When people told her to do things, she usually did them, as long as there wasn't something more interesting to do. To Marcia the man in the clown mask looked interesting, and she was tired of swinging . . . and he had said something about Mommy. She jumped out of the swing and ran toward the man.

Four-year-old Tommy scowled at the man. Maybe this was a surprise like a birthday party or something. No, this wasn't a party. As Marcia started to duck down through the hole in the fence, Tommy grabbed her arm. The man in the clown mask reached out and grabbed the little girl. She screamed, and that was when Tommy knew for sure something was wrong.

He reached up and grabbed the man's mask. . . .

N.F.D.

Dave Pedneau

BALLANTINE BOOKS • NEW YORK

Copyright © 1992 by Elaine Pedneau

All rights reserved under International and Pan-American Copyright Conventions. Published in the United States of America by Ballantine Books, a division of Random House, Inc., New York and simultaneoulsy in Canada by Random House of Canada Limited, Toronto.

Library of Congress Catalog Card Number: 91-92384

ISBN 0-345-36419-8

Manufactured in the United States of America

First Edition: June 1992

In police jargon, N.F.D. means No Fair Deal. It's used in a variety of circumstances, sometimes with a stronger, more profane meaning.

PROLOGUE

THE MAN IN THE CLOWN MASK watched the children from a thicket at the rear of the fenced backyard. Other than the mask, he looked rather ordinary, dressed in jeans, a T-shirt, and steel-toed work boots. He'd found the mask at a department store amid a huge display. It was only mid-September, but the store was already preparing for Halloween. In spite of the choices, the man knew exactly what he wanted. A clown mask. He didn't want to scare the children.

He was crouched in the shadows of the underbrush, and no one could see him. But he saw the kids and the woman who was out in the yard with them just fine. Mosquitoes whined in the man's ears, but he ignored them. A dozen children screamed and laughed and romped in the fenced area. Several, including the one in which he was interested, played on a rusty swing set. She was the only one swinging, going so high that the metal frame of the swing was lurching from the outward thrust at the end of each arc. The girl had been easy to pick out, what with that long pale blond hair, almost platinum, in fact. It shone under the glare of the late summer sun.

He checked his watch and saw that it was 11:45. He planned to wait as long as it took. As if on cue, the woman in the yard froze and glanced toward her house. She said

1

something to one of the older children, a boy who seemed so tall that he was out of place, and headed for the home's back door. Beneath the plastic mask the man grinned and moved out from the shade.

Clara Harrison, the operator of the FunTime Day-Care Center, kept telling her husband that they needed one of those cordless telephones. He promised her he was going to buy one. He just never got around to it—just like he never got around to replacing the shorted-out light fixture in the pantry. Just like he never seemed to have time to paint the front porch.

The phone was all the way in the front hall, and it was on its fifth ring by the time she reached it. The voice on the other end belonged to a woman. "Is this Mrs. Harrison?"

"Who's this?" Clara asked.

"Mrs. Harrison, this is Norma Wyse at the Raven County Department of Human Services."

Clara made a face. "Morning, Miss Wyse. What can I do for you?"

"I'm afraid we have another complaint about your—"

"From who?" Clara demanded to know.

"You know we don't release that information. According to the complaint, you have more than six children that you're—"

"That nosy neighbor, wasn't it?" Clara said. "She's got nothing better to do than stir up trouble for folks that are trying to make a living."

The bureaucrat's voice turned from friendly to very official. "The question, Mrs. Harrison, isn't who filed the complaint. The question is how many children you are providing care for."

"Six, Miss Wyse. Just like always. That's the law, and I know it."

"You're certain of that?"

"The law? Of course I am. Especially since I've got you to remind me so often now."

"I mean the number of children you're caring for," Wyse said in a firm voice.

"Well, one day last week I guess maybe I was over the limit, but you know as well as I do what the law says. It's no more than six on a regular basis. I was keeping two children for a friend of mine. The old reprobate probably counted heads that day."

"I didn't say it was your neighbor, Mrs. Harrison."

Clara stretched the phone cord and craned her neck as she tried to look across the playroom and out the window. "You don't hafta say. I know it was her. She hates kids, Miss Wyse."

There was a pause on the other end. "You do understand, I hope, that it's a misdemeanor to operate a day-care facility without a license when the law requires one."

Mrs. Harrison could feel the heat flushing her face. She wished her husband was around. He usually handled this sort of thing. "Don't you threaten me, Miss Wyse. Me and my husband talked to our lawyer last time you tried to make trouble. She said if you did it again, for you to just call her. Her name's—"

"I remember her name, Mrs. Harrison. When we receive complaints, we have to investigate."

"Well, seems a shame that you gotta harass hardworking people. I take good care of my kids. You just ask their folks."

The man in the clown mask stepped out into the bright sunshine and moved toward the six-foot fence. It presented no real obstacle to him. Late last night he had snipped an opening in the fence with bolt cutters. An overgrown lilac bush hid the hole, but he didn't move directly to it. Instead he went to a point that placed him closest to the blond girl on the swing set. By that time the smaller children had noticed the man. Some of them were pointing. Others just stood and looked at him. One or two were running toward him.

"Marcia," he called out.

The girl on the swing was looking at him. She had stopped pumping, and the swing was slowly losing its momentum.

"Come here, Marcia." He was motioning to her and moving toward the lilac bush and the cut section of fence.

"What do you want?" a voice asked.

The man wasn't prepared to be challenged, certainly not by a kid. It was the tall boy to whom the woman had spoken as she had gone into the office. "Scram, kid. I'm here to pick up Marcia."

"You're not her mother," the boy said.

"What's your name, sonny?"

"Tommy . . . Tommy Fuller."

"Smart kid, ain't ya, Tommy? I'm here for her mother." He glanced at Marcia Winters. She was still sitting in the swing, but it had almost come to a complete stop. "C'mon, Marcia. Time to go."

The little girl was only three. When people told her to do things, she usually did them—as long as there wasn't something more interesting to do. To Marcia, the man in the clown mask looked interesting, and she was tired of swinging . . . and he had said something about Mommy. She jumped out of the swing and ran toward the man.

Tommy Fuller, the taller boy, started to head her off. "You better not, Marcia."

A dark-haired boy came up beside his taller friend. "Who's he, Tommy?"

The man was standing behind the bush. "Over here, Marcia. C'mon . . . Hurry up."

The other kids were moving toward the fence, too. The man used his booted foot to shove at the fence. A gaping hole opened in it. "Come behind the bush and out here," he said to the little blond girl.

"That's not the way we leave," Tommy said. "We go out the front door."

"Not today, kid. C'mon, Marcia. Mommy's waiting, and she's got a surprise for you."

Four-year-old Tommy scowled at the man. Maybe this was a surprise, like a birthday party or something. No, this wasn't a party, and he was supposed to watch the little kids. As Marcia started to duck down through the hole in the fence, Tommy grabbed her arm. She stopped, puzzled by his action. The man in the clown mask reached out and grabbed the little girl. She screamed, and that's when Tommy knew for sure something was wrong.

He reached up and grabbed the man's mask. A rubber band, fastened to the plastic by staples, was all that held it on his face. One of the ends of the rubber band popped free, and the mask fell to the ground.

The man was leaning through the hole in the fence, his face dark with fury. Tommy could smell his breath, and it stank. He looked like one of the men who hung around on the street corners downtown.

"You little bastard. I oughta—" He didn't finish the sentence. He simply wrapped one arm around Marcia Winters and pulled.

"I'm gonna tell," Tommy was saying, backpedaling.

The sleeve of the man's shirt was caught by one of the

sharp severed points of the fencing. He ripped it free as he jerked Marcia through the hole. She was crying, screaming for her mommy. She clung to the fence for a moment, but the man jerked her away.

Clara Harrison didn't want to talk to the woman from the welfare department any longer. "I've gotta go, Miss Wyse. It's time for me to make the children's lunch."

"How many are there today, Mrs. Harrison?"

"I think you better talk to my lawyer . . . or my husband. He should be—"

Tommy Fuller burst through the back door. "You gotta come, Miss Clara."

That's what all the children called her . . . Miss Clara. His face was flushed, and he was gasping for breath.

"Just a second, Tommy." She had cupped the phone's mouthpiece.

"But something bad's happened," Tommy said. He grabbed on Mrs. Harrison's arm and pulled. "It's Marcia. There's a clown back there, and he—"

"I have to go," she said into the phone.

"Is something wrong?" the woman from the welfare department asked.

"A child's fallen," she said, then hung up.

Tommy stopped pulling on her, his face scrunched up in confusion.

"Marcia didn't fall, Miss Clara. A clown stole her."

ONE

WHIT PYNCHON hardly glanced up from the Myrtle Beach real estate guide as one of Raven County's most obnoxious lawyers plodded by his open office door with a distraught young woman in tow. The agent who had mailed the guide to him had circled a few properties in red ink. They were all located in Surfside Beach and Murrell's Inlet, two communities just south of Myrtle Beach. The guides had been arriving at his office on a monthly basis for two years, ever since Whit had visited the agent's office, inquiring about certain listings he had seen in the *Sun News*, Myrtle Beach's daily paper.

Two years ago there hadn't been the slightest doubt in Whit's mind that he would be living in Surfside Beach or Murrell's Inlet within a year at the latest. Whit sighed and pushed aside the slick real estate magazine. What was it they said about the best laid plans? Whit's plan had been chiseled in granite, or so he had thought.

The phone on his desk rang. He tensed at the intrusion and glanced at the blinking red light on the phone. The call was coming over the office intercom. He picked it up. "Pynchon's Bar and Pool Parlor."

"I need to see you, Whit." The unamused voice on the

7

phone belonged to Tony Danton, the prosecuting attorney of Raven County and Whit's boss.

"What's up?" Whit asked.

"Just come on in. I have some people here, and—"

"I saw them. Ardis Harmon and another upstanding client, no doubt. I don't know if I can tolerate Ms. Harmon today." In Whit's book there were attorneys, lawyers, and liars. His boss, Prosecutor Tony Danton, was an attorney. Ardis Harmon was somewhere between a liar and a lawyer. She skirted the edge between right and wrong and kept pushing, expanding the edge further and further. In Whit's book, she was worse than many of the criminals she represented, many of whom walked free because of her tenacity.

"We'll be waiting for you," Tony said, obviously not wanting his audience to know that Whit was giving him a hard time.

"If you insist."

"I do." Even though it wasn't said, Whit, who had worked for Danton for nearly two decades, could hear the word *dammit* punctuating his boss's sentence.

"On my way."

Danton's office was just a few short feet down the hall, but Whit wasn't in any hurry. He retrieved the *Myrtle Beach wish book* and flipped through the final few pages, pausing to study a listing for an executive home in Mount Gilead, a pricey subdivision located on the northern end of Murrell's Inlet. The home's advertised price was just under half a million. He sighed again and closed the slick, full-color publication.

The intercom line rang again. Whit pushed himself up from his desk and ambled down to the prosecutor's office. When he stepped into it, he could read the frustration in

Tony's swarthy features. Nonetheless, Tony stood to introduce Whit to the woman.

"Mrs. Sue Winters, this is Whit Pynchon. He's the special investigator for my office."

Her eyes were red and ragged from crying. The tears had streaked her makeup, and she hardly acknowledged Whit's introduction.

"Ardis, you know Whit," Tony said.

She was a plump, matronly woman in her late forties who looked deceptively harmless. At first glance, her round face and full mouth gave her a friendly appearance, but her brown eyes betrayed her. There was something cunning in how they darted from side to side as if she were constantly scheming. "He's been a worthy opponent . . . at times."

Whit nodded to the woman without making any comment. He'd do everything he could to control himself. He knew that Harmon would take umbrage at even an innuendo of sarcasm, and he'd end up apologizing as she smirked at him. He sat down on a plastic couch to one side of the prosecutor's office.

"Mrs. Winter's child was abducted from her baby-sitter's this morning," Tony said.

Whit stiffened. "Abducted?"

"By my ex-husband," the woman said, her quivering voice full of rage. "The bastard!"

Tony explained what happened.

"We're reasonably certain," Ardis said, patting her client's forearm, "that the culprit is Willie Winters. He's done this twice—once immediately after the divorce and another time several months thereafter. This time he was a bit more inventive with the mask."

Whit glanced at Tony. "What is it you want from me?" he asked.

Not that he didn't care about the plight of the child—or the woman for that matter. It just wasn't the kind of case he handled for Tony's office.

Harmon, who typically tried to control every situation, made the mistake of answering. "We've asked the prosecuting attorney to dispatch someone to secure the child and Mr. Winters."

Whit's head snapped around to the lawyer. "Do you mind if Mr. Danton answers my question?"

Harmon's mouth turned down and she glared at him. Tony rolled his eyes. "C'mon, Whit. Hear us out."

"Christ, Tony. I'm head over heels in work. One of Gil's deputies can handle this."

Sue Winters sprang to her feet. "I'm leaving, Ms. Harmon. I told you we should have gone to the state police."

Whit struggled mightily to suppress a belly laugh. Tony, though, wasn't even smiling. "Please, Mrs. Winters, sit back down. Even if you go to the state police, you will end up back here. I'll have to authorize the trip, even if the state police did make it."

Ardis remained seated, her eyes darting about. "Tony's right, Sue. As for Pynchon here, he's just being his normal obstreperous self."

The fancy word made both Sue Winters and Whit Pynchon blink. Sue didn't know or care what it meant. Whit planned to find out just as soon as the meeting was over. Harmon, who also trafficked in a great many Latin phrases, had hurled numerous incomprehensible insults in her years of practice. She had been fortunate that so few people either remembered or bothered to translate or look up some of the fighting words peculiar to her vocabulary.

Reluctantly Sue Winters settled back into the chair.

"Where did your ex-husband take the child before?" Whit asked.

"Nowhere," Ardis answered. "At that time, Mr. Winters resided in Raven County. Several months ago, however, he relocated. We suspect he made a fast and clandestined trip here, abducted the child, and then absconded back to South Carolina."

Whit glanced at Tony, then back to Harmon. "South Carolina?"

The lawyer nodded. "The Myrtle Beach area."

Whit glanced at his employer. He could see the twinkling amusement in his boss's face. Whit cleared his throat. "And you suspect that your husband—"

"Ex-husband!" Sue Winters snapped.

"That your ex-husband has taken the child to Myrtle Beach."

"I know he has."

Ardis didn't miss the silent exchange between Danton and Whit. "Once your work is done there, perhaps you can sneak in a quick game."

"I hate golf," Whit said, not anxious to let the sharp-tongued lawyer know that he was thrilled by the prospect of a trip to Myrtle Beach, even a job-related one.

The child's mother found no comfort in the lighthearted banter. "Are you going today?" she asked, glaring at Whit.

"I'll be going as soon as I can," he answered.

"Hopefully today," Tony added.

"I'll need some information on your former husband," Whit said.

"What information?" she asked.

"His full name, a description, his address in the Myrtle Beach area if you know it. Oh, and a photo of your daughter."

Sue Winters opened her purse and brought out a bright purple wallet. She pulled a photo from inside and handed it to Whit. "This was taken just a few months ago."

The wallet-sized picture showed a thin-faced child with very blond hair who didn't appear at all pleased that she was being photographed.

"A beautiful child," Whit said.

Ardis Harmon stood up and straightened her dress. "I'll have my secretary prepare a description of Mr. Winters. We have no idea as to his whereabouts in the Myrtle Beach area."

"That will make it difficult," Whit said. He was a frequent visitor to the coastal area of South Carolina known as the Grand Strand and knew that Myrtle Beach was a small town after the tourists left at the end of the summer. From May through September, the area hosted more than eight million tourists and boasted hundreds of thousands of tourist accommodations. For much of the eastern U.S. and Canada, it was a major vacation spot. For law enforcement personnel, it was the place where criminals went to hide.

"Willie had some friends down there," Mrs. Winters said. "I can give you their names. They'll know where he is."

"My secretary will compile that information, too," the lawyer said. "She'll deliver it within the hour."

"You might also include Mrs. Winters's phone number and address," Tony said. "Whit might have more questions."

"He can contact me," Ardis countered.

Whit shook his head. "No thanks, Ms. Harmon. No sense in that. Include Mrs. Winters's home phone and address."

Mrs. Winters was standing by that time. "I don't mind, Ms. Harmon. I just want something done now."

The lawyer shrugged. "Tell you what, Sue. You go on out to the receptionist's office. Give me a few minutes with the prosecutor and Pynchon."

"Are you going to talk about me behind my back?" the woman said, her eyes once again flashing in anger.

Harmon shook her head. "Goodness, no, Sue. I have other clients and other cases. I need to discuss one of them for a moment. I'll be right along."

She didn't seem convinced.

"I won't be but a moment," the lawyer said. Reluctantly the woman exited Tony's office. The lawyer waited until the sound of her footsteps had receded.

"Do we have other cases?" Tony asked.

Harmon smiled. "Not that I know of. I just wanted to tell Pynchon here that when he locates the child and father, I'm sure the extradition proceedings on Willie will take a few days."

"At least," Tony said.

The lawyer turned her smile upon Whit. "You can take a few days and enjoy the trip then. I'm sure Mrs. Winters would be willing to come down after the child. I'll explain to her that you need to remain in South Carolina because of the continuing legal process involving her former husband."

"Don't do me any favors," Whit said.

"Nonetheless, there is a salutary side to the case, Investigator."

Whit shook his head. "Christ, Ardis! You do use some fancy words."

"When's your birthday, Whit? I'll buy you a dictionary," she said as she left the office.

When Whit looked to his employer, Tony Danton was grinning.

"Don't mind her. Weren't you just saying the other day that you wanted to get down to the beach once more before winter sets in?"

The investigator shrugged. "Yeah, but this sounds like a

lot of work. The guy might be pretty hard to find down there.''

''You should take Anna.''

Whit was nodding. ''I was thinking the same thing. In fact, I'm going to call her right now.''

''Of course, the office can't pay her expenses,'' Tony said quickly. ''Or yours either once you locate Winters.''

''No problem,'' Whit said. ''What about warrants for Winters?''

The prosecutor frowned. ''Based on what?''

''Whadaya mean?''

''No one actually recognized the man who grabbed the child. I didn't want to stir up Mrs. Winters, but at this point in time we don't have enough to charge him. You'll be going down as part of the investigation. If he has the child, get back in touch with me. I'll have the warrants issued and copies faxed down to you.''

''Maybe he didn't grab her,'' Whit said.

''He's abducted her twice already, Whit. The family hasn't any money, so it doesn't sound like a ransom situation. Since it was done so brazenly, I think we can assume it was the father.''

Anna Tyree stood behind the new glass wall that separated her office from the newsroom of the *Milbrook Daily Journal*. The glass panels that surrounded her represented one part of the modernization of the *Journal*'s news division. It had started with a new computer system and had gone on to include a remodeling of the newsroom itself, including the office of the executive editor, the position Anna held with the paper. The size of her office hadn't changed, but now that the solid walls had been replaced by gleaming glass panels her work space actually seemed smaller. No question that it was certainly less private. She had insisted on blinds—and had most of them pulled down.

Still, she felt like some zoological specimen on display. The reporters and various editors who worked out in the newsroom seemed to appreciate the upgrade in their work environment, but she sensed that they resented the new glass walls around the editor's office. After all, it implied a certain lack of faith in their work ethic. No one had said that, but she sometimes caught them glancing at her, and she could read the resentment in their eyes.

Anna had been one of them not too many years back, just two in fact. In those days, when she had first started with the *Journal*, she had been known as Anna Tyson-Tyree. That had been the rather ostentatious pen name that appeared above her stories. For some reason, all of her former editors—those at the *Journal* and at the papers for which she had worked prior to coming to Raven County—had loved the hyphenated name. She had detested it, even though it was her full name, minus the hyphen, of course. That had been added by her first editor, who had spouted about how classy it looked every time Anna's name appeared on the front page.

So she knew what it was like to be a reporter. It wasn't a very respected profession—somewhere between a carnival worker and a used-car salesman. Reporters, especially those who worked in the print media, were accustomed to shoddy treatment. In a way it was their badge of distinction, a kind of reverse elitism in which they arrogantly thrived.

Nonetheless, when Katherine Binder, the publisher of the newspaper and Anna's closest friend, had suggested the structural alteration to Anna's office, she had expressed her opposition. Moreover, she had fully expected Kathy to accede to her wishes. Anna had been surprised when Kathy had insisted on the change. In a way it had been so unlike the publisher.

Kathy was about the same age as Anna and had inherited the newspaper from her husband. She had known nothing about the newspaper business and had immediately promoted Anna from the position of reporter to the head of the paper's news department. Over the past two years they had more or less worked as partners. Anna had reorganized and guided the news and editorial functions of the *Journal* with little intrusion on the publisher's part. Kathy, meanwhile, had tried to bury her grief over her husband's death and the circumstances surrounding it by throwing herself into a quick study of the paper's business side. Now, two years later, she was an adept newspaper administrator. The modernization of the paper's editorial division was a source of pride to Kathy, and she was feeling her oats, as Whit Pynchon liked to say. So Anna had gone along with the glass walls, but only after insisting on the bank of miniblinds that she planned on keeping pulled down.

The *Journal* was a morning paper, so most of the editorial work went on in the evening. It was midafternoon, and only a few people sat at their desks in the newsroom. Anna had arrived just after midday and had already written two editorials that would appear later in the week.

A young girl sat at the desk closest to Anna's office. She was on the phone taking down an obituary called in by one of Raven County's mortuaries. That was her sole job. It was the way most young reporters started. On the other side of the newsroom, the sports editor was squinting at the screen of his monitor. He looked busy, but more than likely he was playing one of the computer games he had squirreled away on the system. Anna knew about them, but she hadn't said anything about it. It seemed harmless enough to her, especially compared to one former sports editor who had kept a flask of whiskey in his desk drawer. Besides, the young man came in early every day and got his work done. To Anna, that was all that mattered.

The third person in the newsroom was the reporter assigned to cover the Milbrook City Council. They had met in special session that morning to consider an ordinance that would ban smoking in public places. According to the reporter, the debate had been vitriolic, and the meeting had been adjourned without any action on the ordinance. He was writing the story at that moment.

She was about to leave her office to get a soft drink from the lounge when her phone rang.

"Pack your bags," a male voice said when she answered it.

"What?" Although she and Whit Pynchon had been living together for a year, he didn't call her at work very often.

"Pack your bags," he said, again offering no explanation.

"Am I going somewhere?"

"I am . . . and I was hoping you might go with me."

Anna walked around her desk and sat down. "Where?"

"Myrtle Beach."

"When?"

"If we leave by four, we can be there by eleven."

Anna blinked. "Today? You mean leave today?"

"Why not?"

"Jesus, Whit. This is short notice. I don't think I can just walk out of here."

"Sure you can. You're due a few days off, and we were talking about a trip to the beach just this weekend."

"Yes, but—"

"I have to go down on a case," he said, interrupting her. "It just came up. You can lounge around in the sun for a day or so while I take care of it. Then we'll have a few days to ourselves.''

"What type of case?''

Whit laughed. "Turn off the radar, Anna. It's nothing newsworthy. An ex-husband grabbed his kid. We think he's gone to Myrtle Beach.''

"That's not the kind of case you usually handle.'' She didn't try to conceal her skepticism. She knew Whit too well. It was a minor miracle that she and the prosecutor's investigator had managed to maintain a relationship anyway. Anna had always boasted a healthy dislike for cops, and Whit couldn't abide reporters. Since he usually handled the really big cases in Raven County, it meant that they were often at each other's throats. The professional antagonism frequently spilled over into their personal life.

"Cross my heart,'' he said. "Tony just figured it would give me a chance to get to the beach.''

"I doubt I'll have much fun if you're going to be working all the time.''

"I promise I won't work all the time.''

He sounded like a kid, but, then, when it came to the beach, Whit Pynchon *was* a kid. Anna knew how badly he wanted to relocate there. She also knew that she was about all that kept him in Milbrook; she and Tressa, Whit's daughter by a former marriage, who lived with them and was attending her first year of college.

"What about Tressa?''

"She's got to study.''

"Do you think it's okay leaving her here by herself?''

"Christ, Anna. She's a big girl. C'mon, you know Kathy won't mind at all.''

She couldn't get over the enthusiasm in his voice. He had been talking about Myrtle Beach for the entire duration of their relationship. They'd made the trip once, and several other times they'd been forced to cancel plans, either because of Anna's work or Whit's. This was one time she could probably get away with little trouble. She looked out through the wall of glass and made up her mind.

"I've already called and made reservations. We have an oceanfront with a balcony."

"What should I pack?"

"Your bathing suit."

She laughed. "That's all?"

"They don't allow skinny-dipping in the motel pool."

Two

TOMMY FULLER'S DAD picked him up just around 5:00 that afternoon. Before the boy even had the car door closed, the story about the clown and Marcia Winters started to pour from him.

"Slow down," Jerry Fuller said. "What about Marcia and a clown?"

"He stole her, Daddy."

Fuller hadn't even started the car yet. "When did this happen?"

"Before lunch."

The elder Fuller eyed his son. "Tommy, we've told you about making up stories."

"It really did happen, Daddy. I'm not fibbing."

"Maybe I should go back in and talk to Mrs. Harrison."

Jerry Fuller watched for his son's reaction. Usually, if the boy was making something up, the threat to ask Mrs. Harrison was sufficient to produce a sly smile and the admission from that boy that he was "fibbing."

This time the boy just stared back at his father. "What did Mrs. Harrison do?"

"I dunno," said Tommy. "Mr. Harrison came home and fixed the hole in the fence."

"What hole in the fence?"

20

"The one the clown took Marcia out."

Jerry Fuller shook his head. "Maybe I should go back and talk to Mrs. Harrison."

"I'm not fibbing," Tommy said sharply, convinced that his father didn't believe him.

"That's why maybe I oughta go back and see what happened, Tommy. I believe you."

Fuller was opening the car door when Tommy said, "It was her daddy."

Fuller stopped. "What?"

"Mrs. Harrison said it was Marcia's daddy."

"He stole Marcia?"

Tommy nodded.

Fuller started to ask Tommy if Marcia's parents were divorced. Then he realized that, thankfully, his child wouldn't know what the word *divorce* meant. He closed the door and fired up the car's engine.

"You're not gonna ask Mrs. Harrison?" Tommy asked.

The man shook his head. "I understand what happened."

"Marcia's daddy is mean," the boy said.

How do you explain divorce to a child? And all of the misery that goes along with it? Jerry Fuller decided not to even try.

"Marcia's father probably loves her very much. He won't hurt her."

"He called me a name."

Fuller glanced at his son. "He did? You mean you talked to him?"

"Uh-uh," Tommy said. "I just told Marcia she wasn't s'posed to go with strangers. That's when he called me a name."

"It was her father, Tommy."

The boy didn't say anything.

Jerry Fuller didn't push the point. He was thinking about
something else. "Maybe we should keep this between us two
guys, Tommy. Like, maybe we shouldn't tell your mother."

"Why?"

Tommy's mother had been talking about taking the boy
out of Mrs. Harrison's day-care center. She wanted to place
him in a larger day-care center operated by the Milbrook
Community Hospital. It meant twenty dollars more a week
for Tommy's care, and Jerry Fuller saw no reason for it,
especially with their family budget being so tight at the moment.

He didn't explain all that to Tommy. He simply said, "It'll
worry your mother. Upset her. We don't want to do that, do
we?"

The last really big weekend for Myrtle Beach's summer
season came over Labor Day weekend. It was one of four
times when the small resort town overflowed with beach-
worshipers. The first of the season was Memorial Day, followed almost immediately by the Sun Fun Festival in early
June and the subsequent influx of high school graduates during the first two weeks in June. Activity tapered off somewhat
until July Fourth, when another invasion began. In years past,
the first couple of weeks in July had been the busiest time.
That was when the miners from the coalfields of Appalachia
had headed south and east. It was called, quite appropriately,
the miner's vacation, and occurred at the same time every
year. With the decline in recent years in the coal industry,
the annual migration from the mountains to the beach had
subsided somewhat. Following early July, the traffic into
Myrtle Beach diminished again, then started to pick up again
for Labor Day weekend.

Not that the Grand Strand suffered from a lack of vacationers between the big festivals and holidays. From Memorial Day through Labor Day its streets and beachfront were alive with tourists. That was why Whit Pynchon preferred to visit the area in early May or late September.

He was explaining all this to Anna as he navigated the traffic between Conway and Myrtle Beach itself. Even at that time, almost midnight, the number of vehicles on Highway 501 was surprising to Anna. Their earlier trip to the Grand Strand had been her first, and she'd slept most of the way there. So now she was shocked by the profusion of colorful and sometimes gaudy road signs that sat on both sides of the four-lane that connected Conway, the county seat of Horry County, with the Strand.

"I've seen traffic bumper-to-bumper all the way from Conway into Myrtle Beach," Whit said.

"For ten miles?" Anna asked.

He nodded. "Going in and coming out."

"Coming out?"

"Yeah. One time I got here on the Sunday after the Sun Fun Festival. Traffic was coming out of the beach bumper-to-bumper in both lanes over there. It was solid all the way from Myrtle Beach to Conway. It was like that, too, just before Hurricane Hugo hit. It's just about the only way out of the beach."

"The only way out?"

Whit was moving in and out of traffic as he talked, passing the slower vehicles. "The Grand Strand is really an island; it's separated from the mainland by the intracoastal waterway. There aren't but three bridges over the waterway between the North Carolina line and Georgetown. That's a stretch of almost sixty miles."

"And you wanna live down here?" she asked.

Whit laughed. "Yeah, I do."

"But you despise crowds."

"You can avoid them if you know how."

They had left Milbrook around three that afternoon, driving straight down I-77. By the time they reached Columbia, South Carolina, it was dusk and time to fill up the gas tank. Whit insisted on driving the entire way. It was another of his idiosyncrasies to which Anna had grown accustomed. When he was in a car, he wanted to drive. On the few occasions when he had ridden in Anna's car, he had sat stiffly on the passenger side, braking every time she did—and many times when she didn't. So Anna had dozed on the stretch of lonely road between Columbia and Florence, South Carolina. At that point they'd been sixty miles from the coast, and Whit had started playing tour guide.

"We'll be crossing the waterway in a few minutes," Whit said.

"Good, I'm tired of riding. On the way back I'm going to do some of the driving. It breaks up the monotony." He didn't respond. She asked about the reservations.

"No real problem," Whit said. "If we stay past Friday, we may have to change rooms."

"I told Kathy I'd be back by Friday."

"The paper can get along without you for a few days. I was hoping we might be able to stay through the weekend."

"We'll see. I've told you before. I'm not a big fan of the beach, especially one with a carnival atmosphere."

"You'll love it here," Whit said. As if to prove the point, he rolled down the window. Warm, muggy air, tinged with the smell of the ocean, rushed inside.

"Smell," he said.

"Jesus, Whit; it must still be eighty out there."

"Yeah," he said. "It feels wonderful."

"You do plan on looking for the little girl and her father, I hope?"

"Of course, but with any luck I can wrap that up tomorrow. That'll give us the rest of the week for ourselves."

"You think you can find him that easily?"

"I can always hope."

"Are you going to get the local police to help?"

"Eventually," said Whit, "but I'm going to check out the names the girl's mother gave me first."

"Is that a good idea?"

"The Myrtle Beach police are just like cops everywhere else. They've got their own problems and won't have much time for mine. When I come up with something, I'll make contact with them."

"Always the Lone Ranger."

"There's the waterway."

Anna saw what appeared to be a hill up ahead, but what really attracted her attention was the glare of a multitude of lights on both sides of the roadway. "What's all of this?" she asked.

"A junk outlet," Whit said, now concentrating on the heavy traffic that seemed to slow down as it approached the bridge.

At the top of the bridge the lights of Myrtle Beach proper came into view. "There it is," he proclaimed. Anna noted the exhilaration in his voice. Whit Pynchon hated West Virginia and often declared his intentions to relocate in the resort city before them. So far it had been nothing more than talk, but Anna knew the day would come when the talk would turn into action. She didn't know how she would react. She wasn't as taken with the coast or its mild winters. Nor was she likely to find a job in Myrtle Beach that matched her present position.

On the other hand, she loved Whit, and she knew that each fall he slipped into a depression as the West Virginia winter approached. In a way it was a Jekyll-and-Hyde transformation. The car descended the bridge. Its headlights revealed a sign that announced the Myrtle Beach city limits. Whit had grown quiet.

"A penny?" Anna asked.

He chuckled. "You already know my thoughts."

"About moving down here?"

"Every time I drive in here, I imagine what it would feel like if I knew it was for good . . . permanent."

She recalled how depressed he'd been on the drive home after their first trip. "I bet if you lived here it would be just the same as living in Milbrook. You'd end up taking the beach itself for granted and cussing the cold northeasters during January."

"The hell I would."

The sun lifted like a red fireball above the eastern horizon of the Atlantic. Already, just moments after dawn, people strolled the beach, some of them collecting shells in white trash bags, others sifting with their bare toes through the sand and shale in search of fossilized shark teeth.

Whit sat on the balcony of his second-floor, oceanfront room watching the sunrise as well as the people on the beach. It was his favorite time of day on the coast. When he was there, he made a point of getting up every morning to watch the magnificent sunrise. On those few mornings when it was gray and overcast, he joined those on the beaches. On the clear mornings he preferred to sip coffee and observe, as he was doing that morning.

Not quite 7:00 yet, but already the morning was warm and so humid that the moisture had threatened to condense on his skin when he had stepped onto the private balcony. The sun itself was still low enough to the horizon, still buffered enough by the atmosphere, so that he could stare straight at it. If you watched closely enough, you could see it lifting. The sensation gave Whit a strange sense of time passing, slipping away, as an old country-music ballad put it.

He lit a cigarette and wondered why in the name of God he remained in the claustrophobic mountains of West Virginia. Life was too damned short to miss many mornings like this one.

Behind him the door to the oceanfront apartment opened. Anna peeked out.

"Didn't mean to wake you," he said.

"You didn't." She was staring at the intensifying presence of the sun. "It's beautiful."

"Not as beautiful as you." That was true. Anna Tyree, blessed with a naturally dark skin tone, deep auburn hair, and eyelashes and eyebrows yet one shade darker, woke up looking as if she'd already made up for the day. In the early mornings, her blue eyes seemed to be the color of a cloudless Carolina sky. Her tousled hair only added to her allure.

"Come on out and sit down," Whit said. "I'll get you a cup of coffee."

"I'm in my nightgown," she said.

He pushed himself up. "So what? No one will notice." She shrugged and eased out to the balcony. Whit vanished into the interior of the two-room efficiency apartment and returned with two cups of coffee.

"I hope it's not too strong," he said. "I brewed it on the stove with that old metal coffeepot." The apartment came with a small, modestly equipped kitchen.

She tasted it. "It's fine."

He settled beside her. "The sunrise was spectacular this morning."

She glanced at the sun. "It still is."

"You should have seen it when it first peeked above the ocean. It was like a flaming orange diamond."

Anna was watching the people walk by on the beach. "Is it low tide?"

"Halfway between," Whit said. "Low tides occur just before noon. Are you going to lie on the beach today?"

She shook her head. "By the pool. I never could handle all that gritty sand on my beach towel."

"I can't believe you don't like the beach."

"I do like it," she countered. "I want to go for a long walk on it. I just don't like sunbathing all that much. It's a waste of time."

"Well, I'll try to wrap up the case today, maybe this morning."

"How?" Anna asked.

Whit pulled a small file from the AstroTurf carpet beneath his chair. He opened it up. "I've got the addresses of two places where Willie Winters might be. I'll start with those and hope I get somewhere."

"And if you don't?"

"Then I'll pay a visit to the local police."

"He just grabbed the little girl yesterday, Whit. He may not even be here. I mean, he's got to know that this is the first place the police will look for him."

"It's the only place I'm going to look for him. If he isn't here, or if we can't find him here, then Marcia Winters will join that long list of missing kids who have been parent-napped."

"You mean you'll quit looking?"

"No, not exactly. We'll enter the child's description into the national computer . . . her father's, too."

"I try to put myself into the mother's shoes. I can imagine how distraught she is."

"I don't know a single thing about Mrs. Winters," Whit said. "Very little about her ex-husband. But I do know one thing. More than likely, both of them acted like real assholes when they broke up. I feel sorry for the kid, being yanked one way and another, but those two folks created their own misery. Now they expect—no, actually they *demand* that the legal system solve everything for them. I've had it up to here''—he had his hand level with his forehead—"with people like the Winters."

Anna was shaking her head. "You just said that you didn't know anything about the Winters."

"I also said that, more than likely, they're typical."

Anna laughed. "You are so agile with stereotypes."

He waved her comment off. "Let's not talk about that kinda bullshit right now. I want to spend a few more minutes enjoying this before I have to go to work."

THREE

TOMMY FULLER DOZED in his father's car that morning on his way to the Mrs. Harrison's FunTime Day-Care Center. His parents had put him to bed at his usual time, but he hadn't gone to sleep right away. He had kept looking out his window, expecting to see a clown face looking in at him, or that other face, the one with the breath that smelled so bad. Tommy hadn't told anyone about that face. Everyone said it was Marcia's father. Tommy was glad it wasn't his father, looking mean like that and smelling so awful.

He wished his mother had closed the curtains. He would have done it for himself, but he couldn't reach the string that you had to pull to close them. There was the step stool in his room, the one that he used to get his piggy bank down from the top of his bureau when he wanted to play store, but sometimes that made a lot of noise. He didn't want to get caught.

Neither his mom nor dad had been in a very good mood. They'd shouted at each other again just after supper. His dad had been saying something about not enough money, and his mother had been fussing about his dad's job. Sometimes Tommy couldn't understand his mother. His dad had a fun job. He got to work at a computer all day long. When Tommy went to work with his father, he got to type on the computer. His father even had a game going on the computer, and they played it for a long time. Tommy's mother worked at the hospital in a smelly place she called the lab. He hardly ever got to go to her job, and when he did, she made him sit in a corner and wouldn't let him touch anything. There were the computers where she worked, too, but she wouldn't let Tommy play with them. Her job wasn't any fun at all. Still, she kept fussing at his dad because she made more money than he did. It didn't make any sense to Tommy. What difference did it make? When you needed money, you just went to a place called a bank, gave them a piece of paper, and they gave you money.

He didn't want to make them mad again. So he had stayed in his bed, his head under the covers, except when he peeked at the bedroom window. Finally—Tommy really couldn't remember when—he must have gone to sleep because he had bad dreams about the man in the clown mask. Twice, his dreams had woken him up. The last time, when the clown came back for him in his dream, Tommy had called for his daddy. No one had answered, though. He had started to get out of bed and go to their bedroom, but he was afraid to do that, too. That made his daddy mad, and was when he told Tommy he wasn't a big boy.

The four-year-old was sprawled out in the backseat of his dad's car when it pulled to a stop in front of Mrs. Harrison's house.

"Wake up, Tommy. Whatsa matter?"

Tommy struggled to open his eyes. It was a bright, sunny morning, and the glare jolted him awake. His daddy had the rear door open.

"C'mon, Tommy. Get up."

The boy rubbed his eyes.

"You sick?" his father asked.

"I'm sleepy."

"Well, maybe Mrs. Harrison'll let you lay down awhile. I'll ask her."

"Are you going in?"

Usually, when his father drove him, he had Tommy get out and go to the front door while he waited.

"For a minute," Jerry Fuller said. "I wanna ask Mrs. Harrison if you can lie down for a while."

Tommy didn't say it, but he thought his dad was telling a fib.

Mrs. Harrison opened the door even before Jerry Fuller could knock. She greeted them both with a broad smile and a cheerful "Good morning."

"Tommy's kind of groggy this morning, Mrs. Harrison. Think he might be able to rest for a little while?"

She glanced down at Tommy. "Well, there's cereal on the table. Maybe if he would eat first, drink some milk, then he could lie on the couch."

Fuller looked down at his son. "How's that sound?"

"Fine, Daddy."

"You run on inside, Tommy. Have some breakfast. I'd like a word with Mrs. Harrison."

Tommy did as he was told, but as he eased by the big, rotund figure of Clara Harrison he was disappointed. He didn't like it one bit when his father told fibs.

"I hope he's not sick," Mrs. Harrison was saying to Tommy's father. "There's always one bug or another going around with the kids."

Jerry Fuller peeked around Mrs. Harrison to be certain Tommy had gone on into the kitchen. "I don't think he slept very well last night, Mrs. Harrison. I heard him cry out once. What happened yesterday? He was telling me something about a man pulling Marcia through the fence."

Mrs. Harrison sighed. "Her father, Mr. Fuller. It happened once before. That time, Mr. Winters—Marcia's father—came to the front door. I didn't know that he and Mrs. Winters were separated, so I let Marcia go with him. I mean what was I supposed to do? He was the child's father. This time, he snatched her.''

"Did you see it happen?"

Clara Harrison slowly shook her head. ''I had just stepped inside for a moment to answer the phone. Tommy—he's one of my best helpers—came in and told me what happened. I do hope it didn't upset the boy too much.''

"He'll get over it, Mrs. Harrison. But we haven't told the boy's mother about it.''

"Really?"

"My wife's wanting to put Tommy in the hospital day care, and—"

"Lord sakes, Mr. Fuller. They'll charge you an arm and leg. Tommy's been with me for two years now. Surely Mrs. Fuller—or you—don't think I don't take proper care of him.''

"Oh, no . . . no. That's not it. Please understand, Mrs. Harrison. I want Tommy to stay here, but his mother says the hospital day care is a child development center, sort of like a prekindergarten. She's just got this crazy idea in her head. I just wanted to tell you that we haven't mentioned the incident to Tommy's mother.''

"And you don't want me to mention it?"

"That might be for the best. I mean, if she brings it up, then don't lie or anything like that. I wouldn't expect you to do that.''

Mrs. Harrison was smiling now. ''I understand, Mr. Fuller.''

"Do you think Marcia will be coming back?"

The woman shook her head. ''Even when they find her, I don't think I'm gonna accept her back here. I don't like me or the other kids bein' messed up in family troubles. Do you want me to talk to Tommy about what happened yesterday?''

Jerry Fuller shook his head. ''Let's just let it go for now. The sooner he forgets about it, the better.''

The Grand Strand isn't a single town, but a string of communities running from Little River Inlet at the North Carolina border south to the colonial city of Georgetown. As you drive from Little River south along U.S. 17, you encounter such towns as Cherry Grove, North Myrtle Beach, Atlantic Beach (in the days of segregation, that area of the Strand was reserved for blacks), Myrtle Beach, Surfside Beach, Garden City, Murrell's Inlet, Litchfield Beach, Pawleys Island, the exclusive Debordieu colony, Hobcaw Barony, and finally Georgetown on Wynah Bay.

Myrtle Beach was the hub, the glittering buckle on the Strand belt. As much as it depended on the sun for its reputation, it remained a city of the night. During the day, its visitors flocked down to the beach itself or roasted themselves around the pool decks of hundreds of motels that lined Ocean Boulevard. At night they emerged like bats from a cave to find physical and emotional nourishment in the multitude of restaurants and night spots.

So when Whit left his motel just before 10:00 that morning, the traffic on Ocean Boulevard was light and sporadic. He headed south along the boulevard, following it until it curved inland to merge with Highway 17. He turned left and continued south toward the town of Surfside Beach. The first address he was to check was located at 82 Shell Lane in Surfside. He wasn't familiar with the street's name, but Surfside was much smaller than its flashy neighbor just to the north. It had a few large motels, but cottages dominated its beachfront, most of which were vacation rentals. He suspected that Shell Lane was one of the dozen or so streets that turned toward the ocean from Highway 17. If so, the address should be easy to find.

If all else failed, he could always stop at the Surfside Beach City Hall and contact the local authorities. He carried a certified copy of an order from Raven County's circuit judge giving him authority to take Marcia Winters into his custody and deliver her to the custody of her mother. As a rule, most states would recognize the order. That hadn't always been the case, but with the rising incidence of missing children, many of whom were victims of parent-napping, police officials nationwide were becoming more sensitive and more responsive to the problem.

Most of the community of Surfside was located between Highway 17 and the beach itself. When he reached the highway's intersection with the first of Surfside's streets, he turned left onto it. Whit was familiar with the town since it was one of the places he often scouted on his frequent trips to the Strand. As a result, he knew the first street led to a massive Holiday Inn.

When he was within a few blocks of the ocean, he noted the names of each of the streets running parallel to the coast. He didn't see Shell Lane. When he reached the Holiday Inn, he headed back inland, turning onto the first of the streets running north and south. By driving south he would be able to check all the east-west street lanes. At the intersection he smiled at a small sign that said Shell Lane. He started to turn right and search back inland toward Highway 17, but a large apartment building caught his eye on the opposite side of the street, in the block between the street he was on and the ocean. A signed announced that it was 82 Shell Lane.

''Damn!'' He hadn't been told that the address was an apartment building. At a quick glance it contained at least a dozen apartments. Supposedly the apartment that he sought was occupied by Bobby Stump, another West Virginia transplant who had headed south with Willie Winters. The value of property along the Strand decreased considerably away from the oceanfront itself. This particular structure didn't look much better than an inner-city flophouse.

Whit eased his car to a stop in front of the building and got out to look for a list of tenants or a group of mailboxes. He didn't notice the old man raking leaves at the side of the building, not until he heard his voice.

He came from Whit's left, the rake still in his hand. "Can I help ya, mister?"

"Oh, hi. Didn't see you," Whit said, trying to sound very friendly and casual.

"You lookin' for something?"

"Fact of the matter I'm lookin' for Bobby Stump. The name ring a bell?"

The man sat the business end of the rake on the ground and leaned on the handle. "What if it does?"

"Maybe you can tell me which apartment he lives in."

"Maybe I can . . . maybe I can't."

Jesus, Whit thought. Maybe he should have gone to the local cops first.

The old man was giving Whit a thorough examination. "You look like the police to me, mister."

Some people had a built-in radar about that sort of thing. When Whit had dressed that morning, he had deliberately picked faded jeans and a limp, rather worn safari shirt. On his feet he wore white slip-on deck shoes without socks. It was his preferred beach attire, and he figured it wouldn't shout cop.

"Not here," Whit said.

"A cop from somewhere else then?"

"Sorta."

"You a Fed? A narc? Something like that?"

Whit had to laugh. "No, nothing like that at all. I work for a prosecuting attorney up in West Virginia. I'm an investigator."

From somewhere in his mouth the old man produced a huge wad of tobacco. He spat it on the sandy ground. "West Virginy, huh? I come from Virginy, but that was a long time back."

"You work here then?" Whit asked.

"It's my place, mister. I own it. Bought it with some money I got from a black-lung settlement back in the seventies."

"So you were a miner back in Virginia?"

The old man nodded. "Buchanan County. You heard of it?"

Whit smiled. "Sure have. I'm from Raven County, just over the line."

"Stump in some kinda trouble back there?"

"No, sir. Not at all. I was looking for a fella who might be staying with him . . . or who might visit him on occasion. His name's Willie Winters."

The old man clicked his teeth at the name. "Yep, know him and Stump, but Stump don't live here no more. I booted his sorry ass outta here. The police came to me and said he was dealin' dope. I don't tolerate that kind of stuff, not when I know for sure it's goin' on."

"Did you know for sure?" Whit asked.

"The police did. Good enough for me. I do what I can to help the cops around here. They's a good bunch of fellas. How come you ain't talked to them? They kin tell you all you wanna know about Stump . . . about his buddy, too, more'n likely."

"Well, I'm not down here because of drugs, old-timer. How long ago you give 'em the boot?"

"Jesus, musta been a month at least. Haven't seen hide nor hair of 'em since."

"Any idea where they went?"

The old man spit in the grass again. "What did you say you were after this friend of Stump's for?"

Whit didn't like talking about his cases, but it might help loosen the old man's tongue. "He abducted his daughter back in West Virginia. We think he came down here."

"But it's his daughter, right?"

"He doesn't have legal custody."

"I understand. No, I ain't got no idea where them fellows went. If I knew, I'd sue the bastard for my cleanup money. The cops are keeping an eye out for him. They'll jack him up for me if they see him."

"But they both were here?"

"I rented the place to Stump. He let the other'n come in and stay. I didn't like it, but my lawyer told me there wasn't nothing I could do about it 'cept give Stump notice to get out. I was thinkin' on it when Si Smith—he's a detective in the sheriff's department—told me about Stump's dope deal-in'. That cinched it; gave that no-good notice the next day. Figgered I have to get a court order to get him out, but they was out within a week. Left the place a mess, too. I figger they owe me a C-note for the cleanup."

"So you've already cleaned it up?"

"Hell, yes. Had it rented within a week to one of the local lifeguards—them or members of the beach patrol. They're like cops, too. That's mostly who I try to rent to anyway. They's a good bunch of boys. They like their drink, but then I don't mind a snort myself. I guess they maybe smoke some of that loco weed, and they're horny as bull rabbits, but they don't mess around no hard dope.''

"Sound like fine young men," Whit said, smiling.

"None better."

"Anything else you can tell me?"

The old man slowly shook his head. "Like I said, you oughta talk to the cops. Si Smith. He's a good fella.''

"I will," Whit said, "but I don't want to cause too much stir. The guy I'm looking for might take the kid and make tracks. Know what I mean?''

"Oh, sure . . . sure do.''

"So I'd appreciate it if you wouldn't tell anyone about me for right now.''

"Not even the cops?" the old man asked, a hint of suspicion in his tone.

"Not even them.''

The old man's eyes narrowed. "Say, do you have any identification?''

"If it makes a difference," Whit said, "I sure do." He reached to his hip pocket and realized that it was empty.

"Uhh . . . looks like I left my wallet back at the motel in Myrtle Beach.''

"Maybe I oughta go call the cops," the old man said, tensing.

"Hey, look," Whit said, "I am who I said I am.''

"Just be on your way, fella. I think maybe you're one of Stump's dope suppliers. Si Smith asked me to keep a lookout . . . Let him know if anyone came asking after Stump.''

Whit shrugged. "Look, if it makes you feel better, then just go call Si Smith. Just remember I'm trying to locate a three-year-old girl who was snatched from her mother. I don't want Stump's buddy to know I'm here.''

Whit headed back to his car, but he stopped and looked

back at the old man. ''And thanks for the information. When I find Stump, and you bet your ass I'll find him, I'll be glad to let you know where he is.''

When he pulled away from the apartments, he glanced in the rearview mirror and saw the old man smiling. He also had a pen in his hand, writing something on his arm; his tag number, Whit figured.

FOUR

IF WHIT PYNCHON HAD BEEN a college teacher instead of a cop, he would have been the classic example of the absent-minded professor. It wasn't at all unusual for him to leave home without his wallet and identification. On many occasions he forgot to retrieve the short-barreled .357 he usually carried from its place on the top shelf of his hall closet. The absence of the gun, which he seldom needed, wasn't nearly as disconcerting as the lack of his wallet and identification. It was amazing how naked he felt once he realized the familiar lump in his hip pocket was missing. How had he managed to sit down in the car without noticing it?

After leaving the old man at the Surfside Beach apartments, he headed west toward Highway 17, fully intent on returning to the motel. By that time it was almost eleven o'clock, and traffic on the north-south highway that extended all the way from Maine to Florida was starting to increase. The second address he had to check was at Pawleys Island, a laid-back community located at the southern end of the sixty-mile stretch of resort towns. By the time he returned to the motel and got back down to Pawleys Island, a good part of the day would be lost. Instead of turning north toward Myrtle Beach, he headed south toward the southern Strand.

The highway through Surfside Beach and its sister com-

munity of Garden City was still flanked by a stunning variety
of beach shops, smaller amusement parks, and restaurants.
The cluttered tourist glitter, its southernmost extension recently punctuated by a sprawling enclosed mall, had crept as
far south as the turnoff to Murrell's Inlet. The famous low-
country landscape that Whit loved so much didn't come into
full view until he passed the inlet turnoff. There was still an
occasional restaurant or service station, but coastal forest
now moved in tightly against the road. Spreading live oaks
overhung the right lane, their branches shrouded by the drift-
ing fingers of Spanish moss.

Whit turned off his air conditioner and rolled down his
window. The humid, pine-scented air rushed in to fill the
car. God, he loved it! For a few moments he forgot about
the case on which he was working, the missing wallet and
credentials, and was able to ignore the occasional lapse in
the landscape as he passed through the smaller Strand towns
of North Litchfield and then Litchfield Beach, but as he
neared Pawleys Island, a place known to most people because of the rope hammocks made there, the signs of human
corruption started to reappear. More billboards, including
one for the famous Hammock Shop of Pawleys Island. Then
strips of specialty shops and ever-present real estate offices.

He slowed for a stoplight and turned once again toward
the coast. A two-lane road sloped gently down to the wide
expanse of creeks and salt marsh that separated Pawleys Island from the mainland. As he crossed the bridge over the
main channel, he waved to an old black woman who was
fishing in the saltwater creek. She waved back. The aroma
of the marsh drifted into the car.

When he reached the sandy strip of land on the other side,
he stopped and lifted his notebook from the seat. The island
itself was two miles long and densely packed with vacation

cottages and permanent residences. According to Mrs. Winters, a friend of her former husband's lived on Waccamaw Lane. He had no idea whether to turn left or right. Based on his memory, the road from the mainland came into the island nearly at its midpoint. He decided to drive down to the south end first. Just as he made the turn, he saw a young woman approaching him on a bicycle. Whit stopped his car and got out, waving at her.

"Morning," he called to her. "I've got a question."

The woman stopped, not quite sure what to make of Whit. "I'm trying to find Waccamaw Lane," he said quickly, hoping to allay her obvious suspicion.

"You're on it."

"I didn't see a street sign," he explained.

She finally smiled. "We don't have too many of those. If you're looking for someone, I can probably help."

"Great. Just a second." He reached into the car for his notepad. "I'm looking for 113 Waccamaw Lane."

She laughed. "Sorry, you'll have to give me a name. Like I said, street numbers don't mean a lot there. We like to think of ourselves as people rather than numbers."

Whit checked his note. "Calvin Stewart."

There was nothing subtle about her change of expression. "You're a little late. He doesn't live here anymore." The smile was gone, replaced by a frosty look of hostility.

"Just my luck," Whit said.

"You a friend of his?"

Whit shook his head. "No, ma'am. Don't even know him. I'm looking for someone who might have been staying with him. How long has Stewart been gone?"

"Ever since he died."

"Died? I'm sorry to hear that. Can you tell me anything about him?"

"What's it to you?"

"I'm an investigator for a prosecuting attorney up in West Virginia. This fella I'm looking for is a friend of Stewart's."

She had been sitting astride her bike. She eased off it and lowered it to the ground. "You're a police officer?"

"Of a kind . . . But if you're gonna ask to see my I.D., we might as well end the conversation right now. I'm staying up in Myrtle Beach, and I walked out of the motel room without my wallet this morning."

She ambled over to his car and looked at the inspection sticker. "That says West Virginia, so I guess you're telling me the truth. Not that it matters. I can't tell you much—certainly not anything I wouldn't tell anyone else."

Now that she was closer to Whit, he could see that she wasn't quite as young as she had looked on first glance. She was thin and deeply tanned, her skin starting to show the toughening effects of too much sun. Her hair was a dirty blond. She wore a T-shirt that hyped CLEMSON UNIVERSITY and jogging shorts that displayed her thin, thickly muscled legs. From a distance, she had looked not much older than Tressa, Whit's daughter. Close up she was well over thirty and in very good shape.

"Do you live here?" Whit asked.

She nodded. "For the past five years. On an island this small, you get to know most people. Even the vacationers. Once folks start coming here, they keep coming back. I'm from the western part of the state, and I used to come here with my parents. Eventually I moved here permanently."

"Are you a teacher?" Whit asked.

She laughed, showing white, well-maintained teeth. "I'm a painter . . . mainly watercolors, but don't get the wrong impression. I'm not that good. My parents were just pretty well-off."

"Don't knock it," Whit said.

"Never. I love being able to afford to live here."

"What can you tell me about Stewart? I'm at a dead end."

"What kind of case are you working on?" He hesitated, and she noticed. "Tell you what. You show me your identification and you don't have to answer the question. I'll tell you everything I know."

This time Whit laughed. "You win." For the second time in an hour, Whit described the case.

"How old's the daughter?"

"Three."

"I guess this guy and his wife are divorced then?"

"Yeah, and he's ran off with the child before."

"I live just a few houses down. Follow me. I'll drop off the bike in the yard, and we'll drive back to the mainland."

The suggestion caught Whit off-guard. The woman was certainly attractive enough, but he was looking for answers, not a noon quickie.

"I promise not to bite," she said, grinning at him. "Besides, I'm taking the bigger risk. Maybe you aren't who you say you are."

"Why the mainland?"

"Because that's where you can find some answers to your questions."

What the hell, thought Whit. "Okay, I'll follow you. By the way, what's your name?"

"Maude Adcock. What's yours?"

"Whit Pynchon."

"Whit? What's that short for?"

"Whitley."

She chuckled. "With a name like that, you shoulda been a lawyer. Follow me."

She pedaled about two blocks down and turned into the

drive of a raised cottage that sat on the marsh rather than the ocean. A sign on the front read MAUDE'S MANIA. It was something of a tradition along the Strand to name the cottages. Maude glided the bike into the parking area beneath the house and leaned it against a wall. Whit, waiting in the car, couldn't help but stare at the Mercedes roadster occupying the car port.

"Some car," Whit said as the woman got into his vehicle.

"Another benefit of my inheritance."

"Are both your parents dead?"

"Just Daddy. Mother still lives in Anderson, South Carolina."

Whit pulled back onto the narrow street and headed back toward the causeway. He also took the opportunity to pull his cigarettes from his pocket.

"You smoke?" she asked.

"Like a chimney."

"You seem smarter than that."

"Just as smart as you," he countered.

"What's that mean?"

"You've got a nice tan. That causes skin cancer, doesn't it?"

It brought a smile to her face. "I like you."

"Mind if I smoke?" he then asked.

Her smile turned to laughter. "Be my guest. It's your car."

After lighting the cigarette, Whit asked, "Where are we going?"

"All in good time, Whitley."

"It's Whit, please."

In the close confines of the car her aroma was almost overpowering. It was a strangely erotic combination of a musky perfume and perspiration. As alluring as it was, he hoped it escaped the car before Anna got back into it.

"Stewart was married, and he and his wife had lived on the island for about two years. He claimed to be a writer, and she a painter. She wasn't lying. I've seen her work. It's in oils, and not too bad. Usually we live and let live here on the island, but rumors got started about Stewart actually being a dope dealer. A lot of drugs come in along the coast here, especially between here and Charleston."

"Why did people suspect Stewart?"

"The place he was renting month-to-month cost one hell of a lot of money. If he was making that kind of money as a writer, someone would have known of him. And, as I said, this is a small town. People saw things that made them suspicious. 'Bout five months ago this dude moved in with them. I never knew his full name, but Stewart always called him Willie-Boy."

"Willie Winters," Whit said.

"A month ago they found Stewart's body—what was left of it—washed up on the southern point of the island at low tide. It's like a huge sandy desert down there when—"

"I've been there," Whit said. "It's one of my favorite places to visit when I come down. What killed Stewart?"

"Everyone on the island had it figured this way: Willie-Boy and Stewart's wife—her name is Pam—had a thing going, and Stewart found out about it. We figured they did him in."

"Had they?"

Maude shrugged. "Guess not. The cops questioned them, I hear, but it never went any further. The case hasn't ever been solved. Now, it's the general consensus that some sort of drug deal went bad, and Stewart got terminated. He died from a bullet in the head."

"So what happened to Willie-Boy and Pam Stewart?" The black woman was still fishing on the bridge across the channel as Whit drove back toward the mainland. This time she didn't even look around as the car passed.

"They moved out of the house not long after Stewart's death."

Whit frowned. "Did you just need a lift to the mainland or something?"

"Wouldn't you like to know where they moved to?"

Whit looked at her. "You can tell me?"

"No, but the postmistress can, and she's a friend of mine."

The Pawleys Island post office sat at the southeastern corner of the intersection where the causeway road joined Highway 17. It looked more like a country store than a post office, and Whit wasn't at all surprised that he hadn't noticed it before. A few people, mostly elderly women, stood in front of the small structure talking as Whit and Maude Adcock exited his vehicle. Maude spoke to them, and Whit nodded. He could feel the curious intensity of their gazes as he stepped into the air-conditioned interior of the building.

"That'll give 'em something to wag their tongues about for a while," Maude said over her shoulder.

"What's that?" Whit asked.

"They'll wonder if you're my most recent liaison."

Whit laughed. "Do you have that many?"

"Actually, very few; but far be it from me to dispel their envious fantasies. At their age they're entitled to enjoy what imagination they have left."

A short and obese black woman with unadorned gray hair pulled back tightly against her head stood behind a counter. When she saw Maude, she beamed a bright smile. "You're just in time. Got this big, interesting package for you."

"You should have opened it," Maude answered.

"I was tempted." That's when she first seemed to notice that Whit was actually with Maude. Her eyes went to Whit, then back to Maude.

"Lorleen, this is Whit. Whit, meet Lorleen Freeman, the postmistress for Pawleys Island."

The woman stuck her hand over the counter. "As the saying goes, Any friend of Maude's . . ." She left the rest unsaid as Whit shook her outstretched hand. Then she glanced at Maude. "You been out trollin', Maude?"

Maude glanced back at Whit. "Ignore her. She knows how exaggerated the rumors are about my love life."

"I know you do more wishin' and hopin' than anything else, girl."

"Lorleen!"

Whit laughed and shook his head. He didn't quite know what to say, so he said nothing at all. Maude got him off the hook. "Whit's a special kind of cop, Lorleen."

The mischievous twinkle vanished from the black woman's eye. "A cop?"

"A special investigator," Whit said. "I work for a prosecuting attorney up in West Virginia."

"West Virginia?" the postmistress said.

"Yes, ma'am."

"I have kinfolks up there. You know a place called Powhatan."

Whit nodded. "Sure do. It's about forty miles from where I live."

"I always liked that name," Lorleen said.

"It's a wide place in the road down in the coalfields," Whit explained.

Lorleen grinned. "That's about what my kin says. They also say it's a rather dismal place to live."

"They're right."

"I didn't know you had people in West Virginia," Maude said.

The black woman laughed. "Gawd, Maude. I got kinfolk all over."

"I thought you might give Whit a hand, Lorleen. He's looking for someone."

The good humor left her face. "Now, c'mon, Maude. You know I don't go giving away official information. It's a violation of the law, and—"

"But Whit is the law," Maude quickly countered.

"I haven't seen any identification yet."

Whit sighed. "I forgot my wallet."

"Sure, and I'm a white person with a beach tan," the postmistress shot back. "Wouldn't matter none anyway. I don't give out that kinda information but to the postal inspectors."

"He's looking for Pam Stewart," Maude said, as if that might make a difference.

Another change of expression came over the woman's face. "Pam Stewart?"

Maude smiled and nodded.

"Why didn't you tell me that in the first place?" She looked to Whit. "What's your interest in Mrs. Stewart?"

"None," Whit said. "I'm interested in the man who might be staying with her."

Whit wasn't going to say anything else, but Maude wasn't so restrained. "The guy's from West Virginia. He abducted his child up there."

"I knew he was a lowlife," Lorleen said. "Her forwarding address is 5110 Oak Street, Myrtle Beach."

"You know it off the top of your head?" Whit asked.

"It's one of the few talents I've got, mister. Guess that's why I make such a good postmistress."

Whit, though, didn't have much of a memory for addresses, and she had reeled it off so quickly that he hadn't even been prepared to try to remember it. He started searching for something on which to make a note. The postmistress was ahead of him. She handed him a notepad and pencil. "You write it down. Don't want it in my handwriting."

She repeated it for him, adding, "But you didn't get it from me."

"I understand," Whit said. "The other fellow didn't happen to get any mail at her address, did he?"

Lorleen Freeman shook her head. "No, sir. I always wondered about that, too. How old's the kid he snatched?"

"Three," Whit said.

"No-good bastard. I got a niece who went through that with her old man. In her case the cops never seemed to care too much."

Maude patted Whit on the arm. "This is a good cop. I can tell."

The postmistress reached back and pulled a package from a shelf. "Here's your mail."

Maude checked the return address. "It's my new watercolors."

"I do appreciate your help," Whit said as they turned to leave.

The black woman frowned. "What on earth you talking about, mister?"

Outside, the gathering of old women was moving down toward another small storefront as Whit held the door to his car open for Maude. "Can I buy you lunch?" she asked.

Whit checked his watch. "I oughta check out this address."

"Aw, c'mon. There's a nice little restaurant down there." She nodded in the direction the women were walking.

"Are you looking to make a public spectacle of me?" Whit asked, smiling.

"I'd love making a private spectacle of you, but I'll settle for a public one."

"Why didn't I meet you a few years ago?" Whit said.

"What on earth is that supposed to mean?"

"A beautiful woman—and rich, too—with a place at the beach."

A wistful look came over her face. "Are you married? I've been dreading to ask that question."

Whit shook his head. "No, not married."

There was a sudden resurgence of hope in her expression—that vanished when she saw Whit's pained look. "But there is someone back home?" she said.

"Actually, Maude, there's someone back in Myrtle Beach."

"Oh, well . . . I won't tell if you won't."

Whit laughed as she settled down into the seat. "I'll drive you home."

FIVE

WHIT KNEW he would have little trouble finding the address given him by the Pawleys Island postmistress. For the casual tourist Oak Street might have been unknown. Whit, though, knew it well. It ran parallel and a single block west of Highway 17. During the crunch of summer traffic, the locals used it to navigate Myrtle Beach. They kept it something of a secret, too; Whit had only learned about it three years earlier.

He planned to drive by for a quick study of the layout. Then he'd head back to the motel for his identification and the certified copy of the court order he had brought with him.

As soon as he turned on to Oak Street, he checked the street numbers and saw that he was within a block of the address he sought. That placed the residence of Pam Stewart on the extreme southern fringe of the Myrtle Beach city limits. The buildings along that portion of the street were anything but lavish. Like the old man's apartments in Surfside, they were, for the most part, aging multifamily structures that probably rented to a few of the thousands of young people who came to the Strand to work as desk clerks, maintenance people, waiters, and busboys. Occasionally the units were separated from one another by small homes, many of which were in need of repair and/or paint jobs. It was a part of Myrtle Beach seldom visited by tourists.

The address he sought turned out to be one of the small houses. It sat back from the street in a shroud of dense live oak and coastal pine. Beer cans and weathered bags from a variety of fast-food houses littered the sandy front yard. Quite a comedown from the laid-back luxury of Pawleys Island, Whit thought as he slowed to drive by it.

The unpaved driveway was empty. In fact, from Whit's vantage point the place appeared to be uninhabited. Probably was. In his experience, the underbelly of society tended to be rather transient. Some of them stayed at one address only so long as some gullible landlord bought their argument that the check was in the mail.

He eased his car down to the next intersection and made a U-turn. On his second drive-by he was even more impressed with the suspicion that the house was empty, so much so that he pulled to a stop on the opposite side of the road. Bedsheets covered the grimy windows. A couple of birds rummaged through the thick covering of pine needles on the mossy roof. They took wing when a large, fat squirrel dropped from an overhanging limb to the roof. The place was possessed by an overwhelming sense of abandonment.

Another dead end, Whit figured. He got out of his car and started across Oak Street toward the house. He had just reached the other side when the front door opened, and a lean man with a three-day growth of beard came hurrying out. Whit stopped in his tracks.

The man looked out toward the street about that time and saw Whit. Though separated by at least fifty feet of barren yard, their eyes met. Mrs. Winters had provided the prosecutor's office with a photo of Willie Winters as well as one of the child. The guy standing on the porch, wearing a T-shirt that had once been white and cutoff jeans, was the man in the photo supplied by Mrs. Winters.

"Jesus Christ," Whit muttered, knowing that he'd just fucked up. A series of plausible lies raced through Whit's mind, but the man had that sixth sense universally common to those accustomed to dodging cops and debt collectors. Before Whit could even decide on a lie, Winters was turning back to the door.

"Hang on a second!" Whit shouted.

Winters flung open the door and vanished into the inside of the home.

"Way to go, asshole." The comment from Whit was directed at himself rather than at the man. If he abandoned his position now, the guy might rabbit before Whit could get back, especially if he caught a glimpse of Whit's West Virginia tags. He really hadn't left himself much choice. He moved cautiously toward the front door, now wishing he had his weapon even more than his identification.

As he approached the house, he saw one of the sheets covering a window move. The window went up. He darted toward his left, seeking some sort of shelter in the trees bordering the property. When he looked back to the window, the sheet still covered the window and hung very still. He resumed his cautious advance on the house, staying close to the line of trees to his left. As much as he liked Myrtle Beach, he didn't want to die here, not in the grassless, littered yard of this shabby little house.

When he was within a few yards of the house, he decided to reason with Winters. If the little girl was inside, maybe he could talk some sense into her father. On the other hand, he knew there was a good chance that he'd end up in a hostage situation, and he was hardly prepared for that.

"Winters!" he shouted.

The sheet moved, and the ominous outline of a small handgun came into view. Whit dived toward the foundation of the house just as the crack of a gunshot cut through the still afternoon air.

The 911 call was routed to Detective Mike Shaw. When he answered it, he heard what sounded like an old man's voice whispering something.

"You'll have to speak up," he snapped. "I can't hear you."

"Something's goin' on across the street from me. I heard a gunshot, and there's this guy sneaking around a house."

Shaw pulled a pen from his pocket. A yellow legal pad rested on his otherwise clear desktop. "What's your name?"

"Never you mind my name."

"Sir, if we're to respond, we must have your name." As he said that, Shaw glanced at the display on the specially constructed phone. It revealed the phone number from which the man was calling.

"I don't want to be involved," the voice said. "I got no time for that kind of thing."

Shaw pushed a button beside the display. Almost immediately a name appeared on the LCD screen. "Well, sir, based on my information, this call is originating from the residence of Thomas Green. Would you be Mr. Green?"

"How do you know that?" A hint of panic crept into the man's voice.

"Take it easy," Shaw said. "We won't involve you in anything."

"But how do you know who I am?"

"The wonders of modern technology, sir. Now, about this gunshot—"

"I just heard it. I looked out and seen this guy creeping around the house across the street."

Another push of the button and the address 5109 OAK

STREET was displayed on the screen. "Is that across the street from 5109 Oak Street?"

"Yeah, it is. Your fancy stuff tell you that, too?"

"Yes, Mr. Green. Are you looking out your window now?"

"Yessiree."

"Is the man still there?"

There was a pause. "Oh, yeah . . . He's crouching down at the base of the house."

"You just stay in your home, Mr. Green. We'll check it out. Thanks for calling."

"Wait a minute, sonny. That fancy equipment you got there?"

"Yes, sir?"

"Can anyone get it?"

Whit hadn't any idea where the bullet hit—other than it had apparently missed him. He pulled himself up tightly against the block foundation and realized just how badly he'd fucked up. The situation had escalated far beyond his current authority allowed him to go.

"C'mon, Winters! Don't make things worse than they are."

Whit heard the distant slamming of a door, then the sound of someone crashing through underbrush at the rear of the house. Still keeping low, Whit lurched to the corner of the house. For an instant he saw a solitary silhouette ducking through the dense woods.

"Winters!"

The man kept running, the sound quickly diminishing.

"Shit!" Whit eased up and pressed against the house as he worked his way back toward the front door.

"Anyone here?" He waited for a response.

Then he shouted the young girl's name. "Marcia!"

Still no response. A sandhill hornet, its yellow-and-black body thick and sturdy, buzzed around Whit's face, probably attracted by the salty-sweet drops of sweat on the investigator's face. Out of reflex, he swatted at it, snaring it in his hand. The pain was sharp and immediate, just like the stab of a small knife. Whit winced and cursed. He could already feel his hand beginning to swell. The stiff pain throbbed its way up his arm. When a second and then a third humming insect replaced their fallen comrade, he realized he was in a hornet's nest both literally and figuratively.

"Fuck this," he said, dashing toward the front porch. Lowering his shoulder, he hit the door at full speed, his mind imagining a swarm of the loathsome hornets behind him. The doorframe splintered, and Whit crashed into the house.

The odor made him forget the pain in his hand. It was a nauseating mixture made much worse by the stifling heat contained within the house—a potpourri of unpleasantness, some of which Whit could identify. Trash that should have been emptied days before, body odor, the pungent ammoniacal stench of cat piss. Underlying all that was a sickly-sweet aroma that threatened to turn Whit's stomach. Not because it was that overpowering, not yet anyway, but rather because of its irrefutable source. Only one thing smelled like that—the decomposing body of a dead human being.

Suppressing his reflex to gag, he scanned the room in which he stood. It was a living room, sparsely furnished with ratty, squalid furniture, much of which looked as though it had been salvaged from a city dump. The corners of the sagging couch were shredded. Almost at once his eyes settled upon a cat's litter box, so full of rank-smelling excrement that the poor cat had abandoned it and started doing its business around its perimeter.

Whit swallowed. He wanted to go back out the front door, but when he looked through it he saw several hornets swarming just outside, as if the interior's rancid atmosphere held them at bay.

Instead he cleared his throat. "Marcia?" God help the child if she had been brought to this place. "Marcia Winters?"

He moved toward what appeared to be a kitchen. Dirty dishes and glasses cluttered the table and the double sink. Small piles of feces dotted the grimy linoleum floor. The back door itself, the one through which Willie Winters had fled, was open. It was covered, though, by a screen door through which he could see the deep green shadows of the woods behind the house. Whit started toward it, anxious to get out of the stifling air, but his years as a cop stopped him.

The faint odor of death hung in the air. Whit knew its source was somewhere in the house. In his head he had visions of the child. But she had only been gone since yesterday. Not likely that it was her, smelling like that. On the other hand, in this hothouse atmosphere, decomposition would occur very quickly. It would serve much like an incubator to the microorganisms that reduced flesh to its more basic components.

Whit moved to the back door, flung open the screen, and inhaled deeply. The air outside, though growing very warm, was still much cooler than that inside the house. It smelled clean, too, perfumed by the aroma of the pines.

Somewhat braced, he turned back into the house and moved quickly back into the living room. A gentle tinkling, like glass chimes aroused by an early morning breeze, drew his attention to a glass on a table by the decimated sofa. The sound came from the shifting movement of melting ice. The glass was almost empty. A bottle of Southern Comfort sat beside it. Willie Winters had been having a drink before exiting the house. Whit could understand that. A person couldn't live in this place sober.

A closed door on the other side of the living room appeared to be the only other exit from the living room. Whatever dark secrets the house held were concealed behind that door. As he moved toward it, sweat trickled into his right eye. He wiped at it. His heart raced, and he could feel that light-headed sensation that so often preceded a full-blown, gut-emptying bout of nausea.

The intense heat of the midday sun drove Anna back to the air-conditioned sanctuary of the motel room. While she'd never been a sun-worshiper, she had been blessed with a dark complexion from birth. Most everyone assumed she cultivated it by sunbathing. In truth it was her natural skin color, a gift, according to her mother, from some Cherokee heritage far back in their ancestry. Unlike Whit, she didn't find perspiration sexy. She had been reclining on one of the pool lounges for a little more than an hour, and her body had been glistening with perspiration when she decided to abandon it.

Besides, she'd had enough of the woman lounging next to her. The woman had been quiet at first, her attention on her five-year-old son who had been floating in the shallow end of the pool in one of those inflatable plastic doughnuts. But when the child had moved to the comparative safety of the children's pool, the woman had become talkative, first asking how long Anna was staying at the beach, then where she was from, what she did, followed by a continuing series of questions. Anna had started out being polite, asking her questions in response. After the first few, though, she had started offering monosyllabic responses followed by silence in the hope that the woman might get the message. She hadn't.

"Let me guess," the woman had said. "Your husband is a golfer. That's where mine is at. Golfing."

It gave Anna her opening. "Oh, my. Speaking of my husband, I should go start lunch."

"You cook down here?" the woman asked.

Anna had gathered up her towel. "Oh, yes. He demands it."

"Demands it?"

By then, though, Anna was far enough away from her to avoid a response. Once in the motel room, she took a quick shower to wash off the obnoxious sheen of suntan lotion and sweat that contaminated her skin. Then, donning a white robe, she fixed a cold drink of soda and went out onto the balcony overlooking the beach. A single row of institutional beach umbrellas stretched in an unbroken line from one end of her line of vision to the other. Below the umbrellas, in the gentle surf that was washing up on the off-white sand, a steady stream of people of all shapes and sizes ambled up and down.

Anna loved the beach, but she found it difficult to appreciate its beauty while it was being trampled by such an unending parade of people. The sun was high enough in the sky that the balcony roof provided shade, but even then the heat remained muggy and oppressive. She watched the beachcombers for another few minutes before abandoning the balcony and reentering the room.

She was greeted by the ringing of the phone. She hurried to the nightstand and answered it.

"Whitley Pynchon, please." It was a woman's voice, soft and sweet and heavy with a Southern drawl.

"He's not here," Anna said.

"Oh, shucks! I was hoping he would be back."

"Back?" Anna asked. "Back from where?"

"My name's Maude Adcock. I provided Whitley with some information about the person or persons he is seeking. I've uncovered some additional information and would like to pass it along to him."

Whitley? It almost made Anna want to laugh. Almost, but not quite. The way the woman was saying his name—with a kind of lusty sigh—made Anna want to throttle her.

"Well, I'm sorry he isn't back yet, but I'd be glad to pass the information along to him. I'm sure he will—"

"No, thank you," the woman said. "I'll phone him again. Please pardon the ring, and please be sure to tell him I called."

The woman hung up. Anna slammed the phone down. "Bitch!"

SIX

THE DOOR MOVED as soon as Whit's hand touched the knob. The latch hadn't caught . . . or didn't ever catch. Probably the latter given the battered appearance of the door. His first reaction was to ease it open and peek inside, but he couldn't stand the belly-wrenching suspense. After opening it less than an inch, he wrenched it back as quickly as he could. The banshee wail that emanated from within drove him back from the door.

"Oh, dear God," he said as he stared at the huge black cat. It stood on the swollen belly of a woman, its mouth glistening, drooling a blood-tinged mucous. The animal had been feeding on the corpse. It had its hackles raised. The fur on its tail stood out like a wire bottle brush, and its narrow eyes were filled with hate.

Whit swallowed the bile that lifted into his throat. "Shoo! Get!"

He advanced on the animal, but it didn't offer to yield its place atop the rapidly decomposing body. "Scram!" Whit shouted.

It growled, just like a dog might growl in warning. Whit looked around for something, anything, to drive it away from the body. His eyes settled on a dust mop resting on an interior wall of the room. Slowly, keeping his eyes on the enraged cat, he took a sideways step toward it.

"Nice, kitty," Whit said. "Nice, puss." He tried to keep any hint of threat from his voice. "When I get this mop, nice little kittycat, I'm gonna beat the hell outta—"

His foot bumped against something. He glanced down and saw a syringe lying on the floor. He bent down. The cat, seeing his opening, hissed and unleashed a nerve-shattering screech. Whit, stunned that he was about to be attacked by a house cat, reeled backward. The cat sprang, but it never reached him. The earsplitting sound of a gunshot rang out, and the cat was blown apart in a starburst of blood, guts, and fur.

"Christ!" Whit cried, covering his face against the fallout of gore.

"Freeze!" a voice cried.

Whit dropped his bloodied hands from his face and found himself staring at a 9-millimeter handgun. It was held by a short, stocky man in plainclothes. Behind him, a uniformed cop stood gazing at the mutilated body on the bed.

"I'm a cop," Whit said quickly.

"Just stand up. Very slow and easy. Keep your hands high, where I can see them."

"Thanks for taking out the killer cat," Whit said, trying to give his voice a lighthearted tone that wasn't really indicative of his true state of mind.

The plainclothes cop glanced back at his compatriot. "Go radio for assistance. Get the lab boys down here."

"Yes, sir. Right away." The uniform seemed more than glad to escape the death room.

"Look," Whit said, "I am a cop. A special investigator from West Virginia. I—"

"A P.I.?" the plainclothes asked, the distaste obvious in his voice.

"No, a special investigator for a prosecuting attorney— the Raven County prosecuting attorney."

"Okay, pal. Take it slow and easy, and pull out your I.D."

Whit slumped a little.

"Easy, gawdamn it!"

Whit straightened back up. "Sorry. Look, I walked off and left my wallet at the motel. It's the Wildwood Motor Inn, Room 221. I brought my lady down with me. She'll get my I.D. to me."

The detective was short and stocky and reminded Whit of a quick-tempered bulldog. His head was absent of any hair, and his eyes were a cold, heartless hue of gray. At that moment they were narrowed by a wry grin. "Forgot your wallet, huh?"

"Yeah, I'm here on a case. There was a subject here when I arrived. He fired a shot at me and fled through the back door. This guy supposedly grabbed his daughter up in West Virginia yesterday. I have a court order from a judge in my county giving me authority to take the kid back."

The cop's light gray eyes didn't even blink. "The kid here?"

"I haven't found her. I was just looking around when I came upon her." Whit nodded toward the bed. "The cat had been feeding on her."

Still, the cop's expression didn't change. "You always make it a habit of invading some other department's jurisdiction and carrying on an operation without advising that department of your presence?"

Whit shrugged. "I was just trying to track the guy down. I wasn't looking for a confrontation." At that point he dared to lower his arms a little.

"Keep 'em up," the cop snapped. "I'm not buying your little tale, not just yet."

The uniformed officer reappeared. "The lab boys are on the way. I also called for a meat wagon."

The bald cop nodded, then spoke again to Whit. "That your car across the street? The one with the West Virginia license tag?"

"That's it," Whit said, feeling somewhat vindicated. "You can run a license check, and then send a Teletype—"

"Hold it, pal. I know what I can do. So happens I got a report about someone possibly impersonating a police officer about an hour ago. The same license number, and your description."

"That's because it was me, and I'm not impersonating anyone. My wallet's in the motel."

The detective grunted. "What motel was that again?"

Whit repeated the name and room number.

"What's your name?"

"Pynchon. P-Y-N-C-H-O-N. Whit Pynchon."

The plainclothes cop glanced back at his partner. "Call that room. See what you can find out."

"Thanks," Whit said.

"Who's the guy you claim to be after?"

"The subject's name is Willie Winters. I can give you a complete description and record. Apparently he was having a drink, getting ready to leave, with this lady lying dead in here."

"You know who she is?"

"I have an idea," Whit said. "I'd say it's a young woman by the name of Pam Stewart. From what I've managed to learn, her half unit turned up dead several months back down at Pawleys Island. I'm told he was one of your drug dealers."

"How long you been here?" the cop asked.

"Since yesterday evening," Whit said.

"My, my . . . You done discovered a lot in a short time."

"I'm good," Whit said, smiling.

"Or in this up to your lyin' eyes."

The uniformed cop returned. "A woman answered, sir."

"That's Anna," Whit said.

"What did the woman say?"

"She said she hadn't ever heard of anyone by the name this guy gave us."

"Jesus fucking Christ," Whit said.

The bald cop pulled his handcuffs from his belt. "Okay, pal. Assume the position."

"Let me call her."

"We've bothered the lady enough."

"Christ, man. The guy I came after is getting away!"

"So you say. Now assume the gawdamned position. Or do I have to explain what I mean?"

"No, you don't, asshole."

The bald cop grinned. "Good. So do it, fucker." Whit turned to face the wall, the palms of his hands placed high on it. The cop reached up for one, snapped the cuff on it, and brought it down. He pulled the other down and snapped the bracelet closed.

"Honest," Whit said. "The lady at the motel has a weird sense of humor. I'm sure she's back at the motel laughing her ass off."

"I told her where you would be if she changed her mind," the uniformed officer said.

The plainclothes cop glanced back at him. "Did you get the impression she wasn't being truthful?"

The uniform shrugged. "Well, she was laughing quite a bit, but she insisted she didn't know this guy."

* * *

After the phone call from the Myrtle Beach police officer, Anna had gone into the front room of the motel suite and found Whit's wallet lying on the small kitchen table. She picked it up and turned it over in her hands. She didn't plan on letting him stew in custody too long. Besides, he'd probably manage to convince them of his true identity anyway. All they had to do was phone or Teletype Raven County.

She returned to the bedroom that faced the ocean and dressed quickly. Without transportation she would have to call a cab. She phoned the front desk and asked for them to have a cab come after her.

"Ms. Tyree, this is Eloise Martin," the woman at the desk said. The Martins owned the motel. "Did ol' Whit run off and leave you?"

Anna laughed. "Sort of. Actually I think he's just been arrested."

"Whit?"

"Seems so," Anna said. "I need to go get him out."

"What did he do?"

"They probably charged him with impersonating a human being."

The motel owner laughed.

"I gather it's some misunderstanding," Anna said, then started to explain. "And absentminded ol' Whit went off without his identification."

"The chief of police is a personal friend of ours. I'd be glad to give him a call."

"Thanks," Anna said. "If I can get to the police station, I think I can straighten things out."

"It isn't too far. Why don't I drive you there?"

"I'd hate to put you out, and—"

"Nonsense. Whit's like a member of the family. He's been

staying here with us for ten years or more. I've got plenty of help in the office. You come on down when you're ready.''

Anna thanked the woman and hung up. She finished dressing and stepped out of her room into the sultry Carolina swelter, almost colliding with the woman who had been sitting beside her at the pool.

''On your way shopping, I bet,'' the woman said.

Anna shook her head. ''No. Actually I have to go bail my fellow out of jail.''

''You people do know how to use a Teletype, I hope.'' Whit sat at the balding detective's desk. A nameplate attached to the front indicated that his name was MICHAEL P. HARDY.

Hardy, seated behind the desk, was rubbing his shiny scalp with his hand, studying some documents that had been waiting for him in his desk.

''Did you hear me?'' Whit asked.

''I heard you.''

''Well, do I get an answer?''

The detective looked up. ''I didn't hear a question.''

''I asked if your people know how to use a Teletype.''

''Funny,'' Hardy said. ''I heard you expressing the hope that our people knew how to use the Teletype.''

Whit threw up his hands. ''Great. I've got a kidnapper, you've got a possible murderer . . . getting away, and you wanna play word games.''

Hardy returned his attention to the documents in his hands. ''I can assure you that we have the area into which the man fled cordoned off. We'll find him.''

''You haven't even gotten a description from me for chrissakes. I have a mug shot of him back at the motel.''

''You say his name is Willie Winters?'' Hardy asked.

"I suspect that's the man's name. I got a pretty good look at him as he fled into the woods. He looks like my man."

Hardy dropped the stack of papers on the desk and slid it across to Whit. Attached to the top sheet was a photograph, a mug shot of Willie Winters.

"You've had him in custody?" Whit asked, studying the grainy head shot.

Hardy nodded. "Several times. Never for anything serious. Once because his girlfriend—Pam Stewart—filed a complaint against him for abusing her. Another time, quite recently, for public intoxication."

The phone on Hardy's desk rang. He picked it up and listened for a moment. "I figured that." His gaze flicked over to Whit. "I'll be out with him in a minute."

"Do you believe me now?" Whit asked.

Hardy shrugged. "I guess so—but lemme tell you one thing, Pynchon. Next time you come prowling in my backyard, you best lemme know you're here. I wouldn't come up to West Virginia playing the Lone Ranger, and I don't tolerate it down here. Gets me shittin', pal."

It was a phrase Whit hadn't heard before. Still, he wasn't about to kowtow. "Like I said, Hardy . . . I was just trying to get the lay of the land. It was a case of being at the wrong place at the wrong time."

Hardy leaned back in his chair. "Well, I hate to tell you this, Pynchon, but your man Winters?"

"What about him?"

"He was in the wrong place at the right time. When did you say the kid was snatched?"

"Just before noon yesterday."

"Then you best check out that disposition sheet. Winters was in our jail night 'fore last. He was released yesterday mornin' at ten."

"You're kidding!" Whit snatched up the report, studying the case sheet beneath the photo.

"If he managed to get up to West Virginia in less than two hours, then maybe he grabbed the kid. You think he managed that?"

"Mother of God," Whit muttered.

"So see? . . . If you had let me know you were in town yesterday, then the real kidnapper wouldn't have a full day's head start on you."

Whit, his jaw clenched, stood and started to pace Hardy's office. "I guess I did blow this one."

Hardy was nodding. "Yeah, if you dumb hillbillies had known how to use a Teletype, you coulda saved yourself the trip altogether."

Whit ignored the comment. "Can I borrow your phone? I'll reverse the charges."

Hardy slid the bulky instrument across the desk. "I'll be back in a second."

The short cop marched out of his office. Whit reached for his pocket to pull out his credit card when he remembered he didn't have it. He called the operator and placed a collect call to the Raven County prosecuting attorney. Within moments he had Tony Danton on the other end.

"Don't call the operator, Pynchon. Use your card."

"I don't have it with me," Whit said. "It's a long story, but the short of it is that we read this one wrong."

"What are you talking about?"

"Willie Winters has a foolproof alibi. Looks like we've got an honest-to-God kidnapping." He filled Tony in on the frustrating events of the morning.

When he was finished, Tony asked, "Are you coming back?"

"Yeah. I feel like a gawdamned fool. We better start over at that day-care center. You might get some of Gil Dickerson's guys to start interviewing the neighbors. Maybe somebody saw something.''

Dickerson was the sheriff of Raven County and one of Whit's closest friends.

"The center's in the Milbrook city limits," Tony countered. "I'll have to call on the city guys."

"Fuck the city guys, Tony. They can screw up a wet dream. Just ask Gil's guys to handle it quietly."

"Damn, Whit. You're four hundred miles away, and you still wanna run the show. The city guys can—and will—handle the neighborhood interviews."

"Maybe you just oughta wait until I get back," Whit said, trying to take another tack.

"We've lost too much time already."

"One last thing, Tony. Get hold of Mrs. Winters and ask her if someone else coulda grabbed the kid on her ex-husband's behalf. Do it quick."

"I shouldn't have any trouble with that. She's been calling the office every hour on the hour."

Whit checked the number on Hardy's phone and gave it to Tony. "I'll stay here until I hear from you. I'm at the Myrtle Beach Police Department."

"How's the weather?" Tony asked.

"Too damn nice to leave."

Hardy reentered his office just as Whit was hanging up the phone. Anna, accompanied by Eloise Martin, walked in behind him. Hardy was smiling, brandishing Whit's wallet.

"Nice of you to remember me," Whit said.

Anna settled down on the corner of Hardy's desk. "You had a call at the motel room. I think her name was Maude Adcock."

"Oh, Jesus." Whit had given her the name of the hotel in

case she remembered anything else, but he hadn't expected to hear from her. He shook his head. "What did she want?"

"You . . . from the sound of her voice."

"So, just because you had a fit of jealous rage, you caused Hardy and his guys all this trouble?"

For the first time since Whit had met the Myrtle Beach cop, Hardy was smiling. "Oh, she didn't cause us any problems."

Whit shook his head. "Okay, let's just forget it. It's water under the bridge."

"What about this Adcock woman?" Anna asked. "She's still kinda jammed under my bridge."

Whit looked from Hardy back to Anna. "Can we discuss this later?"

"Something you're withholding from me?" Hardy asked.

"Or from me?" Anna said.

"From neither one of you. I was chasing down an address on Pawleys Island. She had known the Stewarts when they lived there. She got me Pam Stewart's address."

"Does she know her that well?" Hardy asked.

"No, not really."

Hardy pursed his lips, then said, "Then how exactly did she know about the address on Oak Street?"

"She took me to a source to whom I guaranteed confidentiality. I intend to abide by that promise. I can assure you, Hardy, that this person can shed no light on your case."

"I get the impression," the detective said, "that you can be a stubborn son of a bitch, Pynchon. Trouble is, so can I. Why don't you let me decide what's important in my case, and what's not?"

"You're half right in both cases. I'm stubborn, and you're a son of a bitch. As to my source, it could get the subject in trouble," Whit countered. "I have no intention of doing that, not when I know it's a dead end."

"So what's this Adcock woman want with you now?" Anna asked.

Whit threw up his hands. "How the hell do I know?"

"If you don't, I do," Anna said.

Whit looked at her in disbelief. "What's got you so riled?"

"That woman! She kept calling you Whitley."

"That's my name."

"You hate being called Whitley."

Hardy just sat back, enjoying the browbeating Whit was taking.

"Trust me, Anna. It was tough, but I resisted. She's rather attractive, rather rich, and she has a place on Pawleys Island. If ever I was gonna be tempted—"

He didn't get to finish. Anna jumped down from the desk and marched out of the room.

"You two get along this well all the time?" Hardy asked.

"She's a damned journalist. You know how obnoxious they can be."

The phone on Hardy's desk rang. He answered it and handed it to Whit. "For you."

"I talked to Mrs. Winters," Tony said. "She says if her husband didn't nab the kid, then it was his parents doing it for him. I think she's just grasping at straws, but stay down there and see if they catch Winters. Maybe he knows something. I'll get things rolling up here."

"Where do Winters's parents live?"

"Lexington, Kentucky. I'm gonna try to contact them by phone, but I'd say it's a waste of time."

"Ten-four," Whit said. "See you when I get back there."

Whit handed the phone back to Hardy. He dropped it in the cradle. "You heading back now?"

Whit shook his head. "I'm going to wait around to see if you get Winters. His ex-wife thinks someone grabbed the kid for him—like maybe his parents."

"Sounds like bullshit to me, Pynchon."

"Me, too. Will you give me a chance to talk to Winters when—or if—you get him?"

Hardy fiddled with a mechanical pencil. "I dunno. Can you tell me who your confidential source is?"

Whit's face reddened. "You're asking me to break my word."

"If this source is a dead end, I promise it will stop here with me."

Whit eyed the cop. "I guess I don't have a lot of choice. It was the postmistress at Pawleys Island."

Hardy broke down in laughter.

"What's so damned funny?" Whit asked.

"Was that the major state secret? Hell, we get that kinda info all the time from postal authorities . . . on the sly, of course. I'll keep your secret."

Whit stood. "Thanks. Can I get into this search for Winters?"

"You just go on back to your motel and relax. I'll call you when we find him."

Whit shrugged. "Can't blame me for trying. Any idea yet on the girl's cause of death?"

"We're figuring it was an overdose. For now we're assuming it was administered, either intentionally or accidentally, by this fella from up your way."

"You gonna charge him?"

"He's charged already, based upon your statement that you saw him fleeing the scene and recognized him. Who knows? Maybe you'll even get to come back and testify."

"I'll take any excuse to get to the beach," Whit said. He started to leave.

"One thing, Pynchon."

Whit stopped and turned back to the detective. "What's that?"

"The lady there tells me you really like our area."

"She's right. I hope to relocate here before too much longer."

Hardy was still playing with the pencil. "Do me a favor. Check out Hilton Head or maybe even Florida. Maybe you'll like them better."

SEVEN

WHIT FELT LIKE a chained animal waiting to burst out of his cage. Six hours had passed since he'd been released from custody, and as far as he knew Willie Winters was still free. Maybe Winters had nothing to do with the abduction of his daughter, but Whit still wanted a chance to talk to him. He'd called Hardy forty-five minutes ago, but the detective had left for dinner.

He stared down at the remainder of the sausage-and-mushroom pizza they'd ordered for dinner, then over at Anna, who was sitting on the couch with her legs curled beneath her as she read a novel. She'd wanted to go out to dinner, but Whit had insisted they get a take-out meal, just in case Hardy called. They'd eaten in silence, but their disagreement over dinner wasn't the only thing that had come between them. Even though she wouldn't admit it, Anna was still annoyed by the call she'd received from Maude Adcock. When Whit had asked more about what Maude had said, Anna had refused to say anything more about it. He hadn't bothered asking for Maude's phone number. That would've upset Anna even more, and probably wouldn't have produced a phone number, either. The only thing to do was wait for Hardy's call.

"I think I want to go home tomorrow," Anna said, breaking the silence.

"If they catch Winters and let me talk to him, I'll be ready."

"Let's go tomorrow regardless. You said yourself that Winters probably doesn't have a thing to do with the reason you came here."

He didn't want to argue, and just then the phone rang. Thank God. As he reached across the table, he snapped the headset to his ear so fast that the cord caught the corner of the pizza box, sending the remainder of dinner onto the floor.

"Pynchon," he answered, looking down at the mess.

"Well, hello, Whitley," a sexy voice said.

Christ. Just what he needed. "Hi, Maude. What can I do for you?" Whit saw Anna close her book and watch him.

"I hope I'm not disturbing you and your friend. I just wanted to tell you what else I found out about the man you're looking for. I thought you'd be interested."

"Well, the police are on it now. I'm just waiting for them to pick him up."

"Why wait? If he's not at the address you got earlier, I think I know where he is."

"You do? Where? I'll tell the police."

"They're going to have to hurry, because he's leaving."

"What are you talking about?" he barked.

"Calm down, Whitley. I'm just trying to help you."

"Sorry." He glanced up as Anna walked out onto the balcony.

"That's better. You see, I mentioned to my next-door neighbor that Willie was in trouble, and he told me that a friend of his had hired Willie to work on the crew of his yacht."

"You mean he's on the yacht now?"

"I don't know, but they're supposed to leave tonight for the Caribbean."

"Where's the yacht?"

"At the marina. Right here on the island."

"What's the name of the yacht?"

"I don't know. But tell them to check Slip Thirty-two. Like I said, if they wait around, they're going to miss him."

"Thanks. I appreciate this. You've been real helpful."

"Anytime, Whitley. And, look me up the next time you're here. I mean, if you're free."

Whit cleared his throat, glanced out to the balcony, where Anna was staring into the night. "I better go. Thanks again."

Whit got a dial tone, then called Hardy's office. The phone rang five times before it was answered.

"Is Hardy there?"

"He's not at his desk."

"Christ. Take this message. Willie Winters is on a yacht at the marina on Pawleys Island. Slip Thirty-two."

"Pawleys Island? That's out of our jurisdiction."

"Just give him the message, please."

"Who's calling?"

"Whit Pynchon. Hardy is still on the Winters case, isn't he?"

"The search was called off an hour ago. But I'll pass this information on to him."

"Make it fast. The yacht's leaving anytime. You got that?"

"What's your telephone number?"

"He's got it." Whit slammed down the phone. He was furious. "Son of a bitch. Jesus Christ."

He stepped out on the balcony. Anna was staring out toward the ocean, where the waves were rhythmically crashing onto the beach. A breeze was blowing through her hair, and she looked like a goddess. "Well, I think I've found out where Winters is, but I'm not sure what Hardy is going to do.''

''Who tipped you off?''

''Maude. Her next-door neighbor knows Willie.''

''No comment.''

''Listen, I've got to go to the marina.''

Anna spun around, looking at him for the first time since he'd joined her on the balcony. ''Oh, so you are going right ahead and interfering with local police work. Exactly what Hardy told you not to do.''

''Not if they respond to my call. I'm just going to see if I can talk to Winters after the arrest.''

''I'll come with you.''

''No, you stay here. There's no need for you to go. Besides, he had a gun this morning—and there's the outside chance that the cops won't have arrested him by the time I get there.''

Anna looked glumly at him. ''Suit yourself, Whit.''

He reached out and laid a hand on Anna's arm. He started to say that he was sorry he'd joked about Maude Adcock, if that's what was bothering her, but held off.

''I've given them plenty of time to respond.'' He leaned over, bussed her on the cheek, but she didn't react. ''Be back as soon as I can.''

He walked over to his suitcase, which lay next to the bed, and picked up his snub-nosed .357 and shoulder holster. He didn't want Anna to see him arming himself so he wrapped it in a windbreaker and headed for the door.

''Damn him,'' Anna muttered as she heard the door slam. If she'd known how this so-called vacation was going to turn out, she would've stayed home. Whit was so stubborn. And that woman. That horrible, perfect woman. She didn't want to think about her any longer.

Just then the phone rang. "Hello?"

"It's Detective Hardy. Is Pynchon there?"

"He just left. Did you get his message?"

"I sure did. He's *not* going to that yacht, is he?"

"I think he is."

"Can you stop him?"

"Just a second." She laid down the phone and hurried out to the balcony—just in time to see Whit pulling out of the parking lot. "No, he's gone. I hope you sent somebody out to that marina."

"That's just it. The coast guard's been staking out the yacht for the last three hours. I hope to hell he doesn't mess things up. Damn it. I better get over there."

The phone clicked. Anna closed her eyes. "Oh, Whit. You've done it this time."

She had to do something. She couldn't just wait here to find out what happened. She picked up the phone and dialed the desk. Eloise Martin answered on the second ring. "Eloise, this is Anna again. Are you busy?"

"Not at all. It's dead as January at the moment."

Anna tried to think what she should say. "Could I come down and talk to you? It's about Whit again."

"Oh, my. Don't tell me he's gotten himself arrested again?"

"Not exactly. I'll be right down."

He was only a few blocks short of the marina when Whit found himself tangled in a traffic jam created by a minor accident on Highway 17. There were three police cruisers on the scene, and he gritted his teeth at the sight of the patrolmen standing around the fender bender. Why weren't they going after Winters? If the authorities weren't on the scene, he was going to be damned pissed. He wasn't even sure that he had the authority to arrest Winters now that he knew the suspect couldn't possibly have abducted his daughter.

He crept around the accident and did all he could to hold his tongue when one of the uniforms impatiently waved him through the scene. He squeezed the steering wheel and stared straight ahead. As soon as he was past the vehicles, he stepped on the gas, and the tires on the rental spewed loose gravel behind him. He glanced in the rearview mirror, hoping that one of the uniforms would come after him.

No such luck.

He pulled into the marina a couple of minutes later and abandoned the car in the parking lot. Streetlights lit the concrete walkway, and his shadow stretched behind him. He had no idea where to look for Slip Thirty-two, and there was no one around to ask. Cautiously he stepped on to the network of docks. Only the moonlight and an occasional light from inside one of the boats illuminated the docks.

After passing several yachts he stopped by a weathered wood post and ran his fingers over the number Seven inscribed on it. He returned to the main walk and jogged past a couple of docks. He tried again. This time he found number Twenty-six right away. He started to move forward, but hesitated. Something was wrong; he could feel it. Then he saw the woman crouched in the shadow on the deck of the yacht next to number Twenty-six.

He couldn't see what she was doing, but he knew she was watching him. "Can I help you?" she asked.

"Sorry. I didn't mean to stare. Do you know where I can find Slip Thirty-one?"

He intentionally picked a number one off from his target.

The woman was quiet a moment. Then she answered in a low, soft voice. "It's empty. They're gone."

Whit peered down the line of vessels, saw the empty slip. "No wonder I can't get a hold of him." He strolled off, still puzzling over the woman who'd been huddled in the dark. But then he found Slip Thirty-two and focused his thoughts on the matter at hand. The yacht was at least seventy feet long. A single dim light burned from somewhere inside, but there was no one on deck. No cops swarming over it. No handcuffed suspect. Just darkness and silence.

"Figures."

He walked past the vessel, keeping to the shadows, trying not to appear too interested in the yacht. When he was sure no one was on the deck, he decided to take a closer look. Maybe Winters was napping as he waited for the owner or other crew members to show up.

He boarded the vessel, moved across the deck, and cautiously tried the door handle. Locked. Now what? He peered over at the window where he'd seen the light. Why not? He edged along a narrow strip of deck, hanging on to a metal rail, and then peered into the window.

A low-wattage bulb was burning, and in the dim light he glimpsed a neat galley, but no sign anyone was around. He moved back along the side of the vessel, wondering what to do next, when he heard a noise. He stopped, listened. Voices.

Christ. Great timing. Winters was here, and he wasn't alone. He reached under his arm, patted his side. In his rush to get here, he'd forgotten his weapon in the car. First his wallet, now the .357.

He pressed against the side of the yacht as he heard footsteps crossing the deck. Someone tried the door; it rattled in its casing. "Well, where is he?"

"I saw him get on, and he didn't get off."

Goddamn. They were talking about him. He peered down at a puddle of moonlight on the black waters below him. The next boat was a dozen feet away, too far to jump. The water was his only hope, but they'd hear the splash.

Light suddenly exploded in his face. "Hold it right there!" a voice ordered. "Police."

"Okay. But I'm not Winters," Whit answered.

"Damn it, Pynchon!" a familiar voice barked. "Get your ass off this boat before I arrest you for trespassing."

"Hardy, what took you so long?"

He didn't answer until Whit had crawled back to the main deck. "You just fucked up a stakeout. The coast guard's been waiting for Winters to get here."

"You knew about the boat?" He glanced at the man and woman with Hardy and recognized the woman as the one he'd spoken with a few minutes ago.

"Yeah. We've got sources, too," Hardy snapped. "I want you out of here. Get back to your motel and stay there. If I run into you again in this investigation, I'm going to lock you up. You got that?"

"Someone coming," one of the coastguardsmen said.

"Get down," Hardy hissed.

Ten seconds that took at least an hour passed before a figure came into sight on the dock. He stopped at Slip Thirty-two and looked as if he were about to climb aboard. But something stopped him.

"Hold it, Winters. Don't move," Hardy yelled.

The man was stunned, but he didn't try to flee. "I'm not Winters. Who are you?"

"Police."

"My name's Lance Higgins, and you're on my boat. What's going on?"

As Hardy and the guardsmen talked with Higgins, Whit

climbed down to the dock. "I have no idea where Winters is," the yacht owner said as Whit walked away. "He was supposed to be here getting everything ready."

Hardy was right. He'd fucked up again. He'd had enough for one day. He'd go back to the hotel, and tomorrow, if Winters was still missing, he and Anna would leave.

He reached the parking lot, unlocked the car, and was about to slide into the driver's seat when the door of a nearby car opened. He couldn't believe it. "What are you doing here?"

"Eloise Martin drove me over," Anna answered as she walked over to him. She waved to the woman, who pulled away. "I just wanted to make sure everything was okay."

Whit frowned. "Are you spying on me?"

"I was worried about you. Hardy called."

"I told you to stay out of this. Let's go."

"What about Winters?"

Whit slammed the door shut. "What about him?"

"Did they catch him? Did you talk to him? What happened?" she asked as she sat down. "I'm not interviewing you, for God's sake. I'm just asking you a question."

"Several."

Anna reached for something on the floor. "What is this, your gun? You're just throwing it on the floor now?"

Whit turned on the ignition and glanced up into the rearview mirror. He was about to back out when he spotted someone moving under a streetlamp at the edge of the parking lot and recognized him instantly. Willie Winters.

"Give it to me."

"What?"

"Now." He took the shoulder holster and quickly strapped it on.

"What are you doing?"

"My job."

Winters was just twenty feet away. Whit reached for the door handle. He knew he could take him, but Anna grabbed his arm. "You're not supposed to get involved."

"Don't worry about it."

Anna's reaction slowed Whit, and Winters was walking faster than he'd thought. He was already too far away to stop without a chase.

"Gawdamn it to hell, Anna. You're interfering with my duties."

Whit watched Winters move along the walkway. As he disappeared from sight, Whit opened the car door. "Stay here," he told Anna. "Don't get out."

Maybe Hardy didn't want him involved, but he could damn well act as a backup. He hurried across the lot and took up a position at the base of a set of steps leading up to the walkway. He'd no sooner stopped when he heard footsteps pounding along one of the docks. Suddenly Winters burst into view. But instead of taking the steps, he leaped over the wood railing.

Whit crashed into Winters and pinned him to the pavement. He grabbed a handful of hair as he pulled out his .357.

"Don't even think about moving."

"Who the fuck are you?" Winters snarled.

Whit jammed the barrel of the gun to Winter's temple.

"Where's your daughter? What did you do with her?"

"I don't know what the fuck you're talking about."

Just then Hardy and the others reached the railing. "What the hell!" Hardy said, trying to catch his breath.

"This who you're looking for?" Whit asked.

EIGHT

WHIT KNOCKED on the front door of the FunTime Day-Care Center precisely at 9:00 A.M. As he waited for someone to answer, he could hear the voices of children from inside. It sounded as if there were a houseful, each one shouting that someone was at the door. Seconds later, a matronly woman eased it open. She was wiping her hands on an apron as she stared at Whit. "Can I help you?"

Whit displayed his identification. "Are you Mrs. Clara Harrison?"

"What's wrong?" she asked, her grandmotherly face twisted by concern.

"I need to talk to you about Marcia Winters."

"Have you found her father?"

"Yes, ma'am. But we don't think he had anything to do with the kidnapping."

She gasped, covering her mouth with her hand. "Then who on earth would have done such a thing?"

"May I come in?" Whit asked.

The woman glanced back over her shoulder at the gaggle of children who had huddled behind her. Her eyes settled on the biggest. "Tommy, keep your eye on the children."

The boy looked at Whit, then back at Mrs. Harrison. "Yes, ma'am."

She stepped out onto the porch.

"Is he yours?" Whit asked.

"Lord, no. That's Tommy. He's the oldest, and he sorta keeps the others in line."

"How many do you keep?"

She settled down into a swing that hung from chains attached to the porch roof. The rafters to which it was addressed popped and cracked under her weight. "I only have six regular paying ones. But I got a few more than that today, 'cause I'm just baby-sitting for a friend of mine."

Whit leaned against a post that supported the roof of the porch. "As I said, Mrs. Harrison, we don't think Marcia's father was involved in her abduction. So we're going to have to go back to square one. Is there anything you can tell us?"

She thought for a moment. "No, sir. I think I told the city policeman everything. I was on the phone with Ms. Wyse. She's with the welfare department. The kids were out in back playing, and—"

"Do you usually leave the kids alone in the yard?"

She blinked. "It's fenced. The phone rang. I went in to answer it. Happens all the time."

"And then?" Whit asked.

"Usually the kids play in the yard when I'm getting lunch ready. I can watch them from my kitchen sink. I was only on the phone for a few minutes. Tommy came running in about Marcia."

"What time was this?"

The woman shook her head. "My goodness, I'm not sure I can pinpoint it. After lunch, I think."

"I thought you said the kids usually played in the yard while you fixed lunch."

She seemed to tremble. "It's a little chilly this morning. Fall's in the air. Uh . . . now about the time. I'm almost certain it was after lunch that day. I don't really have a set schedule. I mean, I feed lunch at the same time every day, but sometimes the kids go out afterward . . . while I'm washing dishes.''

''So you didn't actually see what happened?''

''No, sir. Like I'm trying to tell you, it was Tommy that came in and told me.''

Whit had studied the sketchy report prepared by the city officer who had answered the call. ''The children say it was a man in a clown's mask. Is that right?''

The woman shrugged. ''I believe so. To be honest, Mr.— uhh?''

''Pynchon.''

''Mr. Pynchon, I haven't talked with them about it. The policeman did. I felt it was best to let them forget it.''

''I'm afraid I'll want to talk with them, Mrs. Harrison.''

At that point Clara Harrison tensed. ''Not here, you won't. Not without permission from their parents.''

Her reaction surprised Whit. ''You don't seem to understand the gravity of this, Mrs. Harrison. We have a child abducted from your backyard. It's certainly possible that the children can tell me something that will help. I don't see what possible harm—''

''Nosiree! I won't allow it! Not without the parents' permission.''

''If you had been as devoted to your duty the day before last, perhaps this wouldn't have happened.''

She lurched up from the swing. ''Now you see here, mister. I run a good program here. You ask any of the parents. Someone cut a hole in my fence and took that child while—''

''While you weren't watching them,'' Whit said sharply. ''I'd like to see the damage to the fence.''

"It's in back. You can go around the side of the house."

"Would you come with me?" Whit asked.

"I'll go through the house and get my sweater. You go around the side." Her attitude had become openly hostile.

"After that," Whit said, "I'll want to talk to the children."

"I've done told you . . . not in my house you won't. Don't you have to have something like a warrant to come in my house?"

Whit shook his head, a weary smile on his face. "Mrs. Harrison, don't you feel the slightest bit responsible for what happened?"

"Nosiree!"

"What if Mrs. Winters decides to sue because you failed to provide adequate protection for her child?"

The woman's face had been gathering more color throughout the conversation. At those words, she almost turned purple. "I don't have to listen to this. You can just talk to my lawyer."

"You *are* going to let me see the fence?"

"Sure, you can go see the fence, but I'm not gonna answer any more of your questions. You come here to my house and treat me like I'm some kinda criminal. Well, I'm not, mister. Like I told you, I run a good day care, and—"

Whit held up his hand. "I'll just go around to the side."

"You wait for me to come back there and open the gate," she said, her anger still festering. "And you just look at the fence. That's all."

When Whit got around to the rear of the Harrisons' home, he was surprised to see a well-installed, six-foot-high chain link. In his mind he had imagined something much less secure. The gate itself was secured by a large padlock. The fence surrounded a large grassy area decorated with a set of swings and a playhouse. Several other toys littered the ground.

Mrs. Harrison, wearing an old blue sweater dotted by snags in the material, came out of her house and unlocked the gate.

"I'm impressed by the fence," Whit said as he stepped into the backyard.

"You should be," she said coldly. "It cost us a lotta money."

"Where's the damage?"

She guided him toward the very back of the play area. "It's there. Behind that bush."

Whit went to the bush to which she was pointing and pulled back some foliage. Whoever had grabbed Marcia had probably used bolt cutters to slice through the thick chain link. The rend in the fencing ran a good four feet. Pieces of metal coat hangers had been used to repair the damage.

He bent down and examined the cleanly severed metal strands. "It took quite a while to do this," he said. "How long were you on the phone?"

"Not more than five minutes before Tommy came to get me."

Whit looked up at her. "You're sure?"

" 'Course I'm sure. You callin' me a liar now?"

"No, ma'am."

He stood up and looked through the chain link at the thick stand of trees behind it. The leaves had yet to start changing, and it was difficult to see more than a few feet into the dense vegetation.

"Had you noticed any strangers hanging around the neighborhood before—I mean, like several days before—Marcia's abduction?"

"No, sir."

"And you're still not going to let me talk to the children?"

She had her hands on her wide hips. "I done told you I wasn't."

"Then please provide me with a list of their parents' names and addresses."

"Me and my husband are gonna talk to our lawyer before we give you anything, mister."

Whit's patience was wearing thin. "Look, lady—as far as I'm concerned, you might have been a part of this kidnapping. If you really want to start playing hardball, I'll haul you down to the courthouse for questioning right now."

Her expression turned from hostility to fear. "You can't do that. I got no one else to stay with the kids."

"Not my problem," Whit snapped. "Do I get those names, or do you come with me?"

"But the kids—"

"We'll call welfare and have the kids turned over to them until their parents can pick them up," Whit said.

"You wouldn't?"

"Try me."

"I'll get you a list," she said, "but you aren't gonna talk to the kids . . . Leastways not in my house, not without—"

"I know," Whit said, interrupting her. "Not without their parents' permission. Just get me the list."

She hesitated, then said, "You go around and wait on the front porch so I can lock up back here."

"By the way, put your name and your husband's on that list, along with your social security numbers."

"Our social security numbers?"

"Just for my report," Whit said.

A few minutes later she came out the front door with the piece of paper in her hand. Whit accepted it from her and counted the names. Excluding the names of Mrs. Harrison and her husband, there were ten others on the list.

"I thought you just kept six kids," Whit said.

"I do. Never more than six paying ones."

"But there are the names of ten parents on here."

"Some come some days. Some don't. I'm careful, mister. I never have more than—"

Again Whit interrupted her. "Okay, I get the picture. What was the name of the woman you were talking to on the phone? The one from the welfare department."

"Why?" she asked.

Whit rolled his eyes. "Christ, lady! Do you know how serious a crime was committed here?"

"Wyse," she said quickly. "Norma Wyse. That's W-Y-S-E, I think."

"What did she want?" Whit asked.

"Just to talk about some welfare business involving the kids."

Whit wrote her name down on the paper the woman had given him.

"I'm gonna call my lawyer about you," she said then, her final act of defiance.

"Good. Maybe he or she'll straighten you out."

"I think you're blowing this all out of proportion, Anna." The advice came to her from her employee and friend, Kathy Binder, owner and publisher of the *Milbrook Daily Journal*. The two women were seated in Anna's newly redecorated office.

The miniblinds that covered the expanse of glass surrounding her office were open, and Anna imagined that all the eyes in the newsroom, a total of three pairs, were on her. Anna stood and started closing them. "I'm going to leave a message to the maintenance people to stop opening these damned things.''

Kathy suppressed a smile. ''Relax, Anna. You're beginning to become as cantankerous as Whit.''

''It's a matter of self-defense,'' Anna said as she returned to her chair.

The two women were as different in physical appearance as they were alike in philosophy and loyalty to each other. Anna's figure was full and lush. Kathy was thin to the point of being bony. Anna could wear anything—jeans, baggy sweatshirts, any evening dress right off the rack. No matter . . . she always looked ravishing. Kathy, on the other hand, selected those styles that offset her lack of a figure. Because of the inheritance from her husband, she was able to compensate for her frail frame. Very blond and fair-skinned, she refused even to open the curtains of her home until she had applied her makeup . . . painted on her face, as she liked to say.

''Did you talk to Whit about it? You-all were in the same car together for what . . . five hours?''

''Seven hours,'' Anna said. ''And no, I didn't. In fact, I don't think we said ten words to each other during the whole trip home.''

Kathy couldn't help herself. She chuckled.

''It's not funny!''

''For God's sakes, Anna! What on earth is the big deal?''

Tears actually welled up in Anna's eyes. ''I don't know. That's what makes me so damned mad. I think I'm as upset with myself as I am with him. In the two years we've been together, I've never once considered the possibility that he might find someone else. Not once, Kathy. I've kidded him about his rare fits of jealousy, but I thought I was above that.''

"Maybe you're getting that marriage bug again."

Anna's eyes snapped up at Kathy. "You and Gil aren't married."

"Gil and I don't live together." Gil Dickerson, the sheriff of Raven County, and Kathy had been seeing each other, thanks to Anna's matchmaking, for over a year.

"Besides," Kathy continued, "Gil and I have this unspoken assumption that very soon we *will* get married. If our past lives had been somewhat less traumatic, I'm sure we would have already made the leap."

Dickerson had lost his wife just a few months before Kathy's husband had died. When Anna had first tried to get the two together, they both were still in their respective periods of mourning. It had been a halting romance at first, but as time passed it had flourished without any further assistance or "meddling," as Whit called it.

"I don't think that's it at all," Anna said in response to her friend's suggestion.

"C'mon, Anna. This is me you're talking to. You have real doubts whether you will ever marry Whit . . . doubts whether Whit will ever want to marry. I have doubts, too. I like Whit, but he's certainly a little eccentric."

"Eccentric?"

"Yes, Anna. He can be weird. He has more moods than I have dresses."

"He only has two moods, Kathy—bad and worse." Kathy laughed, and for the first time since getting back to the office, so did Anna.

"Maybe I am overreacting, Kathy, but you should have heard that bitch's voice on the phone. Then Whit has the unmitigated gall to tell me that she's pretty, rich, and has a house at the beach. Ooohhhh!" Anna clenched both her hands into fists. "I could have kicked him right in the—" The phone on her desk interrupted her. She grabbed it up.

"Yes. What do you want?"

Kathy watched a weary frown come over her editor's face as Anna listened. Finally she said, "Okay, give me about thirty seconds, then send her back."

"What's up?" Kathy asked as Anna hung up the phone.

"I need this like I need a cold sore."

"What?"

Anna massaged her temples. "The girl who was abducted?"

"Yes."

"Her mother's here to see me. She says the police aren't doing anything to find her daughter, and she thinks we should do a story."

Kathy started to get up. "I'll let you handle it."

"Oh, no! You stay put. I want a witness to this conversation. After all, I do have some personal involvement in this matter, and I want the lady to know it up front."

"That's fair," Kathy said.

Since Whit had last visited the local welfare office, the agency had changed its name and moved. He found that out only after he'd made the mistake of driving to the address where he remembered it being located. The building still served people down on their luck, but now it housed a used-clothing store instead of the welfare agency. When he asked where the Department of Welfare had gone, the woman at the counter in the store had looked at him with obvious hostility.

"They don't call it that now, mister," she snapped. "It's the West Virginia Department of Human Services."

Whit shrugged in surrender. "Yes, ma'am. I guess I forgot. It's been awhile since I've had any dealings with them."

"You're lucky," she said. "They ain't nice people to deal with anymore. Better when they was worried about folks welfare, not their human services."

She directed him to one of the many strips of storefronts that were reproducing like rabbits on the outskirts of Milbrook, then added, "Folks who live here in the center of town gotta get a taxi to get to it. I think they moved out there on purpose."

Whit yawned as he climbed back in his car. He'd driven through the night from Myrtle Beach, stopping only for coffee and the rest room. Anna had slept most of the way, which was just as well because she wasn't talking to him. Wasn't talking any more than Willie Winters. But the puzzled expression on Winters's face when Whit had asked about his daughter had told Whit all he'd needed to know. The man might be a murderer, but he hadn't kidnapped his daughter. Whit had slept four hours when they'd finally arrived in Milbrook, and had started his day at noon.

When he arrived at the small shopping plaza, he quickly found the building housing the Department of Human Services. It was the place doing the most business. He parked his car as close as he could and headed into the state agency. The small front lobby was standing-room only. He wedged his way through the old people and the kids to a glass window that separated the receptionist from her agitated clientele. He stood there for a couple of minutes, waiting to be acknowledged. The woman behind the glass, a thin, dark-haired girl hardly out of her teens, kept her face buried in a magazine. Finally he rapped on the glass. She looked up.

"Mister, you gotta take a number."

He flashed his I.D. "I don't take numbers. I need to see Norma Wyse."

For a split second he thought she was going to repeat her surly order to take a number. She seemed to think better of it, though, and said, "I'll see if she's here." She vanished into the building's bowels.

"You a cop?" someone asked.

Whit turned to find an elderly man standing behind. He was short, dressed in a tattered denim jacket and bib overalls. His face was covered with a straggly beard stained and caked with tobacco juice.

"Kinda," Whit said.

"I want you guys to come down to my place. I got some thieves cuttin' trees on my land."

"Not really my department," Whit said.

The man didn't even hear him. He kept detailing his complaint. "Ain't that I mind 'em cuttin' it. They oughta pay me, though. I mean that's the law, right? You take a man's property, you gotta pay."

"Who's doing this?" Whit asked, knowing he shouldn't have.

"Whadaya say?" The old man cupped his ear.

"Who's doing it?" Whit shouted. A sudden silence overwhelmed the room.

"The damned state," the man said, his eyes now afire. "They widening the road, and they sayin' my trees is on their right-of-way."

Whit nodded. "I see," he said. "Then you better talk to the Feds."

"The who?"

"The Feds . . . The FBI!"

The old man turned to a woman behind him. "Told ya,

didn't I?'' He turned back to Whit. "I tried to call them first, but I couldn't get no number.''

Whit reached into his pocket and pulled out a small notebook. He found the number for the Charleston bureau of the FBI and jotted it down on one of his cards. "Here, old-timer. Give 'em a call. My name's on the front. Tell them I sent you.''

The man accepted it, then said, "Tell 'em what?''

"That . . . I . . . told . . . you . . . to.''

The receptionist reappeared and motioned for Whit to come back through a hallway. He nodded.

"Who be you?'' the old man was asking.

Whit took the card back and pointed at his name.

"That's me.''

"Thank ye kindly.''

Whit was pleased with himself as he headed back to meet Norma Wyse. The Feds did that to the local cops all the time. Once they had sent him a guy who saw Communists digging up his cornfield. He never missed a chance to get even.

The receptionist guided him down a long hall bordered on both sides by innumerable small offices. She was almost at the end of the hall when she stopped and pointed at a doorway. Whit stepped inside.

A very tall, attractive woman, her rich brown hair pulled back tightly against her head, stood and extended a hand toward him. "I'm Norma Wyse, head of child services.''

As Whit returned her firm grip, the word *Amazon* came to his mind. Not so much because of her nature, about which he knew nothing, but rather because of her height and appearance.

"I'm Whit Pynchon, Mrs. Wyse. I'm special—''

"I know of you, Mr. Pynchon. I read the papers. Oh, and

it's Miss Wyse . . . or Ms. Wyse. I have no preference. What brings Mr. Danton's special investigator to my doorstep?''

"A missing child, Miss Wyse.''

The woman seemed to sag. "We live in such unkind times. Is it the child of one of our clients?''

"No, ma'am. This child was taken from a day-care center here in Milbrook.'' Whit pulled out his notebook and checked his notes. "The FunTime Day-Care Center. It's operated by—''

"Mrs. Harrison,'' the division head said. "I know it well. It's one of the perennial thorns in my side.''

Her answer surprised him. "Why?''

"Any day-care facility that regularly serves more than six children at a time must be licensed, Mr. Pynchon. In order to qualify for that license, it must meet state requirements. Those requirements are stringent and costly. It's been my opinion for some time that Mrs. Harrison and her husband have been operating in violation of the law.''

Whit was nodding his head. "That explains it.''

"Explains what, Mr. Pynchon?''

"Please, call me Whit.''

"Good; I'm Norma.''

"I visited Mrs. Harrison this morning, and she wasn't at all cooperative. Furthermore, she made every effort to tell me that she had only six children . . . paying children, she was quick to say.''

Norma Wyse laughed. "That's the way she's eluded us. We've caught her with more than six on several occasions, but she always claims it's a special circumstance or that she's simply baby-sitting for a friend or relative.''

"Looks like it would be easy enough to prove otherwise,'' Whit said.

The woman's good humor changed to something else—

not exactly a hostile expression, but one that was circum-spect. "I thought so, too, Whit. Mr. Danton, however, wasn't anxious to prosecute. In your employer's defense, neither was the counsel for my department."

"Why not?" Whit asked, surprised that Tony hadn't men-tioned it to him.

"You know lawyers as well as I do. They like sure win-ners. This case was rather iffy. Cheap day care is difficult to find. Mrs. Harrison's attorney had several of the woman's customers—the parents, I mean—prepared to testify that they only occasionally used Mrs. Harrison's services. The law requires that the clientele be *regular*, a word open to some interpretation."

"Tony didn't mention it to me."

"He's probably forgotten it. This was several years ago, and at that time Mrs. Harrison wasn't using the name FunTime Day-Care Center."

"I would think that parents would want their kids in state-approved facilities," Whit said.

"As I said, the minimum requirements for state approval are strict and expensive. Parents pay much more in licensed day cares."

"You've enlightened me, Miss Wyse."

"Norma. Remember?"

"Okay, Norma. Anyway, I understand that you were on the phone with Mrs. Harrison at the time the child was ab-ducted."

The woman sat up in her chair. "I was?"

"That's what Mrs. Harrison says. She left the children in the yard alone to answer your call."

"I certainly remember the call, and I do remember that something had happened. Mrs. Harrison told me a child had fallen or something."

"A child had been kidnapped."

"Do you know by whom?"

Whit shook his head. "We thought it was a nabbing by an estranged parent . . . her father. Turns out it wasn't. It looks like a straightforward abduction. I don't have to tell you that it doesn't get much worse these days. The child's mother—certainly not her father—doesn't have the kind of money that would imply kidnapping for ransom. The other alternatives are downright ugly."

"Poor child."

"Do you happen to remember what time you phoned Mrs. Harrison?"

"I was getting ready to go to lunch. It had to be around eleven forty-five. I leave for lunch promptly at noon."

Her answer made Whit blink. "Are you sure?"

"I'm certain it was a few minutes before lunch. I can't give you a precise time."

Whit again referred to his notepad. "But you're certain enough to say that it wasn't as late as one-fifteen that afternoon?"

"Absolutely not. Is that when Mrs. Harrison says it happened?"

"That's when she reported it," Whit said.

"Why did she wait so long?"

"I dunno, but you can bet a dollar against a doughnut I'm gonna find out."

NINE

ANYONE WHO REPORTED the news for very long recognized that special kind of rage on people's faces that signaled trouble. They didn't just walk into an office; they stormed in, ready to demolish anyone who dared to question the righteousness of their cause. From Anna's point of view, few people were as entitled to display that unreasoning anger as Sue Winters. For her, the mother of Marcia Winters, it was born of a mindless fear for the well-being of her daughter.

"The police are doing absolutely nothing," the woman was screaming. "Nothing! My child is missing. God knows but what she might be lying dead in some ditch right now."

Neither Anna nor Kathy had yet to experience the mindless devotion of parenthood, but they were women. If they couldn't fully comprehend the reality of the woman's panic, they could imagine it.

Kathy simply sat quietly, her head bowed. Anna tried to talk to the woman. "Mrs. Winters, I know how you must feel—"

"Has your child ever been kidnapped?" she cried.

"I don't have any children."

"Then how dare you say you know how I feel! You don't know how I feel. Obviously the cops don't know. Worse, they don't care."

"That's not true," Anna said softly, trying not to aggravate the woman.

"Just what do you know about it? My child has been missing since day before yesterday, and what have they done?"

Anna traded glances with Kathy. "Please, Mrs. Winters. Listen to me for one minute."

"I'm not interested in any more damned talk. I want something done. I want you to write a story about what the police haven't done."

"Will you listen to me?" Anna snapped.

Her sharp tone caught the woman off-guard. "What is it?"

"Didn't you tell the police that your former husband took your child?"

"I thought he did. Just because I told them that, it doesn't mean they shouldn't have done more checking. They haven't done anything . . . not a damned thing."

"Didn't they send someone to South Carolina to find your former husband?"

The woman laughed. The sound was coarse and sarcastic. "Oh, sure. They sent that damned investigator. He probably went down there and played golf while some monster was abusing my child. Can't they understand?"

Kathy saw Anna's reddening face. She motioned for her friend to take it easy. Anna was trying. "Mrs. Winters, I went with Whit Pynchon to South Carolina. He found your husband. He did not play golf. In fact, he ended up getting himself arrested. He was that determined to find your husband. When he found out—"

Sue Winters's mouth was open. "You went with him?"

"Whit Pynchon and I live together. You should know that up front."

The woman lurched to her feet. "Oh, great! That's really

sweet. He takes you on some kind of illicit romp when he's s'posed to be looking for my daughter.''

"Mrs. Winters!" Anna was on her feet, too.

"I can see I made one big gawdamn mistake coming here.''

Kathy stood and put a restraining hand on the woman, who appeared to be on the verge of hysteria. "Mrs. Winters, I'm Katherine Binder. I own the paper. I can assure you that there isn't a better, more dedicated police official in this county than Mr. Pynchon.''

The woman jerked away from Kathy's touch. "Are you fucking him, too?''

Anna clenched her jaws and restrained herself from ordering the woman to leave her office. "We truly hope they find your child, Mrs. Winters, but we're not going to take the police to task—not yet, anyway. They're doing all they can. I'll check with the police, and if they don't think it will jeopardize your daughter, or the search for her, we'll certainly do a story.''

Sue Winters was trembling. Her eyes were full of tears, but her fury hadn't ebbed. "I'm going to the TV station over in Bluefield. This town stinks. It always has.''

Kathy made a final effort. "Please, Mrs. Winters. Let us try to help—''

"Go to hell,'' the woman said. She fled the office, pausing only long enough to make certain she slammed Anna's door. A glass pane next to it shattered. Shards of plate glass spilled out from under the blinds and onto the new carpet.

Anna looked over at Kathy. "I warned you about those windows.''

Late that afternoon, Whit guided Norma Wyse into the office of Raven County Prosecuting Attorney Tony Danton. He hadn't had a chance to prepare Tony for the meeting, and the prosecutor looked surprised when the woman preceded Whit into his office.

"I don't know if you remember me, Mr. Danton. I'm Norma Wyse. I'm in charge of child services at the Department of Human Services."

"Of course, I remember you," Tony said.

Whit, standing behind Norma Wyse, was smiling. He couldn't tell whether Tony was lying or not, but he knew he had caught his boss off-guard.

Whit stepped forward. "I asked Miss Wyse to meet me here. It's about the Winters girl."

"Have a seat," Tony said to her.

He looked to Whit for an additional explanation. "A few years ago," Whit said, "Miss Wyse attempted to get some action taken against a couple who were operating an unlicensed day-care facility."

Tony frowned. "I remember. We had a marginal case."

"I'm not here to plow that ground again," Norma said, "but the FunTime Day-Care Center is the same facility."

Tony hiked his eyebrows in surprise. "I didn't know that."

"It wasn't going by any name then," she said. "Anyway, given the incident with the missing child, I was hoping we might take another look at the situation."

"Certainly," Tony said. "But what's this got to do with you, Whit?"

The prosecutor obviously felt as if he were the subject of some type of ambush, and Whit knew he was unhappy. "It will help us, Tony. Mrs. Harrison, the woman who operates the center, isn't being at all cooperative. Actually it goes beyond that. It looks as if she has attempted to obstruct the investigation."

"Obstruct it?" Tony said.

"Mrs. Harrison told me she was on the phone with Miss

Wyse when the child was taken. She phoned the city police at one-seventeen P.M. In fact Miss Wyse was on the phone with her slightly before noon. Apparently Mrs. Harrison waited an hour and a half to report the incident."

Norma Wyse was nodding. "I'm certain I phoned her just a few minutes before lunch, and I always take lunch at noon."

"Why would she do that?" Tony asked.

Whit looked to the welfare worker to provide that explanation. "Whit and I have been discussing that. I think it goes back to her problems with licensing." She refreshed his memory on the case.

"The details are sketchy in my mind," Tony admitted, "but that does ring a bell."

Norma leaned forward in her chair. "I think she stalled that hour and a half so she could get rid of some of the kids . . . so when the police came she would be in compliance with the law."

"After a kidnapping, that seems a little extreme," Tony said.

The welfare worker was shaking her head. "Not for the Harrisons. They're very protective of their operation, and they have reason to be. They're making very good money, a lot of unreported income as far as the IRS is concerned."

"Can you verify that?" Tony asked.

The woman smiled. "Of course not. As I said, it's our theory."

Whit rejoined the conversation. "I provided Norma with a list of customers and children given me by Mrs. Harrison. There are a lot more than six families, but Mrs. Harrison says the schedules are staggered. We have a plan, Tony. That's why we're here. We want to run it by you."

"You want me to coerce the Harrisons into closing the center," Tony speculated.

"Jesus, Tony," Whit said, "let me finish. Right now I'm more interested in getting the kid back."

"Good," the prosecutor said. "That's my main concern, too."

"I need to talk to the children who were there that day," Whit said. "They may have seen something to help us. Mrs. Harrison refused to give me access to them this morning."

Tony leaned forward. "Oh, she did?"

"Said I would have to get permission from their parents."

"Go on," Tony said.

"Well, I have an idea as to how to obtain that consent and serve Norma's purpose, too."

A *Journal* maintenance man was languidly repairing the window in Anna's office when she received the call from the Raven County prosecuting attorney.

"I want to see if you'll do a story for us on Marcia Winters, Anna."

The newspaper's editor couldn't contain her surprise. "Golly, Tony, that's a change. I'll wager Whit isn't happy about it."

"It was his idea. He just thought it would be better for me to call."

Anna smiled. "Well, he was right. Actually you're the second person to ask for a story on Marcia Winters. Her mother was in earlier. She's very unhappy with the way the case is being handled."

"We're doing all we can."

"She says you haven't done anything—that Whit went down to Myrtle Beach and played golf."

"You know better!" Tony said.

"Yes, and I tried to tell her so. When I told her how I

know, it only made things worse. She's on her way to the television station over in Bluefield.''

"Then she'll probably get on television. They aren't very picky.''

Anna settled back in her chair, watching as the workman measured the size of the opening for the replacement pane. "I wasn't too hard on her, Tony. She's very frightened.''

"She has reason to be, Anna. The prospects aren't very good.''

"What can we do?''

"We have the photo of the child Mrs. Winters supplied us with. We'd like a straight news story on the abduction. If you could print the picture and ask for the public to assist, we would appreciate it.''

"Tony, I've explained to you before that it's fine to suggest a story, but don't tell me what approach to take, or how to play it. Okay?''

"Sorry. I didn't mean anything by it.''

"Any reason to think running a story will do any good?''

"It's news, Anna.''

"Christ, Tony. I *know* it's news. I'll run it on page one. I was just asking as an interested party.''

"We doubt any information will be forthcoming, but we do have some other reasons.''

"Which are?''

"Do we have to get into that now?''

"It's better that I know up front.''

"Okay. We want to build a fire under the lady that runs the day care where the crime occurred.''

Anna's interest was piqued. "Do you suspect she's involved?''

"No, not at all. But she isn't cooperating. Besides, she's probably running an inadequate day care . . . an unlicensed

one. However, I don't want to go on the record on that point
just yet.''

"Why not?''

"Because my first concern is the missing child."

"So why such a strong interest for a story from you and
Whit? It still doesn't make sense."

"C'mon, Anna."

Anna's voice turned sharp. "You come on, Tony. I don't
mind being used on occasion, but by God I want to know
why."

"We want to create a concern in the community, especially among the parents of those kids at the FunTime Day-
Care Center. We want to interview those kids. At the same
time, we wouldn't mind a bit if they found some better place
to put their kids during the day."

"Whit thought this up?" Anna asked.

"Most of it."

"No wonder he didn't want to call me."

"Will you help us, Anna?"

Anna pulled a notepad over in front of her. "Do you have
any evidence that the day-care center was negligent?"

"Are we going on the record now?"

"I don't recall ever saying we were off the record, Tony."

Tommy's mom and dad were fighting again, not yelling
and screaming yet, just saying bad things to each other.
Tommy was in bed, but he could hear them, and he couldn't
sleep. He couldn't get up, either. So he just stayed in bed,
trying not to look at the window. His mother had closed the
curtains, but the moon was bright. It shone through the
branches of the old dead apple tree in the yard next door.
The branches were moving because of the wind, and they
looked liked a bunch of monsters' arms to Tommy. They had

a book in the school—that's what he called Mrs. Harrison's place—about trees that grabbed kids.

He could hear their voices through the door of his bedroom. They didn't seem quite so mad at each other, but he still didn't want to get up. Sometimes it seemed like they just got mad because he was around—like maybe he did something to make them get mad at each other.

The window in his bedroom rattled a little. Tommy jerked the cover over his head and waited for several minutes before he slipped it down below his eyes. The arms on the trees were going crazy now. They almost looked funny bobbing up and down.

He could see the hall light spilling through the crack at the bottom of his bedroom door. A shadow moved across it, then another one. His mom and dad were going to bed. They were still whispering, but they weren't fighting. He actually smiled when he heard his mother laugh. The light in the hall went out. Then a door closed, the door to their bedroom. His smile vanished. Tommy didn't like it when they closed their door. It made him feel too much alone. They did things, too, when the door was closed. It sounded like his daddy was hurting his mother, but he knew that wasn't it. No, it was something else. Tommy was old enough to know it was something he didn't yet understand. He didn't care much about that, so long as he believed that his daddy wasn't hurting his mother. He just didn't like it when they closed their door.

He covered his head up again and was just about to slip off to sleep when something knocked against his window. It brought him out of that sweet never-never place that he visited just before he went to sleep. Otherwise he might have just buried himself deeper under the covers. Instead, startled and disconcerted by sleepiness, he raised up in bed. The man was standing on the other side of the window, his shadow outlined by the moonlight from behind him. His hands were fiddling with the window.

Tommy couldn't help it. He screamed as loud as he could.

The door to his bedroom flung open. It startled him even more, and he screamed that much louder. Hands grabbed him.

"Tommy! It's me!" His father, stark naked, shook him.

"A man," the boy said, tears pouring out of his eyes. "Coming in the window."

Jerry Fuller looked at the window and saw the swaying branches of the old crab apple tree. "It's just that tree, Tommy."

"No, Daddy! I saw him."

Margaret Fuller, carrying her husband's robe, came into the room. "Put this on, Jerry."

He stood and slipped it on. "Maybe I'd better go check."

Margaret Fuller sat on her son's bed. "What did he see?"

"A man, he says."

"I did!" screamed Tommy.

"You were dreaming," his mother said.

"No. I saw him." He started to cry.

"I'll go check."

Jerry Fuller left the room.

"Are they showing you movies or anything at Mrs. Harrison's?" his mother asked.

Tommy shook his head. "It was the clown, Mommy."

She frowned. "What clown, Tommy?"

"The one that took Marcia."

"Marcia?"

"Marcia Winters."

It always amazed his mother that Tommy knew his friends' last names as well as their first. Before she could ask anything else, she saw her husband's outline outside the window. Tommy jumped.

"That's just your father. Tell me about Marcia and the clown."

Tommy did—and was just finished when Jerry Fuller returned to his son's bedroom.

"Why didn't you tell me about the Winters child?" his wife asked angrily.

Her husband shook his head. "Never mind that now. There *was* someone out there. His footprints are in the flower bed under Tommy's window. I'm calling the cops."

TEN

AS EDITOR of the *Milbrook Daily Journal*, Anna always stayed at her office until the paper was ready to go to press. Her final duty each night was to go to the composing room and review each pasted-up page for glaring mistakes or omissions. On this night she had taken the time to reread the front-page article she had written on the abduction. It was factual without being sensational. She had been very careful not to imply any fault on behalf of the day-care center. Not that she cared about the Harrisons; she just didn't want to be sued. A dark red square the size of a wallet photo marked the place where Marcia's photo would be stripped in, as it was called, later in the process.

When she arrived home a little before midnight, she was surprised to find Whit already in bed. The lights in the living room had been left on, but the television was off. Usually Whit waited up for her, watching Ted Koppel's "Nightline." His car was in the drive, so she knew he was home. Tressa, Whit's daughter, had an early class at a nearby college, so she was almost always in bed and asleep by the time Anna got home.

She moved through the quiet house wondering if this cold, silent war between them was going to be waged for much longer. That, she assumed, was the reason Whit had gone to bed early. Granted she had probably been the instigator of the strife, but it was time to end it. She had hoped to make the attempt tonight.

Maybe tomorrow, she thought. But she wasn't anxious to go to bed again with the bad feelings fermenting. So she walked into the kitchen and quietly opened the refrigerator, where she pulled out a bottle of chardonnay. One glass would help her sleep. She was pouring it when she heard the floor creak. She turned.

Whit stood there in his robe. "I couldn't sleep."

"You aren't used to going to bed this early." She finished pouring her wine, then turned back to him. "You want one?"

"I had a couple of bourbons earlier. I'll pass. I've got to get out of here early tomorrow morning, and after all that driving last night I was beat. But the minute my head hit the pillow I was wide awake."

"Is it about the Winters case?"

"Yeah, but that's all I can say."

She laughed. "Don't worry. I'm not in the mood to play reporter tonight, although I can't pass up the opportunity to remind you that we are running a story at your request tomorrow morning."

"And we appreciate your cooperation," Whit said, a wry smile on his face.

She lifted her glass and went over to him. "I'm sorry I acted like such a nitwit at Myrtle Beach."

"Apology accepted."

She looked at him, a little astonished that he hadn't said something other than that. "On the other hand, that smart-ass crack about the lady being pretty, rich, and having a home down there was also pretty crude."

"But true, Anna. It only served to show—"

She sighed. "You big dumb lummox. What it showed—

or implied—is that you like me even if I'm not pretty, rich, and have a home at the beach.''

Whit thought about it. "Hmm . . . Exclude the part about pretty, and that's still true. For that I apologize; you are lovely.''

"Oh, and you said she was a good investigator.''

"So are you. A better one, in fact.''

"I give up,'' Anna said, easing her way by him. "Let's just forget the whole mess.''

She moved into the small living room and sat down on the couch. ''When that woman called with her come-hither voice, I just got mad. And madder when she called back.''

"She was some piece of work,'' he said, adding quickly, ''and I don't necessarily mean that in a complimentary sense. No matter what she looked like or owned, she wasn't my type. I can assure you of that.''

"So why do you have to get up early tomorrow?'' She asked the question with a sly grin on her face.

"I have a date with this tall, overendowed Amazon.''

Anna was taking a sip from her wine and nearly choked on it. "You *what*?''

"It's true. I'm meeting Norma Wyse. She's the head of child welfare at the local welfare department. It's about the Winters case.''

"I don't know her.''

"You should go talk to her. She really educated me today on the ins and outs of day-care centers.''

"How old is she? And what does she look like?''

Whit smiled. "Aren't we getting a little bit insecure?''

"Answer me.''

"She's maybe thirty-five . . . at least six feet tall . . . big-boned, big-boobed, and not my type. My interest is purely professional.''

Anna reached over and set her glass on the coffee table. "To be very frank, Whit, I guess I am getting a little insecure. We've been living together now for almost two years. I can't help but wonder if it isn't time to take things a step further."

Whit stood up. "I do need a drink."

"Whit! I want to talk about this."

"N.F.D."

"Don't give me that cop jargon. What does that mean?"

He turned on his way to the kitchen. "No fair deal. Not until I get a drink."

"Are you sure that doesn't mean something else?" she called after him.

"Not that I know of."

The city cop who responded to Jerry Fuller's call was illuminating the footprints in the flower bed with his flashlight. "Sure does look like someone was here."

"Is that the best you can do?" Fuller asked. He had dressed as he waited for the police to arrive.

"We'll take a look around the neighborhood, but there isn't much more we can do, Mr. Fuller."

"The man attempted to break into my house!"

The cop shook his head. "Be hard to prove that in a court of law. Besides, can you—or your kid—identify him?"

"What about those?" Fuller asked, pointing down to the footprints. "Can't you take a cast or something of them? They do it on television."

"Yeah, they make it look easy on television. Even if we did, all we could really prove is trespassing. A very minor misdemeanor. You had a prowler, Mr. Fuller. You did what you should have done. You called us. We'll do what we can do now."

"He tried to break in."

The cop directed the beam of his flashlight to the window, concentrating on the bottom of it. "I don't see any evidence where he tried to force it open. We gotta have evidence, Mr. Fuller."

"Jesus Christ! I pay taxes for this?"

The cop turned off the flashlight. "Don't get uppity, Mr. Fuller. I'm on duty until eight. I'll keep this neighborhood under close watch. If you see or hear anything else, just call the station; I'll get here as fast as I can."

Fuller laughed. "That makes me feel much better. It took you twenty minutes to get here this time."

"I was in the middle of a traffic stop when I got your complaint."

"I think I'll just get out my gun and load it. I'd feel a lot safer."

The cop had started to walk off. When he heard that, he turned around. "You best remember, Mr. Fuller. You shoot someone, and you'll be in court proving you were justified."

Fuller was walking back toward his front door by that time. He wheeled on the cop. "What is it you guys say on television? 'Better tried by twelve than carried by six'?"

"Something like that," the cop admitted.

Back inside his house, his wife wanted to know what had gone on.

"Not a gawdamned thing. Christ, those guys are useless." He had gone to the bedroom closet and was rummaging around on the top shelf.

"What are you doing?"

He pulled something from the rear of the shelf. "Looking for this," he said, displaying a small automatic weapon.

"Jerry!"

"Well, I gotta do something. I sure can't depend on those idiots for any help."

"What if Tommy gets his hands on it?"

"Tommy, come here," Jerry called.

The boy was lying in his parents' bed. He came padding out, his face still pale from fright.

"See this?" his father said, holding the gun up.

Tommy nodded.

"You know what it is?"

"A gun, Daddy."

"You ever touch it, and I'll spank your butt so bad you won't be able to sit down for a week. You understand?"

Again, Tommy just nodded.

"Back to bed now."

"Real smart," Margaret Fuller said once Tommy was back in his bedroom.

Her husband was busy checking the weapon's small magazine. "What's that supposed to mean?"

"If the boy shoots himself, are you still gonna spank him?"

"For chrissakes, Margaret."

"And what about this thing at Mrs. Harrison's house? I want Tommy out of there."

"How many times have we hashed this out? We can't afford the hospital day care."

"I'll apply for more overtime," his wife said.

"C'mon, Margaret. That deal with the little girl was a domestic thing. Mrs. Harrison assured me she wasn't gonna let the kid back in. It coulda happened at the hospital day care, too. In fact, I bet it has."

"But if it had, the hospital day care would have notified us, wouldn't they?"

"I dunno. Would they?"

"Damn right they would have, Jerry. We wouldn't have found out about it from Tommy. He needs to understand what happened."

"No, Margaret. He needs to forget what happened."

"Just as soon as they have an opening at the hospital, I'm moving Tommy over there. If you don't like it, then too bad."

Fuller cracked back the action on the weapon, jacking a bullet into the cylinder. "Fine, Margaret. Do what you want."

His wife stood there, suddenly nervous about the ugly little piece of metal in his hand.

He sighted the weapon at a picture hanging on the wall. "Just let that bastard come back here again."

"What is it that you want, Anna? You want to get married?"

"We've never really discussed it, have we? I mean, we've been together for two years and not once have we spoken more than a few words on the subject."

Whit sipped his drink. "Aren't you happy?"

"Most of the time."

"Most of the time? What does that mean?"

"C'mon, Whit. Not every minute of life is supposed to be happy. I love you. Sometimes I don't like you very much, but God knows I love you."

Whit laughed. "The feeling's mutual. I like you when you're not being a reporter."

She smiled, too. "I don't think I'm looking for a proposal tonight, Whit. I'd just like to know that it might be in the cards . . . That it's not an impossibility. I mean, are we just trying each other out for a while—to see if we fit? Or is this the best I can ever expect?"

"Oh, no. I'll get better with age. I promise."

She pounded his shoulder with her fist. "That's not what I meant."

"Gawd, take it easy." He rolled away from the blows.

"Well, I'm trying to be serious. You're obviously not."

"Okay, you want me to be serious? Here goes."

"Seriously," she said, smiling a little, wondering if that's what she really did want.

"Yeah. Why not? Believe it or not, I do think about us being married. This will shock you, but at my age I even think about myself being a father again."

Anna's eyes widened. "You're kidding me?"

"No, ma'am. The trouble is, Anna, I imagine all these things happening somewhere other than the godforsaken backwoods of southern West Virginia."

"Like in Myrtle Beach," Anna said.

"Exactly." He leaned close to her, reached out, and lifted her chin so he was looking her in the face. "I don't think you're ready for my dream, are you?"

"You mean moving down there?"

He nodded. "And giving up your fancy job here. If you wanna work down there, it's okay by me."

That was the crunch. It always came to that. Deep in Anna's mind, she knew it.

"In other words," she said, "I can have one part of what I want, but I have to give up the other part."

He smiled. "It's not an effort on my part to extort anything from you. I'll stay here in West Virginia as long as you don't want to move and as long as I can stand it, but should we get married—maybe have a family—before we resolve this dilemma?"

She leaned closer to him, their lips almost touching. "Why do you have to be so damned logical?"

"Funny, I don't feel logical."

"But under certain circumstances you would be willing to marry me, and maybe even have kids."

Their lips moved closer together. "Absolutely," he said.

"For now, that's good enough."

They kissed.

ELEVEN

IT WAS STILL DARK at ten after six when the man pulled up
to the front of the newspaper office. He'd hardly slept at all.
He'd been keyed up when he'd gotten home. Keyed up and
frustrated. It had taken at least two hours and three or four
beers for him to calm down, and then he'd only slept fitfully.
Finally, at five to six, he'd gotten up, quickly dressed, and
left the trailer. As he neared the newspaper office, he slowed
to a stop. Without bothering to turn off the car's engine, he
walked over to the dark green metal box. He fumbled in his
pocket for a quarter and dropped it as he saw the picture of
the girl on the front page staring out at him through the window of the box.

He picked the quarter off the ground and pulled the door
of the box open as he deposited the coin. He glanced once
at the front of the building. He was tempted to snatch all of
the newspapers, but he knew it would be useless. He couldn't
stop the bastards from spreading the word that the girl was
missing. Besides, she wasn't the one he was worried about.

He looked at the picture of the girl again. Her bright
eyes. Her smile. So she *didn't* always cry. God, what a cry-
baby. He was just glad to be rid of her. But now he needed
to find out what the cops knew.

He stuffed the paper under his arm and returned to his car.

He was about to turn on the overhead light and read the article, but thought better of it. He'd drive over to the doughnut shop and take his time and read it real carefully. He started to make a U-turn, but decided not to take any chances. He drove around the block, then headed to the strip shopping center.

As he pulled up to the doughnut shop a couple of minutes later, the half-light of dawn had arrived with him. That was when he realized he might be making a big mistake. Two of the three cars parked outside the shop were cherry tops. He was about to back out of his parking space when one of the cops turned and looked through the window.

Act normal, he told himself, and turned off the engine. He didn't want to do anything that looked suspicious. Hell, he should have known that there would be cops here at this hour. There were always cops at this place. Cops and doughnuts. It must be something they taught them at the academy. He stepped out of the car, casually walked inside, and took a seat a couple of stools down from the two patrolmen. He ordered coffee and a chocolate-frosted doughnut and unfolded the newspaper.

MILBROOK CHILD ABDUCTED FROM CENTER, the headline read. Maybe he'd comment aloud about the terrible kidnapping. No. Forget that. He'd like to get the cops talking about the case, but that would be stupid. He'd taken enough chances already, and kidnapping the girl had been the easiest of them.

He'd gone back to the day-care center the day after he'd snatched her. He'd parked across the street and watched the parents picking up their kids. He'd known it was dangerous, but he had to take the chance. The thing with the other kid had been eating at him. He'd waited about ten minutes when he'd spotted the boy who'd pulled off his mask. A man, probably his father, was picking him up.

He'd been about to follow the kid home when a cop had pulled up behind him. He'd quickly grabbed a map of Milbrook from the side pocket of the Camaro and acted as if he were studying it. When the cop had asked him what he was doing, he'd said he was lost and had given him the address he was looking for. Foolishly he'd given his own address, because he couldn't think of any others. The cop had informed him he was on the wrong side of town and had pointed the way on the map. He'd driven off, cursing his bad luck and thanking his stars at the same time. Bad luck; dumb cop. Then a few blocks later, he'd spotted the car that had picked up the kid. It was parked at a hardware store. He'd followed the car and found the kid's home.

He shook his head as he finished reading the article for the second time. It didn't say much he didn't know. The perpetrator had worn a clown mask and cut a hole in the fence of the day-care center. It described the little girl and gave the number to contact if you had any information. There was nothing about the kid who'd grabbed his mask. But that didn't mean anything, of course.

There was one thing, though, that bothered him. He read the sentences over again. "The girl's father, William R. Winters, resides in Myrtle Beach, South Carolina. However, after a preliminary investigation, authorities have determined that Winters most likely was not involved in the abduction."

The cops were supposed to think it was Winters and wouldn't believe him. The bastard must have had an airtight alibi. Unless the kid had gotten a really good look at him. The kid was trouble. He wasn't mentioned in the paper, but the cops always kept things to themselves. He wondered what else the little bastard had said. He had to shut that mouth up, and do it fast.

He glanced up in the mirror as the cops stood up. They

reached into their pockets for change. One of them, the one who sported a mustache, caught his eye in the mirror. He shifted his glance from the cop's mustache and pretended he was looking at himself. He ran a hand through his thick, unruly hair. He was twenty-five and ruggedly handsome. At least that's what Randi had said. A lot of women thought so. He liked women. Liked them a lot. He rubbed his square jaw and wished he had shaved before he'd gone out. Act normal, he told himself again. And watch the booze. That was his weakness. Things happened when he drank too much; things he didn't even remember.

The cops were walking behind him. He looked down at the paper. The girl was still staring at him. She'd never smiled like that when she was with him. Not once.

"Paper's out," one of the cops said. "Let's get a copy."

He looked up in the mirror and saw them walk over to a newspaper box. He had an urge to go out and listen to their every word. But he didn't; he knew better. Mustache picked two papers from the box and gave one to his buddy. Fuckin' crooked cops; he'd only put in one quarter.

"More coffee, mister?" the waitress asked.

He jerked his head around. "No. Half a cup."

He watched as the cops walked over to their cruisers without another glance back. He smiled. They didn't suspect a thing. Dumb, fucking cops. It was a miracle the town wasn't full of crooks. You could get away with anything here.

Tough luck, boys. You'll never find her, and you'll never get me.

Maybe he'd celebrate a little today. But then he got hold of himself. He had to do something about the boy. It was just too risky to let him go. He'd blown it last night. But next time it would be different.

TWELVE

THE GRAY LIGHT of impending dawn was just starting to quicken the eastern horizon when Whit arrived at the front of the FunTime Day-Care Center. The clock on the dash of his car read 6:39. He pulled against the curb on the opposite side of the street and waited. He and Norma Wyse had agreed to meet here at 6:45. According to information provided to the director of child services during a prior investigation, Mrs. Harrison's hours of operation commenced at 7:00.

Though still a few weeks before fall officially began, the September morning was crisp. From what Whit could tell, the day was going to be overcast, perhaps even wet. He hoped not. He despised dreary fall days.

Across the street, lights burned in the Harrison home. The same could be said of many of the houses in the middle-class, residential neighborhood in South Milbrook. An occasional car was already out on the street, too. In front of him, in the gradually intensifying light, Whit saw a paperboy riding up the street on his bicycle, tossing the morning paper first to one side, then to the other.

Whit hadn't seen the paper yet and wondered if the boy was carrying any extras. He was about to open his door and intercept the young man when car lights fell in behind him. He looked up into his rearview mirror and saw that it was a new minivan. That's what Norma Wyse said she would be driving. The paperboy peddled by him before he could get out, but as Norma stepped out of the vehicle she held a copy of the newspaper in one hand and a paper bag in the other. She came around to the passenger side of the vehicle and slid inside.

"Morning, Whit."

The aroma of her perfume was light and enticing, but not nearly as pleasing as the aroma of coffee. "I hope you brought two cups."

She smiled. "Sure did—and there's a thermos back in the van for later as well as some doughnuts. We can go back and get them now if you want."

"Just the coffee," Whit said.

She reached into the bag and handed him a cup. "Has anyone shown up yet?"

"Not since I've been here," Whit said as he cautiously removed the plastic lid from the steaming brew.

"I hope they wait for a few minutes."

Their faces were no longer hidden by the retreating night shadows, and Norma Wyse was grinning at him. "You look as if you had a late night."

"I'm just not used to getting up this early. How's the story in the paper?"

"Great. Your ladyfriend did a bang-up job. Haven't you had a chance to read it?"

"I hardly ever read the paper. If you said it's okay, that's good enough for me."

At that moment a car turned on the street and glided into the spacious, graveled pulloff in front of the Harrisons'. "Damn," Whit mumbled. "Looks like it's show time."

Norma glanced at the clock and saw that it was 6:53. "This one's a little early."

Whit had set the coffee on his dash and was already open-ing the car door.

"Here's the list," Norma said, handing Whit a sheet of paper.

Whit took it and hurried across the street. A chubby young woman had gotten out of the car—a small, battered com-pact—and was coming around to the passenger side.

"Morning, ma'am," Whit said.

She stopped, a look of outright fear in her eyes.

Whit had his badge out, displaying it, but the morning light remained poor. "I'm a special investigator with the Raven County Prosecuting Attorney's office. Can I have a minute of your time?"

She didn't seem too relieved. "You're what?"

"I'm a police officer. Here's my identification."

She glanced at it. "What do you want with me?"

"Just a few questions."

"Did I run a stop sign or something?"

Whit laughed. "No, ma'am. Nothing like that. Were you aware that a child was abducted from the center a few days ago?"

Norma Wyse, by that time, had gotten out of Whit's car and was joining them. The woman looked at her, and Whit introduced her.

"A kid was *what*?" the woman then asked.

"Abducted. Didn't Mrs. Harrison make you aware of it?"

"No, she didn't."

"What's your name?" Whit then asked.

The woman took a step back. "So what's this got to do with me? Isn't Julie safe here?"

"Is Julie your child?" Norma asked.

"Yes, but—"

Norma eased the list from Whit's hand and checked it. "Then you are Connie Lawson?"

"Yes, I am. What about Julie? Is she safe here?"

"We have no reason to suspect that she isn't, Mrs. Lawson," Whit said. "We just want to see if your child saw anything that might help us."

For the first time Whit glanced into the car. The sun was probably above the horizon, but it was obscured by thick clouds. He could barely make out the child's form.

"Julie's just two and a half. I don't think it's gonna do much good asking her anything," the woman said.

"I didn't know your child's age, Mrs. Lawson. I appreciate your cooperation."

The woman opened the door and unbuckled the child from the safety restraint seat. When she had Julie in her arms, she hesitated in front of Whit. "Is there something you ain't telling me? Are the Harrisons involved or something?"

"No, ma'am," Whit said quickly. "A man cut a hole in the back of the fence and took a young girl. At this point, that's all we know. There's a fairly accurate report in this morning's paper if you want to read it."

She nodded and hurried into the Harrisons' home. Whit turned to Norma. "You're going to have to excuse my ignorance, but it's been so long. Could a two and a half year old have told us anything?"

The welfare worker laughed. "I doubt it. I'd say we won't get much from any of them under three and a half." Another car pulled in behind the battered compact.

Jerry Fuller was just getting out of the shower when his wife started banging on the door. "What is it?" he asked, flinging it open.

She brandished the paper in his face. "You read this?"

"The paper?"

Margaret Fuller had already showered and dressed. She had to be at work at the hospital lab at 8:00, and she usually delivered Tommy to the day care. She was folding it for him. "This! Right here!"

Fuller wrapped a towel around his midsection as his eyes settled on the photo of Marcia Winters. When Tommy had talked about Marcia, he hadn't been able to put a face to the name. Now, seeing her photo on the front page of the *Milbrook Daily Journal*, he had no trouble remembering her. She was a strikingly pretty child.

"Read it!" his wife commanded.

"For God's sakes gimme a chance." With wet hands he took the paper and started to read the story.

Before he had gone more than a few paragraphs his wife was saying, "Just a domestic thing, huh? The woman lied to you. Some stranger kidnapped that child!"

Fuller ignored her and kept reading. "But it says down here that the police have no reason to suspect any involvement or any negligence on the part of FunTime."

His wife wasn't interested in any defense he had to offer. "It wouldn't have happened at the hospital facility. I told you we should move Tommy out of there."

"Fine," Fuller said, shoving the paper back in her hand. "Go apply today."

"What are we going to do with Tommy?"

"You're going to take him to Mrs. Harrison's," Fuller said, "unless you plan on staying home from work."

"I can't stay home," she protested.

"That makes two of us." He slammed the bathroom door.

"I'm not taking him!" she shrieked.

"Fine again. Leave him, and I'll take him," he shouted through the door.

* * *

Ivan Harrison, a gangly stick of a man, had come charging out of the house even before Whit could approach the young girl who had exited the second vehicle.

"Who the hell do you think you are?" the man cried, charging straight for Whit.

He held up his badge as if he were warding off some evil spirit. "Just cool it, pal. You don't want that kinda trouble."

"I demand to know what you're doing. Mrs. Lawson is in there crying. What right have you got—"

The second customer at the day care was standing outside her open car door, her gaze fixed on the confrontation.

"Your wife made this necessary," Whit said. "I asked for permission to talk to the children yesterday. She said I would need parental consent. That's all I'm doing here."

The man's eyes sparked with anger. His face was crimson, his fists clinched down by his sides. "If you don't get the hell off my property, I'm gonna—"

At that point Whit moved forward. The man was wearing a corduroy shirt and jeans. Whit's fingers dug into the material of the shirt. "Listen, asshole; I happen to be on the gawdamned public right-of-way."

The man was struggling to extricate himself from the hold, but Whit wasn't letting go. "Furthermore, I'm gonna talk to each and every parent that brings their child in today. If you come out here and threaten me again, I'll arrest you for obstructing an officer in the conduct of his official duties."

Whit released him.

"I'll sue your ass off," the man screamed, backing away. "By gawd I'll have your gawdamned job. You can't do this. I know who you are."

Whit smiled. "Have a nice morning, Mr. Harrison. You are Mr. Harrison, I presume?"

"You smart-mouthed motherfucker! You'll find out who I am soon enough."

Mrs. Harrison was on the porch. "Come back inside, Ivan. Don't let him hurt you, Ivie. You come back, and we'll call our lawyer."

But Ivan Harrison was standing at the steps up to the porch, shaking a finger at Whit. "I got a heart condition, mister. You can't grab me and shake me around." His wife came down the steps and pulled him back inside.

Whit turned back to intercept the young woman who had just arrived. She had already gotten back into her car and was pulling out. "Just a minute," Whit said, trying to stop her. She floorboarded the car and squealed away.

"Damn," Whit said.

Norma Wyse was shaking her head. "I don't much blame the poor thing. For a moment I was about ready to do the same thing. I thought you were going to brutalize the man."

"Sometimes it's better to squelch those kind of smart asses before they get a chance to whip up their courage."

She chuckled. "Well, you squelched him."

True to her word, Margaret Fuller had left the house without Tommy. When Jerry Fuller finished his morning coffee, he found the young boy sitting in the living room. "You ready to go to school?"

Tommy nodded and got to his feet.

"Better get your raincoat, pal. It looks kinda threatening outside."

The boy went to the closet and opened it, pulling down the bright plastic coat from its rack. His father grabbed his briefcase, and they headed out to the Nissan Sentra that was parked in front of the house.

Once they were in the car and on the way, Jerry Fuller

looked at his son. "You're awfully quiet this morning. Are you still frightened because of last night?"

The boy shook his head, but kept his eyes down. "C'mon, pal. It's okay to be a little scared. I mean there was someone outside the window."

The boy finally looked up. "I heard Mommy shouting."

"She was just upset."

"How come you shout so much?"

"Me?" Fuller was shocked by what amounted to a challenge from his four-year-old son.

"You and Mommy."

"Gee, Tommy. Sometimes grownups do that."

"It scares me," the boy said.

Fuller found himself squeezing back tears. He hadn't realized his son was as aware as he was. "Tell you what, Tommy . . . Your mother and I will have a long talk about it and try not to do it anymore."

The boy didn't seem very relieved. "Mommy was shouting this morning about Mrs. Harrison's. Was it about Marcia?"

"Tommy, you have to just forget about Marcia. Don't think about it."

"But, Daddy—"

"Forget about it, Tommy."

Jerry Fuller turned the Nissan onto the street where the day care was located. As he neared the residence, he saw the man and woman standing outside. "What the hell is this all about?" he said aloud.

"Thank goodness," Whit said as he saw the boy sitting in the Nissan.

"What is it?" Norma asked.

"I think this is the boy I want to talk to. He looks to be the oldest one here. His name is Tommy."

Norma checked her list. "Tommy Fuller. His father's name is Jerry Fuller."

The man was stepping from the car, eyeing Whit.

"Mr. Fuller?" Whit approached with his badge on display.

Fuller saw it and rolled his eyes. "Whadaya want?"

"Are you aware that a child was abducted—?"

"Sure, mister. I read about it in the paper, and Mrs. Harrison told me about it."

"I see," Whit said.

Fuller marched around his car and opened his son's door. "C'mon, Tommy. Bail out."

Whit stayed with the man. "I understand from Mrs. Harrison that your son came to tell her about Marcia's abduction."

"Tommy's a sharp kid," the man said, guiding him toward the house.

Whit smiled at the young boy, who kept his eyes averted. "I'd like to talk to Tommy for a few minutes," Whit said, still walking beside Jerry Fuller.

At that point Fuller stopped. "Forget it. I don't want my son upset by all this. He saw a man in a clown mask. That's all."

"Maybe he can tell us how tall the man was," Whit said. "How about it, Tommy? Can you—"

"I told you," Fuller said, "he's told you all he knows."

Tommy was tugging on his father's trousers. "Daddy, I—"

"Quiet, Tommy."

Whit had returned his attention to the father. "We have a

child kidnapped, Mr. Fuller. If it had been Tommy, wouldn't you want the other parents here to cooperate?''

''Sure! Sure I would. Tommy's cooperated. We've cooperated. He saw a man in a clown mask.'' Fuller looked down at his son. ''How tall was he, Tommy?''

The boy blinked and pointed to Whit. ''Tall as him.''

Fuller glared at Whit. ''There, does that help?''

''Just a few minutes with your son,'' Whit said, his voice flat and cold.

Fuller slowly shook his head. ''I'm late for work as it is. I don't want you hassling my son. C'mon, Tommy.''

His father's hand guided Tommy toward the steps and into Mrs. Harrison's house. The boy was looking back over his shoulder at Whit.

Norma came up to join him. ''Sometimes, Whit, I do not understand people.''

''I do. I understand them all too well. By and large they just don't give a damn.''

THIRTEEN

TONY DANTON received the summons to appear in Judge David O'Brien's office precisely at 9:00 A.M. It came in the form of a call from the judge's secretary. He'd checked his schedule while she was telling him that he was supposed to go to the judge's chambers. "I don't have a thing on my calendar for this morning. Did I forget something?"

"This is an emergency matter," she said. "The judge is waiting."

He had climbed the flight of stairs to the second floor, and, upon entering the judge's outer office, was immediately ushered into the inner sanctum by the secretary who had called him. He found O'Brien chuckling at a joke being told by Ardis Harmon.

The judge didn't bother to rise. "Have a seat, Tony. Want some coffee? Tea maybe?"

"No, sir."

Ardis nodded to Tony.

O'Brien was in his shirtsleeves, leaning far back in his chair with his feet propped up on the desk. The jurist had been talking retirement for years, but according to the general consensus he wasn't going to step down from the bench until he had a good chance of picking his successor. The most obvious candidate for the job was Tony Danton, not that Tony was interested. O'Brien, though, was thought to favor Marshall McComas, a country-club lawyer who was serving as a state senator. Of the two men, Danton much preferred O'Brien, so he wasn't about to tell the aging judge that he wasn't going to challenge McComas for the judge-ship.

"What's up?" Tony asked.

"Read that story this morning on the missing child," O'Brien said. "Nasty thing to have happen around here."

Tony glanced at Ardis. "If the counselor is here to com-plain about our efforts to locate the child, I can assure you that we're taking every conceivable step to—"

"Whoa!" bellowed O'Brien. "Ardis's here complaining about some of those steps you're taking. She represents a Mr. and Mrs. Ivan Harrison who claim—"

Tony couldn't contain himself. "The Harrisons? For God's sake, Ardis—"

O'Brien popped up to a sitting position. "Tony, we might not be in the courtroom, but I still don't take kindly to being interrupted."

"I apologize, Dave, but did Ardis bother to tell you that she also represents the mother of the missing child."

"She did, and I've taken that into consideration. Now, if you will please let me continue."

Tony sagged into his seat, and Ardis smiled pleasantly at him. Her round face, framed by short hair, looked nearly angelic.

"As I was trying to say, Tony, Ardis's clients are asking for an injunction enjoining Pynchon from interfering with the operation of a day-care center they operate."

"A center they operate outside the law?" Tony said.

O'Brien banged a fist on the desk. "Mr. Danton . . . if you please!"

"I apologize again, Your Honor."

"According to Ardis, Pynchon manhandled Mr. Harrison this morning. You know anything about that?"

Tony shook his head. "I haven't talked to Whit."

Ardis Harmon spoke for the first time. "My client isn't a well man. He suffers from angina. He's prepared to sue. I think Pynchon's gone off the deep end."

Tony leaned forward. "He's trying to find the child of your damned client, Ardis."

O'Brien banged on his desk again. "Can we please keep this civil?"

Tony turned back to the judge. "Your Honor, yesterday Whit went to the day-care center to attempt to interview some of the children. They were witnesses to the abduction. Mrs. Harrison, the owner of the center, refused to allow Whit to do so unless he obtained parental consent. He went to the Harrison home this morning with Norma Wyse of the—"

"I know who she is," O'Brien said.

"With her, then, to obtain that permission from parents as they brought their children to the center."

Ardis attempted to say something, but O'Brien stopped her. "Hang on a second, Ardis. Let Tony finish. Then you can respond."

"Thank you," Tony said. "We also have reason to believe that the Harrisons are operating an unlicensed day-care facility in direct contradiction to state law. . . . That is, they are regularly—and for remuneration—providing day-care services to more than six children."

"Categorically untrue!" declared Ardis. Her eyes darted about and the angelic features had been replaced by a look of wily determination.

"Well, by counting them as they go in today, we will know, won't we?" Tony countered.

O'Brien looked quizzically at Ardis Harmon.

"Your Honor, Pynchon is intimidating my clients' customers. His presence and his manner are suggesting that my clients are somehow involved in the kidnapping. As Mr. Danton was so quick to point out, and I hasten to add that I had already made it known to this court, I do represent the missing child's mother, and she has no animosity toward the Harrisons. Moreover, Pynchon assaulted Ivan Harrison when Ivan challenged his right to conduct these gestapo-type activities."

Tony threw up his hands. "For chrissakes, Ardis."

"It's true! I'm prepared to produce my clients as well as witnesses to Whit Pynchon's strong-arm tactics."

The judge checked his watch. "It's almost nine-fifteen. Can I assume that Whit has talked to most of the parents who will be using the facility?"

Tony shrugged. "I can't say."

The gesture struck O'Brien wrong. "Well, Mr. Prosecutor, *I* can say. I'm going to issue the temporary injunction. If you want to pursue the investigation in this manner, I'll schedule a full hearing on the issue of a permanent injunction."

Tony knew it was coming. He could read O'Brien like a book most of the time. "Your Honor, may I inquire as to what we will be enjoined from doing?"

The judge looked to the other lawyer. "You have something prepared?"

Ardis fished into a notepad and offered a typed order. O'Brien read it and nodded in approval. He then read the relevant passage. " 'The office of the prosecuting attorney, its employees, and its agents, limited but not included to any and all police officers in Raven County, may not harass, annoy, or interfere with, Ivan and Clara Harrison, doing business as FunTime Day-Care Center; nor shall they harass or annoy those individuals who have retained the services of Ivan and Clara Harrison, doing business with FunTime Day-Care Center.' ''

Tony was shaking his head. ''Much too broad, Your Honor. We have the right to question individuals pursuant to a criminal investigation. We probably will find it necessary to visit the parents at their homes as part of that investigation.''

But Ardis cried, ''No! No! No!''

''Tony has a point,'' O'Brien responded.

''Your Honor, Pynchon will go to these people's homes and try to poison them against my clients. This Wyse woman—she's been out to get my clients for years.''

''Nonsense,'' Tony said.

The judge pondered the document. ''Okay, this is what it will say. Tony, you're enjoined from confronting or questioning customers of the center at the center. Furthermore, you're enjoined from interfering with its operation, absent some due process of law.''

''What's that mean?'' Ardis asked.

O'Brien smiled. ''C'mon, Counselor. If the prosecutor has reasonable grounds to believe your people are violating the law, he can pursue the proper courses of action—criminal prosecution, search-and-seizure, etc. I can't issue an injunction absolving them from the duty to obey the law.''

Ardis's customary smile wasn't in evidence. ''Fine, Your Honor. May we get this served with all possible dispatch . . . before Pynchon hospitalizes my client?''

''Spare us the hyperbole,'' O'Brien said.

''I have one other request,'' Tony said. ''We may want to question Mr. and Mrs. Harrison. We certainly would encourage Ms. Harmon's presence. If we can't do it at their home, because of this order, then where may we conduct the interview?''

O'Brien looked at Harmon. ''Counselor?''

''My office,'' the lawyer said.

Tony stood and turned toward the door.

''One more thing,'' the judge said. ''Keep me posted on the child. I have a granddaughter that age.''

By 10:00 that morning, a total of eleven children had been delivered to the FunTime Day-Care Center.

Norma was checking the list provided to Whit the prior day by Mrs. Harrison. ''According to this thing, she still has three other 'regular' clients. Either Mrs. Harrison is giving away more day care than she's selling, or she's in violation of the licensing law.''

Whit was leaning against the fender of his car. ''I don't get the impression that the Harrisons give away much of anything. If this can be done for another morning or two, perhaps on a random basis, I don't see any reason why they can't be prosecuted.''

''It hasn't helped you much with your case.''

The morning, which had dawned under the gray overcast, was turning sunny. The thick clouds had started to break apart, unveiling broad vistas of azure skies. When the rays of the sun found one of the openings in the overcast, its warmth was a reminder that summer hadn't abandoned the Central Appalachians quite yet.

As comforting as increasing sunlight was, it did little to dispel the dark chill of apprehension within Whit. ''I'm afraid we're going to find that child in a drainage ditch somewhere, or buried under leaves just off a highway. It's that kind of kidnapping.''

"Maybe not," Norma said. "You need to keep a positive attitude."

Whit laughed. "That's not something I do very well. Too many years in this business; too many layers of crusty cynicism."

The street had been quiet for several minutes. Most of those who were going to work had already left their homes. The housewives in the neighborhood were just beginning to stir. When a black Chrysler pulled onto the street several blocks south of them, both Whit and Norma noticed it.

"That's Tony Danton's car," Whit said.

"Checking up on you?"

Whit shrugged. "Something must be going on."

Tony pulled his car in front of Whit's and got out. "How's it going?"

"The lady's packing them inside like sardines in a can," Whit said.

The prosecutor nodded to Norma Wyse, who said, "So far, Mr. Danton, she has eleven children in there."

"Any information on the kidnapping?" Tony asked.

Whit slowly shook his head. "The few kids we were able to talk with just said it was a clown."

"What happened between you and Harrison?"

"I guess he's been on the phone," Whit said, smiling.

"Actually I've been before Judge O'Brien with Harrison's attorney."

The news made Whit chuckle. "That didn't take long. Who is his lawyer?"

"Ardis Harmon."

The amused look vanished from Whit's face. "You gotta be shittin' me?"

" 'Fraid not. The court has issued a temporary injunction

against us. We're to cease and desist. Now, back to my question: What took place between you and Harrison?''

"He came out and got in my face. I got in his face. No harm done. Is that why they got the injunction?''

Tony shook his head. "They would have gotten it anyway, I think.''

"Really, he didn't hurt the man," Norma said, coming to Whit's defense. "What does the injunction mean?''

"It means, Miss Wyse, that we can't interfere with the operations of the Harrisons' business.''

She flushed. "But they're in violation of the law!''

"We can pursue that, and we will," Tony said.

A white Cadillac rolled down the street. "That's Harmon," Tony said.

The Cadillac pulled to a stop on the other side of the street, in front of the day-care center. Even before the attorney was out of the car, the Harrisons were coming out of the house.

Harmon stepped out of her car and greeted her clients. The shoulder pads in her dress seemed to square off her squat figure and give her a harder than normal appearance.

After a moment of consultation, Harmon, followed by the Harrisons, crossed the street. The lawyer had a piece of paper in her hand.

"Here she comes," Whit said.

Tony cast a look of warning at his investigator. "Just stay cool, please.''

"May I assume, Danton, that you have informed your investigator of the injunction?''

"I have, Ardis.''

Surprisingly it was Norma Wyse who spoke next—and not to the lawyer, but rather to Mrs. Harrison. "Who's minding the children, Clara?''

"None of your business!" Ivan Harrison snapped.

Harmon put a restraining hand on her client. "I think it's best, Tony, if you and these other two people adjourn from the scene."

Whit smiled at Norma. "Don't you just love the way she talks. She can talk that way outta both sides of her mouth. It's a real talent."

Norma laughed.

Ardis glared at Whit. "You should be aware, Pynchon, that my client intends to file a criminal complaint charging you with assault and battery."

"Take your best shot, Counselor. Tell me, does your other client—Mrs. Winters—know that you are obstructing our efforts to find her daughter?"

Harmon shoved the paper at Tony. "Here's the injunction signed by O'Brien."

Tony accepted it.

"I have one question," Whit asked. "Why did it take you more than an hour to notify us of Marcia Winters's kidnapping?"

For a moment Ardis Harmon seemed shocked by the question, but before Mrs. Harrison could respond, she did it for her. "I've instructed my clients not to make any statement. In my opinion, they are targets of a possible criminal prosecution."

"For once," Whit said, "your opinion is right."

"We want to question your clients," Tony said. "What time is convenient?"

Ivan Harrison lurched forward. "Question us? You mean beat us, don't you? Just like that bastard's already done."

"Easy, Ivan," Harmon said, stepping forward to position herself between her client and Whit. She looked at the prosecutor. "I'm sorry, Tony. Given the circumstances, the Harrisons will be offering no statements. If you have grounds to arrest them, then do so—but they stand on their right to remain silent.''

Tony looked to Whit. "We got enough to arrest them?"

Whit grinned. "Yeah, we can arrest them for violating the law regarding licensing of day-care facilities, but I think I'd rather wait. I'd rather nail them for being accessories to kidnapping."

"How dare you?" Mrs. Harrison cried. "We didn't have a thing to do—"

"Please, Mrs. Harrison," said her lawyer, "please allow me to handle this."

"But we didn't have nothing to do with any kidnapping," she protested.

As far as Whit was concerned, it was a good time to leave. "I'll see you back at the office, Tony. I've had about as much of these people as I can stomach for one day."

The prosecutor said, "Wait one second, Whit. How many children have been brought here this morning?"

Whit looked to Norma, who said that eleven children had been left in Mrs. Harrison's care. "That doesn't include the names of three parents of children Mrs. Harrison has declared as regular customers."

"I'm baby-sitting for friends," Mrs. Harrison snapped. Harmon shushed her.

Tony was smiling at the lawyer. "I can play games, too, Ardis. This afternoon I intend to seek a temporary injunction closing the FunTime Day-Care Center down until a full hearing can be scheduled on the matter. I think we've got more than enough reason to believe that the center is being operated outside the requirements of the law."

"He can't do that!" bellowed Harrison.

"Stand back and watch me," Tony said.

Norma Wyse was clapping.

FOURTEEN

ANNA ENTERED Kathy Binder's office just after 1:00 P.M. to tell the *Journal*'s publisher that she was going home for a few hours. When she saw that Kathy was on the phone, she started to ease her way out of the office. The publisher, though, motioned for her to stay.

"Anna just came into the office. Give me a moment to talk to her, then I'll get back to you." Kathy hung up the phone, her usually pale complexion tinged by an angry flush.

"What's up?" Anna asked.

"That was the receptionist out front. You and I both have visitors."

Anna eased down into one of the plush leather chairs in front of the publisher's desk. "What now?"

"A television crew. They want to talk to us both about the Winters case."

Anna closed her eyes in frustration. "Myra Martin," she said.

"The one and only."

Anna stood up. "Well, you can do what you want. I have no intention of talking to her. I came in to tell you I'm going home."

"How do you plan on getting by her? She and her crew are stationed outside the front door. Even if you go out the back way, they'll see you when you come around the front and go across to your car.''

"I'm not going out the back door. I'm going out the front door. If she's smart, she won't shove a microphone in my face.''

Kathy laughed. "My God, Anna. Whit's personality is rubbing off on you.''

Anna had started to pace. "It's ludicrous, Kathy. It doesn't matter what I say, Myra will probably make it look like Whit and I were screwing our brains out in Myrtle Beach instead of—'' She stopped. "I'd like to punch her lights out.''

Kathy picked up the phone and dialed the receptionist.

"What are you going to do?'' Anna asked.

Before Kathy could answer, the receptionist picked up the phone. "Please inform the TV reporter that neither Ms. Tyree nor I wish to make any comment at this time. Let me know when they leave.''

"Good for you,'' Anna said as her employer hung up the phone.

Kathy shrugged. "If the Martin woman is intent on making the *Journal* look bad, and I assume she is, then I don't see why we should help her.''

Anna dropped back down into the chair. "I guess I'd better cool my heels here until they clear out. I often wonder if people think of me in the same way I think of Myra.''

Kathy smiled. "A few, I'm sure, but then you've managed to neutralize one of the county's biggest media critics by sleeping with him.''

Anna frowned. "Not funny, Kathy.''

"But true nonetheless.''

"It is not true nonetheless. I might be sleeping with him, but I haven't managed to silence him.''

Kathy was still smiling. "I don't know, Anna. Based on

my recent observations, Whit Pynchon is definitely mellowing.''

Anna, though, was still fuming over Myra Martin. ''I really think that our friend Myra is after me more than she is anyone else.''

''You sound paranoid.''

''I'm serious, Kathy. It's just the vibrations she puts off. Furthermore, haven't you noticed how she always tries to put a new spin on any story we've already covered—generally a totally opposite spin?''

Kathy shook her head. ''I never watch television news— at least not the local news—and it sounds to me as if you'd get more piece of mind if you didn't, either.''

Anna laughed for the first time since entering the office. ''*Now* who sounds like Whit Pynchon? That's his constant hue and cry.''

''I always figured that was just macho bullshit. How could someone not read the paper? Or watch at least some news— the national stuff—on television?''

''It's not bullshit, Kathy. He really doesn't read the paper. Sometimes he does watch the national news, and he never misses 'Nightline.' ''

''Not even the local weather?''

Anna shook her head. ''He has a weather radio at home that he keeps tuned to the National Weather Service. When he's not listening to that, he's watching the Weather Channel on television.''

Kathy threw up her hands. ''Jesus, the Weather Channel.''

Anna once again pushed herself up from the plush chair. ''Well, I'd better go before I get too comfortable and fall asleep. I still haven't fully recovered from that whirlwind trip to Myrtle Beach.''

"Whit's been hyping the joys of Myrtle Beach to Gil. Now Gil wants to go down for a long weekend."

Anna was already at the door. She turned. "Well, don't let the blond bombshell find out about it. She'll make it the stuff of news promos: SHERIFF, PUBLISHER TRYST AT BEACH. Film at eleven."

Kathy grinned. "I don't think she's interested in my sex life as much as yours. Maybe she has a thing for Whit and this is her way of getting his attention."

"I suspect the only people she has things for, as you put it, are station managers who can increase both her salary and her visibility. I'll be back around six-thirty or seven."

Anna hurried through the noisy, bustling business offices of the *Journal*. The newspaper was really two separate operations. On this side, strictly Kathy's domain, advertising salesmen were in and out all day long. Several female employees were constantly on the phone accepting classified ads. The circulation department was forever trying to manage the complaints about papers not received and paperboys who mangled screens with their errant tosses. All of that went on during the daytime. On Anna's side, it would remain relatively quiet until about four o'clock, when the news department started its day. The sound of news Teletypes would spread throughout the building as the business folks headed home.

The receptionist, who also served as the paper's switchboard operator from 8:30 until 4:30, wasn't at her desk in the front lobby, so Anna quickly jotted down a note saying she would be at home until early evening. She placed the note on the receptionist's chair.

Bright, early afternoon sunlight spilled through the glass front door of the *Journal*. Anna shielded her eyes as she stepped out and onto Milbrook's Main Street. She almost collided with the lens of the television camera that was thrust at her.

Sunbeams filtered into the woods behind the Harrison home where Whit searched through dry brown leaves left over from the previous fall. Off to his right he could hear and see at least a dozen children playing in the backyard of the house. Whit had returned to the courthouse after the street meeting with the Harrisons and Harmon had broken up. But after a restless hour puzzling over the case, he'd made up his mind to quietly return to the site of the kidnapping.

Gnats no larger than a pinhead danced in front of his eyes. He lit a cigarette to keep them at bay. The patch of forest, which separated the Harrisons' home and the next three from an alley, formed an irregular triangle. Whit had started his search on the side of the triangle near the alley. He had been moving from one end of the woods to the other, and each pass was getting shorter as the triangle narrowed. So far he seemed to have escaped observation, but he knew that he would soon be close enough to the Harrisons' backyard to be in sight.

Most of the time he kept his eyes to the ground as he moved through the oak and pine woods. At the outset he had found a sun-bleached beer can. It seemed unlikely that it was relevant evidence, but he retrieved it anyway, placing it in a plastic Ziploc bag.

He reached the edge of the forest and turned around for the fifth time when he heard a small child cry out. At that point he was within a few yards of the backyard. The child, who he recognized as Tommy Fuller, was pointing at him. The others kids were gathering around. Whit stepped to the edge of the woods and smiled. "Don't pay any attention to me, kids. I'm just looking around."

But that was asking the impossible. As Whit moved back into the mottled shade and resumed his search, the children formed a huddle that moved with him. Some of them were laughing, but all of them were watching him. A strange, bowllike form caught his eye. It had white edges and was partially concealed among the remains of last season's leaves. Whit bent down and picked up a small twig. He used it to lift the object.

"You got your nerve," a woman's voice said. Whit looked up. Mrs. Harrison was standing at the fence.

"I'm not bothering you, Mrs. Harrison. I just wanted to have a look in the woods one more time."

"The judge said you can't come around here." The object he was extracting from the leaves captured his attention. He forgot all about Mrs. Harrison as he turned it over and saw that it was a mask—a clown's face.

"You hear me?" the woman said.

Whit looked over at her. "Mrs. Harrison, would you happen to have a paper bag I could borrow—a grocery bag, perhaps?"

His request stunned her. "A grocery bag?"

One side of the mask's rubber band was loose. Carefully Whit tied it to the end of the twig he held and then stood up. "Yes, ma'am. A paper bag. I think I've just found our clown."

He exited the woods holding it up in the air. Mrs. Harrison seemed surprised. "Was that just laying out there?"

"Almost in plain view."

"The cops looked in there the day it happened."

"Obviously not very well . . . If you have a paper bag in which I can place this . . . ?"

Her hostility was gone. "Oh, sure." She turned to Tommy.

"Would you run in and get the man a bag? You know where I keep 'em?"

"Yes'm."

"Wait up a second, Tommy," Whit shouted.

The boy stopped and looked back.

"Is this the mask you saw the other day?"

The boy nodded furiously, then dashed into the house.

"Can you get fingerprints or somethin' off that?" Mrs. Harrison asked.

"There's a good chance," Whit said, eyeing her to see if that produced any kind of reaction.

When it didn't, he continued to examine the mask. His gaze came to rest upon a small orange sticker. "I'll be damned," he said.

The woman was leaning over the fence. "What is it?"

"The price tag, Mrs. Harrison. The kidnapper bought the mask at the local department store. Paid three ninety-five for it."

"For that piece of junk?"

"Ridiculous, isn't it?"

Tommy bounded out of the house with the bag in hand. He gave it to Mrs. Harrison, who handed it over the fence to Whit. "Don't you tell my husband I gave you this."

"Where is Mr. Harrison?"

She blushed and smiled awkwardly. "Well, he's gone to see if he can get a warrant for your arrest for assaulting him."

"I see."

"Maybe if you'd stop trying to shut us down, he'd consider dropping it," she offered hesitantly.

"No thanks. I'd rather be arrested. It won't be the first time on this case, either."

* * *

The Dollar Mart was Milbrook's only major downtown retail outlet. All of the others that had once flourished in the main business district had relocated either to the mall or to one of the small shopping plazas that had sprouted like mushrooms on the highways radiating out from Milbrook. The department store, along with the small grocery across the street, survived because of their lonely singularity. They existed on the fixed income of the elderly and the poor who now inhabited Milbrook's core.

It was the second time in as many days that Whit found himself downtown. But unlike the Department of Human Services, the Dollar Mart had neither moved from the slightly sordid center of the county seat nor changed its name.

The afternoon had grown pleasantly warm. After parking in the spacious lot of the store, Whit exited his car and removed his lightweight sports coat. As a rule, he didn't like walking around in his shirtsleeves. Not that he stood on formality. He was simply uncomfortable walking around in public with his .357 S&W in plain view. He considered removing the weapon and dumping it into his trunk, but decided against it. Unlike most law enforcement officers, Whit didn't feel especially naked without it. On the other hand, considering the part of town he was in, there was always that infinitesimal chance that he might need it. He retrieved the paper bag containing the clown mask and entered the store.

Several customers stood at the only checkout lane that was in operation. They eyed Whit and the weapon on his belt as he approached. The clerk was ringing up the purchases and didn't see Whit.

"Excuse me," he said. "Is the manager in?"

The clerk, a hefty woman with graying hair in a tight bun, emitted a low curse and whirled around. "Can't you see I'm busy waiting on—" At that point she noticed the weapon.

"Just tell me where I can find the manager," Whit said.

The woman glared at him. "She's out to lunch."

"So who's in charge?" Whit asked.

"Mrs. Muldoon, I guess. She's back in the office. Straight at the back of the store."

Whit smiled. "Thanks for your help."

The clerk didn't answer as Whit moved toward the rear of the building. The aisles of the store were narrow and cluttered. As he passed through them, he kept a lookout for the Halloween masks. They were nowhere to be seen. When he reached the rear of the building, he saw the word OFFICE above an opening in the wall. He moved to it and stepped up to the worn counter. Two women were sitting inside the cubicle. They looked up at him over the counter.

"I'm looking for Mrs. Muldoon," Whit said.

The older of the two women stood. "That's me, but if you're selling something, you'll have to come back."

Whit displayed his badge. "Not selling a thing."

The woman studied his badge. "You're not one of the city cops."

Whit introduced himself.

"Is there some kind of problem?" Mrs. Muldoon was tall and thin, probably approaching sixty, and she looked as if she had worked in what everyone called the five-and-dime for most of her adult life.

Whit opened the bag and allowed the mask to slide onto the counter. "Please don't touch it," he said.

Mrs. Muldoon actually stepped back from it. "Why? Is it dangerous? Infected or something?"

"I'm going to have it fingerprinted. According to the price tag, the mask was purchased here, probably very recently."

The younger woman, who was nearly as broad as she was tall, stood up and examined the mask. "We carry those, mister—and if it was bought here, it wasn't before Monday. I put them things on the floor late Saturday evening, just after closing."

Mrs. Muldoon was nodding. "Right; we didn't get the Halloween stuff in until last Friday."

"Then it had to be purchased on Monday morning, sometime after you opened. I'd like to see if any of your employees remember selling someone this mask," Whit said.

Mrs. Muldoon turned to the young woman. "Who worked the front register Monday morning?"

"Musta been Stel. I was off Monday morning."

"Stel?" Whit said. "What's her full name?"

"Stella. Stella Howell."

"Is she here?"

"Right up front on the register," Mrs. Muldoon said. She turned to the other girl. "You go relieve her and send her back here."

But the young girl hesitated. "Is this about that missing kid?"

The question surprised Whit. "Yes; how did you know?"

The girl shrugged. "Read about it in the paper this morning. They said the guy wore a clown mask. Gee, I guess he bought it here, huh?"

"Looks that way," Whit said.

"Shoo, girl!" the older woman said. "Go fetch Stel."

"Yes, ma'am."

"I'm the assistant manager, Mr. Pynchon. The manager is going to be sorry she missed this."

"Not to be complaining," Whit said, "but the woman up front—Stel—didn't seem especially friendly when I came in."

Mrs. Muldoon smiled. "That's Stel. She's a good worker,

dependable and honest as the day is long, but she's a bit cranky. Doesn't have much use for the police, either.''

"I noticed."

"Well, her youngest got into some trouble a while back, and they sent him to prison. She ain't gotten over it. It was the boy's first time in trouble, and she can't figure—'' The woman stopped. ''Here she comes.''

Stella Howell looked even less pleased than she had when Whit had met her just a few minutes before. She marched toward him, her lips clinched and her eyes narrowed. ''If this is about my boy, mister—''

Whit held up his hand. ''Whoa, lady! I don't know anything about your son.''

"You people did him damned dirty, mister. He got caught with some pills—my pills, mind ya—and they sent him to prison. I see all kinda scum walk in here day in and day out done a lot worse than my boy. They ain't in prison.''

Whit had learned long ago not to try to defend the inconsistencies of the judicial system, especially when he didn't know all the facts. ''Well, Mrs. Howell—''

"*Miss* Howell,'' the woman said. ''Not married . . . never have been. Not proud of it, but not ashamed, either.''

"Okay, Miss Howell then. I don't know anything about your son. I just need to know if you sold a mask like this on Monday morning.''

The woman frowned, not even looking at the piece of molded plastic on the counter. ''How the devil would I remember?''

"It might help if you took a look at it,'' Whit said.

"Look, mister. I got no time for you people. I got no time to be tied up in your damned courts. I gotta work to pay off that damned lawyer that didn't do no good.''

"Stel!'' This time Mrs. Muldoon spoke up. ''There's no

sense taking your problems out on this man. He's trying to find a missing child. I know you well enough to know that you care about children.''

The clerk nodded. ''Yeah, I do care about chil'un.'' She moved toward the mask.

''Please don't touch it, Miss Howell. I haven't had a chance to have it checked for fingerprints.''

The woman looked at Whit. ''Fingerprints?''

''Yes, ma'am.''

''You can get them from something like that?'' she asked. Whit nodded.

''Well, then you might get my prints. I sold that mask—leastways one just like it—on Monday morning. I 'member the one who bought it, too.''

FIFTEEN

ANNA DESPISED TELEVISION NEWS. She despised television cameras. Most of all, she despised the woman who was snapping questions at her as she tried to cross Main Street to the safety of her car. What would she look like on television? At the moment of confrontation, she suspected that she had appeared at first startled and then angry.

Myra Martin was talking into the mike. "The person exiting the offices of the *Milbrook Daily Journal* is Anna Tyree, the newspaper's editor. According to the mother of the missing child, it was Miss Tyree who accompanied Whitley Pynchon on his wild-goose chase down to the resort area of South Carolina."

By the time Martin had gotten around to shoving the microphone at her, Anna had regained her composure.

"May we have an interview, Miss Tyree?"

"Any and all news I know I put in the newspaper," Anna had said, trying after that to brush by the television reporter.

The crew had been prepared for her action. As Anna stepped into the street, the cameraman dashed to keep in front of her. The reporter moved along beside Anna. "Is it true that you were with Investigator Pynchon in Myrtle Beach?"

"As I said, Miss Martin, any news I have to report will

be available through the pages of the *Journal*." If Anna had been able to cross the street at that point, the confrontation might have been otherwise uneventful. However, as she started to move into the street, a huge truck loaded with gravel came barreling toward her. She had no choice but to stop.

"You do respect the public's right to know, don't you, Miss Tyree?"

"More than you do," Anna snapped.

"Were you in Myrtle Beach with—"

"Tell me something, Myra. Any truth to the rumor that you fucked your station manager to get your job?"

The cameraman laughed, and the blond reporter pulled the mike away from Anna and back to her own mouth. "Miss Tyree, are you refusing to answer?" Back came the mike.

"I asked you a question, Myra. Don't you want to answer it?"

Martin had lost some of her control. "Do you want me to tell the people of Raven County that the *Journal* is intimately involved in an effort to cover up police incompetence, perhaps even official misfeasance?"

"I'd rather you told your audience how you managed to screw your way into your job given your level of incompetence. It's bimbos like you that give local television news such a bad name."

Martin turned back to her cohort. "Kill the camera, Kenny."

"Keep the camera going, Kenny. I might do something that'll make you rich on 'America's Funniest Home Videos.' "

Kenny kept the camera rolling.

"Damn it, Kenny!" Martin ordered. "I said kill it."

This time he did. Then he lowered it from his shoulder.

"You know we can edit out all that bullshit," Martin said.

Anna shrugged. "Sure, I know that. What's your motto, Myra? All the news that makes me look good? Where the hell do you get off pulling this kind of crap? Is it ratings week or something?"

"It's news, and—"

"You wouldn't know news if it bit you on one of those implanted boobs of yours."

Kenny laughed again. "I'd sure like to get this on film."

Martin whirled on him. "If you dare, I'll get your ass fired."

Anna winked at Kenny. "Maybe you oughta try sleeping with the boss."

"The issue isn't who I've been sleeping with," the TV reporter said.

"Yeah, that would be pretty hard to detail in a thirty-second sound bite. Just for the sake of argument, you do know that Whit Pynchon went to Myrtle Beach because of the child's mother. She was the one insisting that her ex-husband, who now lives in Myrtle Beach, had snatched the child."

"That's not what she says," Myra countered.

"Then she's not telling the truth, Myra."

"It's not up to me to decide who's telling the truth. I have the accusation Mrs. Winters made on camera. I'm honor-bound to give the other side a chance to respond."

Anna laughed. "Honor-bound? You tarnish the very concept."

Martin straightened her back. The muscles in her neck and face tensed. "You can be damned sure of one thing, Anna. You won't be looking very professional on the news tonight, and you have no one to blame but yourself."

"Wrong," Anna said. "I know who I'll blame—and you can be assured of one thing yourself: I never forget."

"Is that a threat?" Martin asked.

Anna looked at the cameraman. "Is she always this quick?"

He snickered.

"Go ahead," the TV reporter said. "Have your fun. I'm just doing my job."

"I know that," Anna said. "That's why I have so little use for you. You're paid to look pretty and act ugly, and you do the latter very well."

"What'd the guy look like?" Whit asked.

Stella Howell had eased up on her hostility. Like the other cashier, she had heard about the missing child. If there was any way she could help, she wanted to do so. After all, she knew what it was like to have a child taken away—even if her child had been nineteen when the law had taken him from her.

"I 'member him because he didn't look like the type to be buying a kid's mask. I wondered if maybe he was gonna go use it to rob a bank or something."

"Can you describe him?" Whit asked again.

"He was tall . . . over six feet. He was wearing jeans and a gray T-shirt with a hole up by the shoulder. He had big hands with calluses, like he did some physical work, you know."

"What about his face?"

The woman pondered the matter. "Ya know, I can't really remember. He needed a shave. I remember that."

"What about his hair?"

The woman shrugged. "I think it was kinda dark, but he had a cap on—one of those kinds advertising chewin' 'bacca—maybe Red Man. The hair stuck out a little in the back, but not real long.''

Whit contained his frustration. Here was a woman who probably had seen the kidnapper and who had cause to remember him. The best she could do was provide a description that fit half the males in Raven County. ''Would you know him if you saw him again?''

''I think so. Won't rightly know until I do see him again.''

''Did he say anything?''

''I think maybe he grunted when I said good morning. I made some comment about how his kid sure was gonna like that mask, and he didn't say anything.''

Huge panes of unobstructed glass formed the front of the Dollar Mart, so Whit asked, ''Did you happen to see what kind of vehicle he was driving?''

She shook her head. ''I 'member there was someone else behind him in line. When I finished with him, I paid attention to the next customer.''

''You happen to remember who that was?'' Whit asked.

''Landsakes, no. Only reason I 'member so much about the fella buying the mask was 'cause of the mask.''

''I wish you remembered a little more,'' Whit said.

''Did the best I could,'' Stella Howell said, a hint of animosity returning to her voice. ''If it hadn't been a kid involved, I guarantee you I wouldn't 'member that much. I got little use for the law these days.''

''If I can make the arrangements, would you stop by the sheriff's office at the courthouse and take a look through the mug shots? There might be a chance you can pick the fella out from those photos.''

The woman tensed. ''Wonder if Lonnie's picture is in there.''

''They take photos of anyone who has been arrested, Miss

Howell. Sometimes they even use photos of police officers if they have to prepare a photo lineup. If your son was arrested, then he's probably in the books. Was your son arrested by the sheriff's department?''

She shook her head. ''Damn state got him. Some grungy undercover cop.''

''The state police handle things a little differently. You aren't likely to come across your son's photo in the sheriff's file unless he was arrested by the city or the county.'' In truth Whit planned on asking the woman to visit the local state police detachment to go through their mug shots, also, but he was working with the woman one step at a time. If she could make no identification from the sheriff's photo records, then he would bring up the issue of the state police. Not until then.

''When should I go?'' she asked.

''This afternoon if you can.''

Mrs. Muldoon, the assistant manager, was monitoring the conversation. ''Go now, Stel. I'm sure no one will mind.''

Stella Howell shrugged her consent, so Whit made a quick call to the sheriff's department to make them aware that she was coming.

''You gonna be there?'' she asked as she prepared to leave.

''I have some other things I need to check,'' he said.

He pulled out his badge case and withdrew a business card from it. ''If you happen to remember anything else, will you call me?''

She looked at the card for a few seconds before accepting it. ''Yeah . . . if I 'member anything else. You sure I won't come across Lonnie's picture in them books?''

''Not unless he was arrested by the deputies or the city police for something else.''

''I done told you that was his first time. Never heard of

anyone getting sent to prison for their first time. You tell me, mister. You ever heard of it?''

Whit nodded his head. ''Yes, ma'am. It does happen.'' He didn't add that it was usually only in cases of first-degree murder.

Whit drove over to the state police detachment and quickly arranged for a county-to-county relay to get the clown mask to the Criminal Investigation Division in Charleston. By the time he borrowed an office to phone the fingerprint lab, the mask was already en route. A secretary answered the phone, and he briefed her on the situation. He hoped the urgency in his voice would be enough to get the matter handled as soon as the mask arrived.

''I'm just filling in this afternoon,'' the woman replied in an unenthusiastic voice.

''Let me talk to someone in the lab,'' Whit said impatiently.

''No one's here.''

''What do you mean no one's there?''

''They're all out. At a party.''

''A what?''

''A party for one of the guys. He got a job in Washington, D.C.''

''Wonderful. Tell him congratulations. So when can I get the report on the mask?''

''I can put a rush on it.''

''What's that mean?''

''Noon tomorrow maybe. I'm not sure.''

''N.F.D.''

''What?''

''Do I have to spell it out? We're dealing with the life of a little girl. You call up the party boys and girls and tell them I want the results tonight. You got that?"

"Yes, sir."

He slammed the phone down. "Christ."

Whit headed to the courthouse to tell Tony Danton about the mask. But as soon as he stepped through the front door of the building, bright lights blinded him. Through the glare he saw a blond-haired vision coming at him. He shielded his eyes from the lights just as the microphone was pushed close to his face.

"Investigator Pynchon, have you found Marcia Winters yet?"

"Back off," Whit said, unable to contain his fury at the ambush.

"The mother of the child claims that the prosecutor's office isn't even looking for her child."

Whit pulled himself together and saw an obnoxious smile on the face of Myra Martin. It wasn't his first encounter with the shapely but aggressive star from the Bluefield television station.

"No comment," Whit said.

He tried to sidestep her, but she headed him off. "Mrs. Winters claims you went to Myrtle Beach allegedly to find her child, but you in fact went down in the company of a woman and played golf."

"I hate golf," Whit said.

She pulled the mike back to ask something else. Whit saw his chance and literally shoved her aside. As he fled into the sanctuary of the prosecutor's office, she heard the woman saying, "Obviously Investigator Pynchon doesn't want to answer—"

He didn't hear the rest of it . . . didn't even want to hear the rest of it.

The office secretary had an expression of sympathy on her face. "I would have warned you, but—You really should get a police radio in your car."

"That would be a worse fate," Whit said.

She handed him a stack of phone messages and said, "The sheriff wants to talk to you right away."

"Call him and tell him I'm here, but warn him about that she-brute in the hall. He may want to wait."

"Anna called, too. I gather Myra Martin paid her a visit before coming here."

"Oh, shit," Whit said. "Did she want me to call her back?"

"She didn't say, but sounded angry."

"I can imagine. Did she say whether she was home or at the newspaper?"

"At home."

Whit went to his office and immediately dialed the number. "I hear you had an encounter of the infuriating kind with the charming lady from the television station," he said when he heard Anna's voice.

"Damn her! She's actually going to report that you and I went on some kind of Love Boat excursion to the beach when you were supposed to be searching for the missing child."

"Tell you the truth, I don't care what she reports," Whit said.

"For chrissakes, Whit; I care. She's going to make it sound—well, tawdry."

"It wasn't. You know that, and I know that. What difference does it make?"

"First of all, I happen to believe that the press has a duty to be responsible. She's prepared to broadcast a total lie. Second, I don't like being accused of—of . . . well, you know what I mean."

Whit laughed. "As far as I'm concerned, there are more reporters like her than you, so I'm not surprised at what she's doing. As to the other, what the hell can you do about it? People will think what they want to think. If they know you or me, they'll know better."

"I wish I had your thick skin. I don't. It bothers me."

"Don't watch it."

"Oh, sure. You know I'll have to watch it."

"Fine, suffer then. Just don't bother telling me about it. Ignorance can be blissful."

Anna knew better than to pursue the matter. "Any progress on the child's case?"

"Not much."

"What's that mean?"

"Not much."

"I gather that. Can you at least tell me what you were doing this morning? Must have been something really spicy to get you up and out so early."

He chuckled. "Yeah, it was loads of fun. Norma Wyse and I planted ourselves in front of the FunTime Day-Care Center and interviewed the parents as they dropped their kids off. Aside from the fact that cheapo day care is in great demand, it was a waste of time."

"Wow! I bet the Harrisons were pissed."

"You could say that. They managed to get an injunction to stop us."

"An injunction?"

Gil Dickerson, the sheriff of Raven County, stuck his head around the corner of the door. Whit motioned him to come inside. "Yeah, an injunction. I'll tell you about it later. Gil's here."

"The injunction sounds like news to me," Anna said.

"Forget it. I've had enough of you damned reporters today."

He hung up.

Gil hobbled into the office. Two years earlier, a bullet had shattered his knee. It left him with a limp and frequent bouts of severe pain. "Miss Martin cornered me earlier and asked if we were involved in the search for the Winters kid. I assured her that my department was investigating any and all leads."

"Bitch," Whit muttered.

"Watch it," the sheriff said, his eyes twinkling. "It's okay to talk nasty about male reporters, but take it easy with the ladies."

"I haven't seen any ladies in that business."

Gil hiked his eyebrows. "Oh, we *are* touchy. Better watch where you say that line. Anna might take serious offense."

"With regard to Martin, Anna agrees." He told Gil what Anna had said to him.

"Ouch!" Gil said. "Anyway, I had one of my detectives search through his case files as well as our more recent criminal records. We can't find a single individual likely to grab a kid like this."

"Not one?" Whit asked.

The sheriff shook his head. "There was Tiny Bright. He liked to take pictures of naked little girls, but he's still in stir up in Moundsville. We also pulled Dayton Caldwell's file. He was a suspect in those parking lot rape-cases a few years back. He's on his deathbed with cancer."

"Maybe there *is* a God," Whit said.

"Anyway, we've pulled some files on guys we're gonna check out, but none of them seem to fit our idea of a child molester who actually kidnaps his victims."

The sheriff sat on a plastic couch that filled one corner of

Whit's small office. He had his bad leg extended and was massaging it just above the knee.

"Your leg giving you trouble?"

"Don't even ask about it. I was getting out of the cruiser this morning and wrenched it. Damned seats are too low."

"You need to be more careful," Whit said. "I found the mask."

"You did?"

"The price tag was still on the mask. It came from the Dollar Mart downtown. I located a clerk there who remembers selling the mask to an adult white male. She gave us a partial description, almost useless. She's going through the mug shots at the sheriff's office right now."

"Where's the mask?"

"On its way to CID in Charleston. Maybe we'll get a print, maybe not. You hear about the injunction?"

"What injunction?"

Whit waved a hand. "Never mind. Anything from the Teletypes?"

Immediately after he had returned from South Carolina, Whit had enlisted Gil's department to send Teletypes nationwide about the missing girl. They had sent a regional Teletype to other police agencies asking if any other departments had experienced similar abductions.

"We got a response from a department over in Kentucky. A child got separated from his parents in a shopping mall and hasn't been seen since. That was three months ago. They're sending me the case file."

Whit rubbed his hand through his thick, graying hair. "I wouldn't hold my breath on it."

"I know. It's a tough one," the sheriff said. "It's like a serial killing. More than likely, the choice was randomly made. The perp has no prior connection with the family. He saw the little girl and saw a chance to grab her.''

"He did a little more than that, Gil. He must have planned it. That fence wasn't cut in a hurry. I've been thinking. Could one of your detectives check out the hardware stores? See if anyone bought a pair of bolt cutters within the past week or so?''

"Sure.''

"I know it's a long shot, but if the guy was passing through town, odds are he wasn't carrying a bolt cutter with him.''

"Did the city boys interview all of the neighbors?''

Whit rolled his eyes. "They claim they did, and no one saw anything out of the ordinary. But considering how they missed the mask . . .''

"Want my guys to do a follow-up?''

The offer surprised Whit. "If the city boys find out about it, they'll be like a bunch of angry hornets.''

"Screw 'em,'' said Gil. "When it comes to a missing three-year-old kid, there's nothing wrong with double-checking.''

"Great, then. Do it. Be sure they ask about any suspicious vehicles hanging around the neighborhood—not just that day, but for a week or so before that.''

Grimacing in pain, Gil pushed himself to his feet. "Will do.''

"Oh, and warn your deputies to stay away from the day-care center. They've got an injunction.''

Gil nodded. "What's this about an injunction?''

Whit explained the morning's events. Gil shook his head in disgust. "It's lawyers like Ardis Harmon who give the legal profession a bad name. Isn't it a conflict of interest for her to represent the day-care people and Mrs. Winters?''

The answer came from Tony Danton, who appeared in the

doorway. ''Not until Mrs. Winters decides to sue them for negligence.''

''Who will she represent then?'' Gil asked.

''The one with the best insurance,'' Whit said.

''No doubt,'' Gil said. ''Gotta go. By the way, at Whit's recommendation, I've sent deputies to the Harrisons' neighborhood.''

Tony bristled. ''You *what*?''

''Take it easy, Tony. There's good reason. Whit will explain.''

Tony stepped back to let Gil leave and then came into Whit's office. ''This better be good.''

''They're not going to bother the Harrisons. They're going to talk to the neighbors.''

''The city boys already handled it.''

''You mean like they searched the woods behind the center?'' Whit said.

He told Tony about the mask.

By the time Whit had finished, Danton had made up his mind. ''Okay, I'm going to notify the judge and Harmon about Gil's intentions . . . just in case. Otherwise Harmon will file a contempt motion in the blink of the eye.''

''Forget Harmon and her fucking motions.''

''I wish I could. You don't have more zingers for me this afternoon, do you?''

''Well, there is one.''

''What?'' Tony growled.

''Myra Martin.''

''What about her?''

''She's probably going to run a story about me lollygagging in Myrtle Beach with Anna instead of looking for the girl.''

''How'd she find out Anna went along?''

"Mrs. Winters."

He explained the circumstances. Tony jumped to his feet. "Damn it to hell! The woman is crazy."

"She's scared, Tony. I can overlook her behavior. But Martin . . ."

"What did you say to her?"

"No comment—until she accused me of playing golf."

"You hate golf."

"That's what I told her."

"What about Anna?"

"I don't know what Anna said."

The prosecutor's eyes became as large as saucers. "Christ, Martin talked to Anna, too? I meant, what did you say about Anna?"

"Yeah, she talked to Anna. I didn't mention her."

Tony started toward the door. "Sometimes, Whit, you're more damned trouble than you're worth."

Whit fell to his knees. "Oh, please, boss man. Fire me! C'mon, make my day."

The commotion turned Tony around. "I wouldn't give you the satisfaction." The prosecutor was smiling when he said it.

SIXTEEN

WHIT DIDN'T REALLY PLAN to arrive home in time to see the six o'clock local news on television. It just happened that way. As he stepped into the house, he stripped off his jacket and hung it up in the closet in the house's small foyer. He removed the gun and holster from his belt and tucked the weapon away on the closet's top shelf. He could hear the sound of the television set coming from the living room. He recognized the music as the intro to the news from WWWA-TV, the Bluefield station. When he entered the living room, he found Anna and his daughter, Tressa, sitting in the living room.

"Just in time to see me make a fool out of myself," Anna said.

Whit kissed Tressa and cast a wary eye at the screen. "You? You mean me, don't you?"

"Both of us probably," Anna said.

Tressa laughed. "Anna told me all about it."

Whit felt his face warm with a touch of embarrassment. Tressa and Anna often talked about things that made Whit a little ill at ease. He still wasn't quite able to accept that Tressa was an adult.

The local anchor, a skinny young man with an obvious overbite, opened the newscast with details of a fatal accident in Bluefield. Whit settled down on the couch beside Anna. "You worried?"

"I really laid into her, Whit. But I'm sure that'll all be cut."

Whit cringed. "I've told you not to bother defending me. See what happens?"

"Defending you? What about me?" Anna retorted.

"Shh!" Tressa said. "Here it comes."

Whit scowled. "I don't need this."

With an outline of Raven County superimposed on the screen behind him, the anchor was saying, "In Milbrook, authorities still aren't saying if they have any leads on the mysterious abduction of a three-year-old girl from a day-care facility, and some people, including the mother of the missing child, are beginning to question the manner by which police officials are conducting the investigation. Myra Martin has the story."

"Why am I watching this?" Whit asked as the blonde's painted face appeared on the screen.

The reporter was standing in front of the Harrisons' house. "On Monday of this week, three-year-old Marcia Winters was pulled through a hole in a fence in the rear of this day-care facility by an unidentified individual wearing a clown's mask. Her abduction took place in front of half a dozen of her stunned playmates."

Myra's face was replaced on the screen by a tight shot of the opening cut in the fence. She continued with a voice over. "Whitley Pynchon, special investigator for the prosecuting attorney's office, was assigned to head the investigation. According to Sue Winters, the child's mother, Investigator Pynchon . . ."

A shot of Whit, frozen in action, appeared on the screen. His face was contorted into an angry leer as the reporter went on. ". . . Investigator Pynchon, seen here as he refused comment on the case, promptly left Raven County for Myrtle Beach, South Carolina, where William Winters, the child's father and Mrs. Winters's ex-husband, lives. It's unclear at this point what evidence the authorities had to implicate Winters in the kidnapping. However, while authorities are not commenting on the case, we have learned from a source that William Winters has been cleared of any involvement in the child's abduction.''

Anna was on the edge of her seat, expecting her own face to flash up on the screen. It didn't. Instead, the face of Sue Winters came on. A label at the bottom of the screen identified her as Marcia's mother. "The police, and especially Whit Pynchon, are doing nothing to find my child.'' Her eyes were full of tears as she spoke. "Some pervert has stolen my daughter, and instead of looking for him, Pynchon spent the morning right here . . .''

The camera pulled back to show the day-care center. ". . . harassing the people who run this facility. I just want Marcia back. I'm so afraid that this pervert . . .'' She shook her head and covered her face with her hands, unable to go on.

The cameraman kept the lens on her as Myra Martin started into another voice-over. "This woman weeps for her child. She doesn't know what the authorities are doing. Neither do we, for that matter. If they're doing anything, they're not saying. We have learned one thing. Late this afternoon, a Raven County magistrate issued a warrant charging Whitley Pynchon, the investigator with the Raven County Prosecuting Attorney's offices, with assault upon Ivan Harrison, along with his wife, Clara, who operates this day-care center.''

Tressa gasped. Anna slowly turned her head to Whit. He was sitting there, his jaws clamped tightly shut as Myra Martin concluded her report. "We will stay on top of the situation here in Raven County as events continue to unfold in this bizarre incident."

"Why the hell didn't you tell me about the warrant?" Anna said.

Whit grabbed the remote control and switched off the television. "Because I didn't know about it. I mean, I didn't know one had been issued. Mrs. Harrison told me her husband was going to file a complaint."

"Are you going to be arrested?" Tressa asked.

"That's what a warrant does," Whit said, pushing himself up from the couch. "I'd better go call Tony."

"I've got to get to the office," Anna said.

Just as Whit reached the phone, it rang. He picked it up and grumbled an impatient "Yeah" into the handset.

"Whit?" It was Tony.

"I was just going to call you. Did you see the news?"

"Yes. I guess you didn't know about the assault charge."

Whit flushed mad. "And you did? Why the hell didn't you tell me?"

"I just found out about it moments ago. It's not a warrant. It's a summons to appear ten days from now."

Whit shook his head. "So why did we have to find out about it so late?"

"The magistrate was in a trial. He took Harrison's complaint during a recess and went immediately back into trial. He called as soon as he finished."

"Then how the hell did that bitch over in Bluefield get hold of it so damned quick?" Whit asked.

"Ardis Harmon probably called her just before she went on the air."

"That figures. Did you file a case against the day care?"

"Yeah, but now it'll just look like sour grapes. Like we're doing it just to negotiate you out of an assault charge."

"The hell with what it looks like! Did you get an order to shut them down pending the investigation?"

Tony shook his head. "Ardis convinced the judge there was no immediate danger to the children. We lost on that one, but—"

"Chrissake, Tony! It seems like whatever Harmon wants, Harmon gets."

"I can't argue with you there. Just be glad there's only one of her."

"That's for damn sure," Whit muttered.

"Anything on the mask yet?"

"Not that I've heard." Whit tried to shake the image of a smirking Ardis Harmon from his mind.

"What about the clerk?"

"Nothing. She could not find him in the mug shots."

"Can she I.D. him if she sees him again?" Tony asked.

"I wouldn't bet a bundle on it."

There was a moment of disappointed silence on the other end. "So we don't have a lot."

"I'm hoping the fingerprints boys and girls will come up with something. If they don't we're at a—" He started to say dead end. That didn't seem appropriate. "We're at a standstill."

Dewey Johns crushed the can of beer in his hand. It was nearly full, and the beer fizzled over his fist. "Fuck you, bitch. I ain't no pervert." He hurled the can at the television set as the uppity blonde finished her report. "Better get that straight, too."

He slouched further down in the couch and turned off the TV with his boot. Rolling over on his side, he snatched up the phone, which was on a coffee table next to a half-empty bottle of Wild Turkey. He punched a number. "Randi, it's me. Did you see the TV?"

"I told you not to call me," the woman replied in a firm voice.

"I said did you see the TV?"

"If you mean the news, yes I did."

"They called me a pervert. The bitch."

"So what?"

"I ain't no—"

"I know you're not." Her voice softened and sounded the way he liked it. "Let them think what they want."

"I don't like it, Randi," Johns grumbled. "I ain't no molester."

"What are you going to do, go down to the TV station and tell them you're a good guy?"

Johns didn't answer.

"Now don't call me again until things calm down. Just lay low like I told you. Everything will be okay."

"What about the other kid, the one who pulled off the mask?"

"Forget about him," the woman said in a comforting voice. "Believe me. He's too young to identify you."

"I don't know about that."

"Dewey, don't mess this up. We've got a good thing going, you and me. In another couple of months—when it gets cold—we'll head down to some island in the Caribbean, and it'll be great. Just you and me."

He grunted and twisted the cord in his hand. "Yeah. Okay."

The phone clicked. Johns pushed off the couch. He needed another drink.

He didn't like how bossy she was getting with him. She

seemed different now from back when he met her when he was in jail. She was one of those women who felt sorry for guys who were locked up, but when they got out, things changed.

He was glad he hadn't told Randi about his failed attempt to silence the boy. But he didn't buy her argument that the kid was too young. What if the kid saw him somewhere and recognized him? Then it would be all over.

No, he had to finish what he'd started, and she'd be glad he did it when it was all over. Then they'd be safe.

SEVENTEEN

TOMMY FULLER EYED the spoonful of pink medicine with obvious distaste. "That stuff looks yucky."

"It will help you sleep," his mother said. "Besides, you're sniffling."

The four-year-old was coming down with a cold, but, like most kids his age—especially those in day care—that wasn't anything unusual. They spent their lives coming down with a cold, sick with a cold, or getting over one. Margaret Fuller sometimes thought her only function at this point in her son's life was to wipe his nose and deliver him to the pediatrician. The sniffles, though, were a pretext for the medicine. Tommy hadn't slept much at all the night before, frightened as he was by the prowler, and she knew he'd been worrying all day about going to bed tonight. So Margaret had phoned their pediatrician, who had recommended that she pick up some Benadryl at the local drugstore. "But that's for colds," Margaret had said.

The doctor had chuckled. "True, but it has the same basic ingredient as those adult sleep-inducers. It's dyphenhdramine—DPl. It should make Tommy sleep."

That's what was in the teaspoon she was offering Tommy. "It doesn't taste that bad," she said, not even stumbling over what amounted to a blatant misrepresentation. She had never tasted the stuff herself.

"Then you take it," Tommy said, crossing his arms in front of him.

His mother had to suppress a smile. She loved his independence and did little to stifle it. Public school would do that soon enough. "Take your medicine, Tommy, and don't get sassy."

"Can I have some ice cream?"

Margaret Fuller nodded. "Just as soon as you take your medicine."

He finally relented and opened his mouth. "There. Was that so terrible?"

He made a face. "It tastes bad."

"Now, what kind of ice cream do you want?"

"Choc-choc."

"Say it right. Chocolate chocolate chip."

"Choc-choc."

"That *is* easier," she said, and laughed. As she scooped the ice cream into a dish, Margaret heard television voices in the background. Jerry Fuller was in the family room watching one of those true-life mystery programs that had become so popular in recent years. Margaret saw nothing entertaining about them. At least with the more traditional television programming, you knew it was just the product of someone's imagination. Working at the hospital, she saw more than enough real-life dramas.

She placed Tommy's ice cream at the kitchen table and helped him into a chair. Then she went into the family room, where Jerry was spread out on the couch, a can of beer in his hand.

"I called the hospital day care today," she said. He didn't

respond for a few seconds, not until a commercial interrupted the program. Then he sat up. "So what did they say?"

"They put Tommy's name on the waiting list."

"A waiting list?"

Margaret shrugged. "It's a popular place. The director told me it would probably be a month or so."

Jerry had struggled against it as long as he dared. "That'll help a little. Don't we pay off the washer and dryer next month?"

His wife nodded.

"Then we should be able to afford the extra cost."

"I was talking to the director, Jerry. In the long run it might not cost any extra money. We can deduct it from our taxes. You haven't been doing that, you know."

He hadn't deducted it, because they were paying the Harrisons in cash. That was part of the agreement they had, and because of it the Harrisons had given him a better deal. "We'll see," he said. "I'm gonna wait until we're ready to move Tommy before I tell the Harrisons."

Tommy came into the living room. "Move me?"

Margaret laughed. "You've got big ears for a little boy."

"Sometimes," his father said. "Unless we're telling him to clean up his room. Then he seems to be deaf."

"Where are you gonna move me?"

His parents traded glances. It was Margaret who answered. "We're not moving you anywhere right now, Tommy. We were talking about when you move up to kindergarten next year."

"I don't wanna go to kindergarten."

Tommy had been in a defiant mood all night, displaying a feistiness bordering on disobedience. Margaret thought he was behaving in such a fashion to conceal his overwhelming fear of going to bed. She had asked her husband to overlook it. Jerry Fuller had shown amazing patience, but it was wearing thin. "You'll go where you're told to go, young man."

Tommy looked his father straight in his eyes and said, "No, I won't."

Margaret sighed in exasperation as her husband pushed himself up from the couch. "That's what you think, young man. You'll do as you're told—and right now that means going to bed."

The boy reacted as if he'd just touched something searing hot. His face twisted into a mask of fear. Tears filled his eyes. "It's not bedtime!" he shrieked.

Margaret saw her husband's face flush. She reached out and put a hand on his arm. He looked at her, then settled back into his chair. The anger was gone from his face. "Come here, Tommy."

The boy moved closer to Margaret. "I want my mother."

Margaret, though, eased him back toward his father. "Your daddy wants to talk to you." She had been married to him long enough to read that signal. Jerry Fuller had that look on his face, the same one he had when he was getting ready to tell her that they were going to have to cut back on groceries for the month . . . or maybe give up a planned weekend outing.

"Over here, son," his father said again.

The boy moved slowly toward Jerry Fuller, tears still streaming down his face. When he was within his reach, Jerry Fuller gathered the four-year-old into his arms and lifted him onto his lap. He brushed the tears from his son's cheeks. "You know, when I was a lot older than you, I was afraid to go to bed, too."

That admission lifted the boy's face. "Older 'n me?"

Jerry nodded. "I used to go see those scary movies they

showed down at the theater. It's gone now, the theater I mean, but they made me afraid to go to sleep at night.''

''Because of monsters?''

Jerry grinned. ''Yeah, but when I grew up, I found out that there wasn't any such thing. When I went home from school, there was no one at the house. My mom and dad, your grandparents, they both worked, so I was even afraid then—afraid something terrible was hiding in the closet or in the attic.''

''Was there?'' Tommy asked.

''You know there wasn't, Tommy. I was just scared of silly things. You're a lot braver than I am.'' The look of confusion on the boy's face prompted Jerry to try to say it again another way. ''I was a lot more scared than you are.''

Phrased that way the boy understood it. ''You were?''

''Sure. I mean, you tried to keep that bad man in the clown's mask from taking Marcia Winters, didn't you?'' Tommy nodded.

''That was very brave of you. You weren't scared, were you?''

''A little,'' Tommy admitted.

Margaret listened to her husband without interrupting. At the same time, she wasn't certain she liked her husband's approach to this problem. After all, there had been a prowler last night. That wasn't a figment of her son's imagination. In some ways fear was a good thing. Nonetheless, she kept her doubts to herself.

''But you tried to help anyway,'' her husband was saying.

The boy nodded.

''Sometimes, Tommy, we have to do things even when we are scared. Like tonight, I know you're scared to go to bed because of what happened last night.''

There were new tears in the boy's eyes. "I wanna sleep with you and Mommy."

Jerry Fuller slowly shook his head. "Big boys don't do that, Tommy. Big boys—brave boys—sleep in their own beds even if they are a little scared."

"What if the man comes back?"

"He won't, Tommy. I bet he's the one who's scared now."

"He won't come back?" Tommy asked.

Jerry Fuller tossled his son's thick brace of brown hair. "I promise, Tommy. He won't come back tonight."

Whit's life had undergone a major reconstruction over the past two years. First, he had met Anna. Their relationship had been stormy at first, more like *typhoonish*, if there were such a word. It was still stormy at times. Some months later she had moved in with him. He'd lived as a bachelor for so many years that it had been difficult learning to live with someone else again. After all, his first effort at cohabitation, nearly two decades earlier, had been an absolute disaster. It had ended in divorce, but not until after Tressa had been born.

His daughter had been the second big change in his life. Not that she hadn't spent a lot of time at his house. In spite of the divorce, he and Tressa had managed to stay close throughout her childhood and adolescent years. Then, not too many months ago, Whit's first wife had died. Tressa moved in with Anna and him. The two women, years apart, had become best of friends even before the tragic death of Whit's ex-wife. Now they all but consumed his life.

Getting used to Anna had been hard enough. Getting used to two women had been a trial. Not that he wasn't happy to have them here. It just took some adjustments. With Tressa, the biggest change that she brought with her was the constantly ringing telephone. Whit hated telephones. There had been a time when his seldom rang. Now it rang all the time, and generally it was for Tressa. As he sat on the back porch of his small house, enjoying the warm September night, he had been counting. He'd been on the porch for about forty minutes, and the phone had rung five times. Anna had already returned to the newspaper, and Tressa had been fielding the calls. It had just sounded again, prompting Whit's assessment of the recent upheavals in his life-style.

He'd been thinking about the Winters case. As a rule, crimes in his jurisdiction weren't big mysteries. Most killings grew out of domestic arguments or beer-joint feuds. In those cases, the culprit—more often than not—was standing over the body with the smoking gun in hand when the cops arrived. There were, of course, the occasional armed robberies at the all-night convenience stores. In Raven County they occurred maybe a dozen times a year. About a third of them were cleared.

While Milbrook and Raven County weren't crime-free by anyone's standards, its children had generally been safe. Crimes against children just hadn't been a big problem, not until this week. Sure, estranged husbands grabbed their kids and absconded. As had many states, West Virginia had adopted new laws to address parental kidnapping, but that was a little different than a cold-blooded, random childnapping. When one of the parents snatched a child, you didn't lie awake all night worrying that the phone was going to ring with news that the decomposed body of a child had been found under a thin cover of leaves.

Whit heard the screen door squeak and looked around. Tressa was poking her head out. "The last call was for you," she said.

He remembered hearing it ring a few minutes earlier. He

started to get up, assuming it was Anna calling from the office, and that Tressa had been talking to her. "Anna?"

"It was a newspaper in Charleston. I told them you weren't here."

Whit dropped back into the lounge chair. "Thanks."

She stepped out onto the rear deck and took a seat beside him. "You seem down in the dumps. Is it that warrant or whatever?"

Whit chuckled. "Naw. That's an occupational hazard, I guess. It'll work itself out."

She was silent for a moment, waiting. When he said nothing else, she said, "So?"

He glanced at her. "So what?"

"So, how come you're down in the dumps?"

"I hate having a case I can't do anything with." He leaned his head back and stared at the faint pinpoints of light in the night sky. "Do you remember the time I took you to that carnival that came through here?"

"Not really."

"You were four, I think. Anyway, it was early evening, and there was a carnival in town. I went over to your mother's and picked you up. I was with the sheriff's department then. It was before I went to work for Tony."

"Why are you thinking about that?" Tressa asked.

"Patience," Whit chided. "Just have some patience. I'll get to the point. We were walking along the midway, and the place was jammed with people, a lot of them real scums. Anyway, there was this shooting gallery where you could win one of those huge teddy bears. I asked you if you wanted one, and you started to clap and jump up and down. I thought I was a real hotdog with a gun back then, so I dragged you over, paid the carny his money, and started shooting."

"Did you win?"

"I didn't finish shooting. I took two shots and looked down for you, and you were gone. I called your name. You didn't answer." The memory of it still made Whit cringe. "I don't think I've ever panicked like that before or since. There was a steady stream of people walking along the midway. I started shoving them out of the way, screaming your name. One guy was standing there. I grabbed him and shook him, demanding to know where the little dark-haired girl went. He just stared at me like I was crazy. I dunno. I guess maybe it was a minute or so before you peeked around the edge of the tent that housed the shooting gallery. It seemed like a lifetime to me. I remembered wanting to go to somebody for help. Go to who? I was the damned law."

"What did you do?"

Whit laughed. "I busted your behind. You kept saying, 'Daddy . . . I was playing seek.' That's what you called hide-and-seek."

"Scared you, huh?"

Whit nodded. "Like I said, I can't ever remember such a feeling of helpless panic. It must be how the mother of the Winters girl feels. I felt that way for only a minute, and it was the worst one minute of my life. She's been feeling that way since Monday."

He glanced over at his daughter. The lights from inside the house spilled out the screen door. Whit could see the sheen of moisture on her eyes. "There was a time," he said, "when you'd be telling me to cheer up . . . When you would be saying, 'Don't worry, Daddy. You'll find her.' "

Tressa lowered her head. "I've grown up, Daddy. It doesn't mean I love you any less. I just know how many kids vanish and are never found. It's terrifying."

"That it is, Tressa."

"I'm sorry I scared you like that," she said, sounding very serious.

It made Whit smile. "Oh, you didn't ever do it again. You learned your lesson. I learned mine, too. Whenever I had you around a crowd like that, I never let go of your hand."

The phone rang again. Tressa brushed at her cheek and stood up to go answer it.

"We do have that answering machine," Whit said.

"Yes, with that horrible message you put on it. It actually scares my friends at school."

"Good," Whit called after her as she disappeared into the house.

Seconds later she returned to tell him that Gil Dickerson wanted him on the phone. He hurried inside, praying that Gil wasn't going to tell him that his deputies had found the girl's body.

He picked it up at his desk. "Yeah, Gil."

"Somebody from the lab just phoned the jail about your mask."

"Any prints?"

"Lotsa smudges, Whit . . . And two clear prints."

"Two?"

"Yeah, but according to the lab guy they belong to the same person, probably a small child."

EIGHTEEN

THE HOUSE in which Tommy Fuller lived with his parents sat on a quarter-acre lot and was flanked by other identical houses built by the same contractor some ten years earlier. Over the years the owner of the houses had done what little they could to make their own abodes a little different from that of their neighbors. Just south of the Fullers, the Hinkles, who had owned their home since the subdivision was constructed, had turned their spacious backyard into a garden. With summer coming to an end, the garden was faded and withering. Rain hadn't been too plentiful that year, and throughout the months of July and August, Samuel Hinkle had faithfully watered the garden three times a week. Now, with everything but two pumpkin vines and a few tomatoes harvested, there was no reason to continue the practice.

The garden was separated from the Fullers' backyard by a sagging grape arbor. As decrepit as it appeared with its leaning timbers, it was Sam Hinkle's pride and joy. In late summer its twisted vines were laden with sweet grapes. He used them to make homemade wine that he gave to his friends and relatives every Christmas.

After many seasons, it still bore fruit, much of it hidden among the broad green leaves of the grapevine. The leaves hid something else that night: the dark figure of the man searching among the leaves for bunches of grapes. When he found a small cluster, he used a sharp fingernail to separate it from the woody main vine. As he ate each grape, swallowing its meat and its tough skin, he quietly spit the seed out onto the ground. Who knows? Maybe next spring, one of the seeds would sprout, starting another grapevine.

Inside the Fullers' house, Tommy hadn't gone to sleep in his own bed after all. He had climbed onto his father's lap and fallen asleep there some time between the beginning of the television program "Cheers" and its first commercial. At that point, Jerry Fuller had carried his son into the boy's bedroom and tucked him into bed. The young boy hadn't stirred. The Fullers themselves hadn't gone to bed until after the eleven o'clock news.

Dewey Johns didn't know whose grapes he was eating and he didn't care. He didn't know what had gone on in the house, either. He had simply monitored the place from his arbor sanctuary. The lights had been going on and off in the house since he had arrived, shortly after ten o'clock, but it wasn't until eleven-thirty that the entire house was dark and still. He settled back to wait a little longer and to eat a few more of the grapes.

Just after midnight he eased his way out of the jumble of leaves and vines and moved quietly through the open backyard. In the distance a dog barked. He could hear traffic noises, too, coming from a busier street some three blocks away. The Fullers' neighborhood was very quiet. That had been one reason for his visit on the prior night, a dry run of sorts to see if the Fullers or their neighbors had any dogs that were likely to cause him grief. There had been none. He had managed to make it right up to the house and had decided to see if he could break in and get it over with when he heard the child scream. It had been a stupid mistake on his part, and he had raced away before anyone could react.

He reached into a pocket of the lightweight jacket he wore and withdrew a small .22 caliber pistol. He jammed it down into the belt. From the other pocket he pulled out a compact packet of tools, one of which was an old credit card. When he reached the house, he ducked down low and crept slowly around the house, being careful to stay well below the windows. The moon was just coming up, and he didn't want to do something stupid two nights in a row. When he reached the front of the house, he checked the street for any signs of activity. Seeing none, he quickly scurried to the front door.

The credit card easily opened the screen door, but the inside door required the use of his miniature tools. Before he even started the operation, he pulled a small can of spray oil from the case and squirted some into the lock. He worked sitting down on the porch, his back holding open the screen. A small penlight flashlight provided barely enough illumination for him to see. He jiggled the picks in the lock until he heard the tumblers fall into place. Flicking off the light, he eased the door open an inch or so, flinching when it squeaked just a little. He stopped then and slipped the tools back into the case. Before opening it any more, he studied the other side of the door and sprayed a small amount of oil into those points in the minute crevice where the hinges should have been located. He eased the door open a little more, then sprayed a little more oil, continuing the process until the door stood wide open.

When Anna arrived home at fifteen minutes past midnight, Whit was sitting in the living room, reading a book.

"I figured you would be in bed," she said.

"I'm not sleepy. You're running a little late."

"We spent a lot of time putting together the front-page story on your big case. You should know now that there's going to be an article on the charge pending against you."

Whit smiled. "Figures. You probably know more about it now than I do."

Anna settled down into a chair across from him. "I talked to Harrison himself. He says you manhandled him."

"No, I didn't. I wanted to, but I didn't. A damn shame, too. If I had known I was going to be charged with it, I might have gone ahead and enjoyed myself."

"What about this woman from the Department of Human Services?"

"Norma Wyse."

"I couldn't reach her tonight."

Whit sat up. "Why would you want to talk to her?"

"She was a witness."

"Hell, I was a witness. Don't you believe me?"

"You mean you would have given me a comment about it?"

"Hell, no."

She grinned. "That's why I didn't waste my time asking. Anyway, Harrison was furious when he discovered that the magistrate issued a summons to appear rather than a warrant for your arrest. He gave me some rather hostile comments about how the system protects its own, even the rotten ones. He was referring to you, of course."

"What are you saying about the missing kid?"

The humor vanished from her face. "Just rehashing the old news. We're going to run her picture again. It might interest you to know that Tony did give us a comment about your trip to Myrtle Beach. I called that Myrtle Beach detective, and he gave me a comment, too."

That surprised Whit. "Gawd, what did he say?"

"He will be quoted as saying that as a result of your efforts in South Carolina, Marcia Winters's father is being held on a charge of voluntary manslaughter in the death of the woman. He's also saying that your investigation in Myrtle Beach cleared her father of any involvement in Marcia's abduction."

Whit shook his head. "C.Y.A., huh?"

Anna frowned. "What?"

"You're covering your ass."

Anna was incensed. "Whit Pynchon!"

"Well, with all that background Myra Martin can hardly claim that you and I spent all that time in Myrtle Beach rolling in the hay, can she? Did you mention the fact that you were along for the ride?"

"I didn't write the piece, Whit. One of the reporters did. I'm not mentioned at all. I wasn't there in any official capacity."

Whit nodded. "Just like you weren't mentioned by Myra. Honor among thieves and reporters."

She lurched to her feet. "I can't believe you."

"Take it easy, Anna. I'm just ribbing you. Can't you take a joke?"

"I don't think it's funny."

Whit did, though. He was laughing. "You reporter types are real hypocrites. You think it's fine to drag everyone else's name through the mud. When someone threatens to do it to you, though, you go stark raving berserk."

"That's not fair!"

Whit shrugged. "Earthquakes aren't fair, but that doesn't stop them from happening."

Tressa, dressed in her pajamas, opened her door. "Can't a person get some sleep around here?"

"I'm sorry," Anna said. "I didn't mean to be shouting. I

spent half the night doing your father a favor, and he doesn't appreciate it. He thinks I was just acting in my own behalf.''

Tressa, rubbing her eyes, moved into the living room. ''What kind of favor?''

''I was trying to establish that his trip to South Carolina had some official purpose.'' She wheeled back to Whit. ''By the way, Tony also gave me a quote saying that you traveled down there because of Mrs. Winters's conviction that her former husband was somehow behind Marcia's kidnapping.'' Tressa settled down beside her father. ''What was on the eleven o'clock news?''

''Didn't you watch it?'' Anna looked from Tressa to Whit, who was shaking his head.

''He wouldn't let me,'' Tressa said. ''Was it bad?''

''A shorter version of the six o'clock version,'' Anna said. ''This time they did report that the magistrate had issued a summons for Whit to appear rather than an arrest warrant. Of course, there was some implication that the magistrate was showing some favoritism toward your father.''

''Some favor,'' Whit said. ''He should have told Harrison to go to hell.''

Tressa yawned. ''Did you tell her about the fingerprints, Daddy?''

Anna's eyes snapped toward Whit. ''What prints?''

''On the clown mask I found today.''

Anna's jaw dropped. ''You found it, and you didn't tell me.''

''No, I didn't—and don't you get your bloodhound nose outta joint. There weren't any useful prints on the mask. Well, there were . . . but they were the prints of a child.''

''The Winters girl?'' Anna asked.

Whit stood and stretched. ''Probably. But we don't know.''

''Maybe the mother had her child printed. A lot of organizations now sponsor that sort of thing, just in case this happens."

Whit started back toward the bedroom. "What if she did, Anna? How will that help?"

Anna cast a look of utter frustration at Tressa, then looked back at Whit, who was walking away. "Christ, Whit. Why do these groups bother then?"

He turned. "Those prints are primarily kept so they can be used to positively identify bodies, Anna."

Anna blinked. "I didn't realize that."

"Any more questions before I go to bed?"

A dull glow greeted Dewey Johns as he entered the Fullers' house. At first he thought someone was still awake, but he realized very quickly that it was just a night-light illuminating the hallway that ran down the center of the one-story structure. Based on the incident of the previous night, he had a pretty good fix on the location of the child's bedroom. He also figured that the last lights he'd seen go out came from the parents' bedroom. That meant he didn't have to go by their room to get to the kid.

He paused to slip on a pair of rubber gloves, the kind women used to wash dishes, before he eased his way down the wall, treading very lightly. He was just about to open the door to what he believed to be the kid's bedroom when he froze at a sound from the rear of the house. He yanked the gun from his belt and held his breath. The sound repeated itself, the noise of something falling. Sweat oozed from his forehead and trickled down into the corner of his eye. It stung, but he didn't dare wipe at it. Instead he stood still, listening, waiting. The house was once again quiet.

He waited for a few more seconds before slipping the gun back into his belt. The door to what he assumed was the little boy's room was just ahead of him and to his left. He stepped across the hallway and slipped down toward the door. It was only partially closed. The perspiration continued to form on his forehead and roll into the hollows of his eyes. He used the sleeve of his jacket to wipe it away and then forced his gloved hand into the right-hand pocket of his blue jeans. He pulled out the small switchblade. Covering the blade with the other hand to minimize the noise, he pushed a button, caught the blade in the palm of his left hand, and allowed it to open slowly.

Inside the room Tommy was awake. His eyes were riveted on the slit of urine-yellow light created by the open door and the night-light in the hall. Someone was in the hall. He had been watching its shadow. His breath came quickly, and he could feel his heart beating.

Maybe it was his dad . . . or his mother . . . or . . . He had been awake for several minutes, long enough to hear the noise from the kitchen. He had known what that was. It came from the refrigerator. His daddy said it happened when the freezer made ice.

Whatever had been moving in the hallway wasn't moving anymore. Tommy stared so long and so hard at the strip of light that his eyes started to act funny. He squinted them closed and opened them. That's when he saw the funny-looking hand. It touched the door and began to push it back. Tommy pulled the covers up to his nose, but was careful not to cover his eyes. He wanted to see.

The door squeaked a little as it opened. Johns thought about using some oil on it like he had the hinges to the front door, but decided against it. If he moved quickly, the barely audible squeak wouldn't matter. It shouldn't be too hard.

Dash in. Cut the kid's throat. Dash back out. Maybe his folks wouldn't even know anything happened until morning. If he could get to the kid's throat quickly enough, the kid wouldn't make a sound.

Johns didn't really want to kill the kid, but he didn't have any choice. He'd gone over and over it, and he wasn't going to think about it anymore. He was just going to do it. Besides, he'd warned the kid. He'd told the little bastard to butt out. If the kid had minded him, like kids were supposed to do, then this wouldn't be necessary.

He eased his head around the door and peeked into the room.

Tommy saw the shape of the head. He had planned to bury himself under the covers, but that wasn't what he did. He screamed. The sudden cry seemed to freeze the man at the door, but only for an instant. The door crashed open, and the dark, shadowy figure lunged for Tommy's bed.

The boy rolled out on the other side, his knees cracking against the floor. Tommy didn't even think about the pain. He just kept his hands and knees working as he pulled himself under the bed.

The man pounced on the bed, then Tommy heard him hit the floor beside him. He kept crawling until he was out on the other side, on his feet . . . running out of his room, still screaming.

The shrill howl shocked Jerry and Margaret Fuller awake at the same moment. Jerry realized what it was a second or so sooner than Margaret. This time, unlike the prior night, he at least had on his underwear. He literally hurled himself out of the bed and flung open the bedroom door. He saw

Tommy race toward him, then the silhouette of a man in the hallway.

"Call the cops!" he shouted to Margaret.

Tommy grabbed his leg, but he pulled him away. He blocked the hallway, trapping the intruder. He was going to catch the bastard and hold him for the cops. He never saw the gun. He never even heard the shot itself. He just saw a flash of orange and then felt something slam into his chest. There was no discomfort. Just a sense of falling . . . followed by nothing.

NINETEEN

SAM HINKLE had spent the evening at the local Elk Lodge dropping more than a hundred dollars in the regular Thursday night poker game that followed the lodge meeting. He'd also had a few stiff drinks, enough that he wanted to get safely into his driveway before a cop pulled him over.

He'd just about reached the sanctuary of his driveway when a small figure darted toward the street. At first the object appeared to be little more than a blur, but as he slammed on his brakes, he saw that it was Tommy Fuller, running hellbent into the street. His tires squealed, and the boy kept coming.

"Jesus!" Sam cried, trying to decide which way to swerve.

Then he saw the saw the second figure, a man—not Tommy's dad—chasing the boy. The car started to slide, and he lost control. But as the car skidded to a stop, he knew that he'd somehow missed the kid.

Sam let out his breath, then drew in a deep one. The boy had tumbled over the curb and was trying to get on his feet as Sam opened the car door. He heard pounding footsteps and saw the man running down the sidewalk away from him. Sam's legs were trembling as he hurried over to the boy.

"Tommy, are you okay?"

"He shot my daddy!" the boy cried.

Sam gaped. "What did you say?"

"That man shot my daddy."

Sam told Tommy to stay right where he was. He ran for his car and jumped behind the wheel. The engine was still running. He dropped the gearshift down into drive, cranked the wheel, and stepped on the gas pedal.

Sam hadn't given it a second thought. When he had been in the service, some thirty years earlier, he had been an officer with the military police. After the service, he had always wanted to become a cop, but in those days men with college degrees did better things with their lives. Still, Sam often dreamed of being a police officer. This was the next best thing. He gunned the car down the street and tried to catch a glimpse of the man.

By that time, the assailant wasn't running along the sidewalk. He was standing at the door of a vehicle on Sam's right, fumbling with his keys. For the second time that night, Sam slammed on his brakes. The man lifted up his hand as if he were pointing at Sam. For a split second Sam wondered what the hell the guy was doing. Then he knew. His foot slid off the brake as he ducked down. A split second later, his windshield exploded as he heard the crack of the small-caliber weapon.

"Dear God," Sam said, blindly stabbing at the brake as the car rolled forward.

He heard an engine start, but he didn't dare look up until he heard the screech of tires and glimpsed a car race past him on the right. Sam stomped his foot on the gas pedal again and was within a few yards of the vehicle when its rear windshield shattered. The bastard had shot back at him, straight through his own windshield. He couldn't keep up with the black Camaro, didn't want to, either. He was done playing cop.

Sam braked as the car disappeared around a corner, then reached into his glove compartment. His hands were shaking; his breath was coming in gasps. He'd given up on the chase, but he'd managed to get a glimpse of the license tag.

"Tommy!"

His mother's cry echoed across the neighborhood. Lights had come on in several houses. Porch lights were spilling their illumination out into the yards, and doors were opening.

"Tommmmyyyyy!"

The small boy hugged the dew-dampened grass on the far side of the road. His mother couldn't see him because of the shrubs that decorated their front yard.

"He's here," someone shouted from very close to Tommy.

The boy started to whimper.

Warm hands reached down and touched his face. "Tommy?"

The boy looked into the face of Mr. Morton, the man in whose yard he had fallen.

"Are you hurt, child?"

"Tommy!" It was his mother. She was close to him. He rolled over and jumped up, bounding into her arms.

"My God! What're you people doing over there?" Morton's tone indicated that he thought it was a domestic fight.

Margaret Fuller was clutching her child, bawling almost as hysterically as he was. People were spilling out of their houses, some gathering in the Fullers' front yard, but most forming a circle around the frenzied mother and son. Sam Hinkle pushed his way through the crowd. "Mrs. Fuller, Tommy says someone hurt his father."

"He's dead!" the woman bawled. "They just shot him down!"

"I'll go check," Sam said.

"They?" someone said. A murmur of growing panic spread through the crowd.

"Has anyone called the police?" someone cried.

Another voice answered, "I did."

Mrs. Morton worked her way to Margaret and Tommy. She put an arm around the woman. "Is there anything we can do?"

Through her tears, Margaret nodded.

"What, Margaret?"

"Somebody call an ambulance for my husband."

Whit wiped the sleep from his eyes as he walked up the front walk toward the house. He'd just fallen asleep when the call came. He thought he had answered the phone on the first ring, but he couldn't be sure. All he knew was that he was suddenly listening to the voice of the dispatcher from the Milbrook Police Department. At first he had been prepared to be his usual cantankerous self. After all, who could blame him, being awakened like that at one o'clock in the morning? Anna had stirred and groaned, but hadn't woken up. He decided to count his blessings and had listened quietly as the Milbrook officer told him that there was a homicide on Henry Avenue. He'd gotten the address, slipped out of bed, and had actually managed to exit the house without waking either Anna or Tressa.

Lieutenant Terry Watkins stepped out the front door and greeted Whit. "It looks like a burglary gone bad."

"Is the scene secure?"

The city officer nodded. "And we haven't let them move the body."

"Good for you, Terry. You're learning."

"The victim's wife and kid are still inside. I wanted to warn you."

"Isn't there someplace we can put them out of the way?"

"You may want to talk to them first. They're still pretty upset. I haven't gotten much out of them, but they may be witnesses."

"Where are they?"

"In the family room. I don't think the intruder got in there, so they're not tainting the scene."

Whit sighed. "Let's hope you thought right. What's the victim's name?"

Watkins checked a notepad in his hand. "Gerald Kirk Fuller."

"Fuller?"

Watkins nodded.

The name rang some distant bell in Whit's head. "Let's go take a look."

"He doesn't look too bad," Watkins said. "I mean, he looks dead, but Christ, the wound is hardly noticeable. Not much blood at all."

Several uniformed officers milled about the foyer of the house as Whit entered. "You guys doin' anything in here?" he asked.

"Waiting on you," one said.

"Then wait outside," Whit countered as he brushed by them.

He saw the body almost at once. It rested crossways in a hallway that divided the house. The man's head leaned against the wall; his feet were against the woodwork on the other side of the hall. If it hadn't been for the grayish color to his face, the victim might have been asleep with his chin pressed down against his chest.

A small spot of blood was evident just to the left of the

sternum. "Looks like he got it in the heart," Whit said, pulling a pencil from his pocket as he knelt down.

Watkins was standing behind him. "Definitely small caliber."

Whit studied the wound, then looked at the face. He frowned. "What'd you say the guy's name was?"

"Fuller."

Whit used the pencil to shift the head's position. It rolled away from the woodwork, coming to rest on the floor. "I know this guy. Christ, I just talked to him this morning."

"You did?"

Whit's knees popped as he pushed himself up. "And he's got a boy—a four-year-old boy."

"Yeah, the kid's in the family room. . . ."

"Which way?"

Watkins led Whit toward the front of the house. He opened a door and nodded. "In here."

Whit peered inside. The boy was in the arms of his mother, who was sitting on a couch. An older woman stood behind her, massaging her shoulders. Watkins went into the room first. "Mrs. Fuller, this is Whit Pynchon. He's an investigator with the prosecuting attorney's office. He'll be handling the case. Whit, this is Margaret Fuller."

But Whit was looking down at the boy. "Hi, Tommy."

The woman's eyes were red-rimmed and weak from her tears, but when Whit spoke directly to her son, she looked up at him. "You know my son?"

"I saw him at the day care this morning. Mrs. Fuller, I'm very sorry about what happened. Did you see the person who did this?"

She shook her head. "I saw him from the back, but that was after he'd shot—" Her voice faltered.

"I saw him," Tommy said.

Whit knelt down in front of the boy. ''Are you sure, Tommy?''

The boy slowly nodded his head.

''Can you tell me what he looked like?''

''He was trying to get me.''

Whit frowned. ''Get you?''

''Uh-huh. Just like he got Marcia.''

Margaret sagged. ''Tommy, please!'' She looked at Whit. ''I'm afraid my son is upset. He thinks the man came in the house after him.''

''But he did!'' the boy shrieked.

Margaret Fuller put a hand around her son's shoulders. ''I've told you—''

''He came to get me just like he came and got Marcia.''

Whit tensed. ''Did he have a clown mask on?''

The boy shook his head. ''But he was the same man.''

Her mother pulled the boy tight against her. ''Tommy has a vivid imagination. He—''

Whit held up his hand to stop her. ''Tommy, how do you know it was the same man that took Marcia Winters?''

''I saw him,'' the boy said flatly.

''Tonight?'' Whit asked.

''When he took Marcia, too.''

Whit felt his heart starting to race a little, but he kept the excitement out of his voice. ''The day the man took Marcia— on that day, Tommy—you saw his face?''

The four-year-old nodded. ''He smelled bad, too.''

''Tonight?'' his mother asked.

''When he took Marcia!'' the boy snapped, frustrated because everyone seemed to be asking him the same thing.

Margaret Fuller was looking at Whit. ''If Tommy's right, is that why that man came here tonight?''

''It makes sense, Mrs. Fuller.'' Whit turned his attention

back to the boy. "Just a few more questions, Tommy. Did you tell anyone that you saw the man's face?"

The boy lowered his head. Whit reached over and lifted his trembling chin. "You didn't, Tommy?"

"Answer!" his mother commanded.

The boy shook his head.

His mother jerked him around to face her. "Why? Why didn't you tell someone?"

Tommy's face reddened. Huge tears filled his eyes. "Daddy told me not to talk about it."

"Did your father know you saw the man's face?"

"No. He just said not to talk about it."

The woman started to cry again as her son pulled away from her. He was crying, too. Whit's knees were starting to ache, so he stood up. He put his hand on top of the boy's head. "Let's leave your mother alone a few minutes. Why don't you come with me?"

The boy kept looking back at his mother as Whit guided him from the room. He shielded the boy from the view of Fuller's body as they moved across to the formal living room on the other side of the hall. Watkins stayed behind in the family room for a few seconds and then followed Whit and the boy.

Whit guided Tommy to a large leather couch. The boy continued to weep. "Can we get you something to drink?" Whit asked.

"Some milk?" Tommy asked.

"I'll go see if there's any in the kitchen," Watkins said.

Whit followed Watkins to the door. "Tell the ambulance crew to move the body," Whit whispered.

"I shoulda told him," the boy said when Whit sat down on the couch beside him.

"You said you tried to tell your father."

"Uh-huh. He just told me not to talk about it. He said it was Marcia's daddy."

"It wasn't her daddy, Tommy."

"My daddy said it was."

"At first we all thought it was, but it turned out to be someone else, and—"

"The man that made my daddy dead," the boy said.

"Can you tell us what he looks like? Or maybe you could look at some pictures of people and see if he's in those pictures."

If Tommy could identify the man from mug shots, it would be a mixed blessing. Under West Virginia law, children under the age of seven were automatically presumed incompetent to testify. That didn't mean they could never offer testimony. It simply required that the side wanting to use their testimony had to establish that the child knew the difference between right and wrong and knew that it was wrong not to tell the truth. Tommy seemed unusually advanced for his age, but Whit knew that Tommy's identification, if he could make one, would be questionable as evidence. The court would be extra careful before allowing that identification to be heard by a jury.

Watkins came back into the living room with a glass of milk. He gave it to the boy and then motioned for Whit to follow him outside.

"It's our lucky night," the lieutenant said.

"It certainly wasn't his," Whit said as the ambulance crew lifted Jerry Fuller into a plastic body bag.

"We've got a fella outside—a neighbor—who got the guy's tag number. One of my boys already called it in."

The news produced a broad grin on Whit's face. "As soon as you get a name, let me know."

Watkins offered Whit a slip of paper. "Presto!"

Whit snatched it away from the city officer and read the name. "Dewey Johns. With a post office box address. His name doesn't ring a bell."

"He's crossed our path a few times. A B and E a couple years back. He was our guest for six months in the county lockup. Then a DWI last year, and a couple of domestic complaints about the same time. The latest thing was a welfare fraud charge, but that was dropped."

"The neighbor didn't happen to get a glimpse of the guy, did he?"

Watkins shook his head. "He was too busy ducking bullets. Johns, if that's who it was, shot out his windshield."

Whit shook his head, but even as he did so the wheels were spinning inside. "If you guys arrested Johns a few times, then you probably processed him."

"Most likely," Watkins said.

"That means you have a photo, and hopefully a damned street address. Wonder if the boy can pick Johns from a photo lineup?"

"Tonight?" Watkins asked.

The ambulance crew wheeled the packaged body of Jerry Fuller toward the front door, and Watkins and Whit stepped aside. "Definitely. If the kid's right, and I think he is, then this guy knows where Marcia Winters is. Let's hope she's fared better than Fuller."

TWENTY

"WHAT GOES AROUND comes around," Whit mumbled as he dialed Tony Danton's home number. Usually it was Tony who called Whit in the wee hours of the morning. The prosecutor seemed to find some perverse glee in getting Whit out of bed. Well, it was almost 2:00 A.M., and Whit smiled at the opportunity to return the favor.

Tony answered the phone on the second ring.

"Top of the morning, boss."

"Who the hell is this?"

"Time to wake up, Tony. Smell the roses."

"Whit?"

"Damned annoying, isn't it?"

"Are you drunk or something?"

"I thought you might be interested in knowing that we I.D.'d the guy who snatched Marcia Winters."

Tony's voice came alive. "You've got him?"

"No, but we've made him. He's a small-time punk by the name of Dewey Johns."

"What about the child?"

"Wake up, Tony. All I said we did was I.D. the guy."

There was a moment of fumbling on the other end. Then Tony said, "What the hell's going on? It's two in the morning. Something must have happened."

"Yeah, you might say that. The suspect—Johns—went after one of the other kids from the day-care center. He failed, but he did manage to kill the kid's father."

"Christ, Whit. Was he trying to abduct another child?"

"We don't think so. Looks like he was just trying to silence the boy. Seems the boy got a look at the kidnapper's face. I guess the asshole was afraid the kid could identify him."

After a long pause, Tony said, "You mean one of those kids actually saw the kidnapper?"

"Yeah."

"How come we didn't know that?"

Whit sighed. "That's the sad part. The kid's father figured it was best for the boy to forget what happened, and—"

"He told the kid not to tell?" Tony asked, incredulous.

"It wasn't like that. The boy's only four, Tony. Every time he started talking about the incident, his father put a stop to the conversation. He never told his father that he saw the man's face. It's one of those things. Anyway, the kid's father paid rather dearly. He interrupted Johns before he could hurt the kid, but he got a bullet in the ticker for his efforts."

"What time did all this happen?"

"Maybe two hours ago."

"How did you come up with a name so quickly?"

"Stroke of luck. A neighbor managed to get a tag number from Johns's car. We ran it and got Johns's name. I'm down at the city police station with a picture of him. We've got the kid here, too. Do you see any problems with a photo lineup? That should give us a positive identification."

Tony whistled. "That's mighty tricky, Whit. What if the kid can't I.D. him from a photo? It'll blow our chances at a regular lineup later on."

"That's why I'm calling, Tony. I figured this is one call

you might wanna make. This kid's pretty damned sharp for a four-year-old. He certainly didn't have any trouble recognizing the bastard in a dark house tonight.''

''If you're gonna do it, Whit, be sure the other photos are similar enough to make the identification valid.''

Whit was sitting at Watkins's desk. The photo of Dewey Johns was one of five in front of them. Each photo depicted a white male in his late twenties. Johns appeared to be a little better-looking than the other four, but like the others he had dark hair, a square jaw, and rugged facial features.

''I've already picked out the panel, Tony. Actually they look a little too much alike. We can wait if you wanna come down and look them over for yourself.''

The prosecutor thought about it for a moment. ''Hell, Whit; you can handle it. It's what I pay you to do.''

Whit chuckled. ''Not very funny to be roused from a sound sleep, is it, Tony?''

''If you don't think you can handle it, I'll be there,'' the prosecutor said, his voice now tinged with a hint of anger.

''I'll handle it, Tony—but if the kid can't make Johns, then I don't wanna hear any second-guessing on your part.''

''You can still go after him based on the tag number,'' Tony said. ''One way or another, I want that guy in custody. Where does he live?''

Whit paged through the file on Dewey Johns provided by the city police. ''According to this, at that time he lived at Rt. 3, Box 111-C. I'm told that's a mobile-home park west of Milbrook.''

''Check it out. Just in case the little girl's there.''

''I plan to . . . just as soon as we finish showing the kid these photos.''

''Keep me posted. No matter what time.''

''Count on it,'' Whit said.

* * *

Babs Duncan was beat when she got home from the diner in Milbrook where she waited on tables. She'd gulped a couple of sleeping pills and laid down. The pills made her forget, and that was good. Everything was put on hold. She stopped worrying about her boss and the threats he made to fire her for coming in late, and the way the cook grabbed her ass when she walked by. The pills chased away memories of her past, too. Every so often she remembered being beaten up and abused by her father and uncle, and it made her want to throw up. And the pills let her forget what Dewey had done to her—and her worries about what he might do to her next time he was drunk and blew up.

The furious pounding on Babs's door jolted her from the pill-induced sleep. It was him. Dewey. Had to be. The thumping on the fragile trailer door continued as she roused her drugged body from the bed. She looked at herself in the mirror and ran a hand through her long dirty-blond hair. She was twenty-five, but felt ancient.

"I'm comin' for chrissakes," she yelled as she walked into the living room in her oversized T-shirt.

Before opening the door she pulled back the frayed curtain that covered the small window. Dewey scowled at her. "Open the fuckin' door," he shouted.

"Bastard," she mumbled as she slid back the bolt lock.

The door flew back, almost knocking her down. "Dammit, Dewey. You drunk or somethin'?"

"You on those fuckin' pills?" he said, glowering at her.

"The doctor gave 'em to me."

He turned to slam the door closed. "Dumb bitch. You got anything to drink?"

"Beer," she said.

He made a face. "I need somethin' stronger."

She could see that his hands were shaking. He looked white around the mouth, like maybe he was going to faint.

"Whatsa matter with you?"

"Nothing. I just need a drink."

Dewey drank a lot, but Babs didn't think his current condition was caused by the need for a drink. "You in some kinda trouble? If so, I don't need you bringin' it here, Dewey Johns."

He went to the couch and plopped down on it. Babs turned back to the door and opened it. She peered out at the graveled driveway. Her car was there, but not Dewey's.

"Shut the gawdamn door," he said.

"Where's your car?"

"It's down the road. I had some car trouble. Gawdamn piece of shit. That's what got me so riled."

She closed the door. "You're lyin' to me, Dewey. You're in some kind of trouble. You gonna end up in jail again?"

"I told ya, hon, I had car trouble. You go on back to bed."

Babs studied him. Funny thing; he didn't seem like he'd been drinking at all. When he had a few belts in him, he either wanted sex or he wanted to beat up on her. Besides, she hadn't smelled anything on him when he came in. It usually wasn't difficult to tell when Dewey had been drinking.

"What you gone and done, Dewey?" The edge was gone from her voice. The question was asked in the same tone that a mother would use in talking with a child.

"Get to bed, Babs. I got some thinkin' to do." She went to the couch and started to sit down beside him. He caught her and shoved her back up. "Dammit, woman. I told you. Get on in bed."

"Damn you!" she shrieked. "You don't come into my

house and tell me when to go to bed. I'll go to bed when I please.''

He lurched to his feet. She saw his hand go back, but the blow came so quickly that she didn't have time to react. His open palm caught her just in front of the ear. She collapsed to the floor.

He loomed over her, his face twisted with rage. ''Don't push me tonight, bitch. Just get your scrawny ass to bed. Now!''

She looked up at him, pain racking the side of her face. Tears spilled from her eyes as she crawled away from him. ''Don't hit me again,'' she whimpered.

He reached down for her, and she cringed. He worked one of his hands under her right arm and pulled upward. ''I don't wanna hurt you, Babs. Just go to bed like I said.''

With his help she got to her feet. She was still crying, and she held her hand to her bruised face. ''You almost broke my jaw.''

''I'm sorry.'' He put an arm around her. ''Look, Babs— just go take another pill or somethin'. Go on back to bed. I'm gonna get me one of those beers. I'll be along in a little while.''

He guided her down the narrow hall to her bedroom. She continued to cry as he helped her into bed. He started to leave, but she caught his hand. ''You done somethin' bad, ain't ya, Dewey?''

He didn't answer, but she thought she saw something glisten in his eyes. Dewey closed the door behind him. She heard him open the refrigerator door and pop the top on a beer can. For the next few minutes the trailer was quiet. The side of her face ached, and she knew the skin would darken overnight. She got up to look at it in the mirror over the dresser.

That's when she heard his voice. She tiptoed to the bedroom door and eased it open.

Dewey was on the phone. "C'mon, sweet thing. I had no choice," he was saying. "What? . . . Yeah . . . I know. I know . . . So you coming with me or not?"

Babs pushed the door closed. She forgot about her pain. By the time she got back to the bed she was furious, mad enough to do what she should have done months ago. She could take the abuse. She could even tolerate him fucking around. She couldn't, however, allow him to take off with another woman—not after all the misery she had gone through because of him. Sweet thing. The bastard.

Tommy Fuller looked with adult care at each of the five photographs spread out in front of him. He started to pick one of them up, but Whit stopped him. "Just look at them," he told the boy. "Take your time. If one of those men is the one you saw at Mrs. Harrison's, just point it out to me."

The boy looked up at him. His eyes were swollen from his tears. He had been crying off and on since arriving at the police station. Margaret Fuller stood behind him, her eyes even more ragged. She was looking at Whit. "Will Tommy have to testify in court?"

Whit put a finger to his lips. For the moment he wanted the young boy to concentrate on the photographs.

They were in a small but comfortable conference room used by the city administration. Terry Watkins was the only other person in the room besides Whit and the Fullers. He stood at the door, his attention also riveted on Tommy.

Whit glanced at Watkins, who gently shook his head. Both of the men had gone through this sort of thing before. As a rule, if the witness didn't immediately react to the proper photo, it meant trouble. More often than not, it meant they were trying to guess.

Whit waited another few seconds, then said, "If you aren't certain, Tommy, just say so. Remember. We want you to tell us the truth."

Before they had spread the photos out in front of Tommy, Whit had spent five minutes talking to the boy about telling the truth. He'd started out by asking Tommy if he knew what it meant when someone was telling the truth.

"Not fibbing," the boy said.

"What's fibbing?" Whit asked.

The four-year-old hesitated. He said, "Making stuff up."

Whit asked, "Do you know what a lie is?"

"A big fib," Tommy replied.

"What happens when people tell lies?"

The boy lowered his head. "They get in trouble."

His mother joined the conversation at that point. "Tommy's a good boy, Mr. Pynchon. He doesn't tell lies."

Whit then explained to her Tommy's legal status as a witness. He told her that's why he was asking Tommy the questions. In the wake of her grief, she probably hadn't realized immediately that Tommy might be called upon to appear in court.

Now, as the boy frowned at the photos, it looked as if the issue of his future as a witness was already settled. "No one's going to be mad at you—or upset with you—if you aren't sure," Whit said to the boy.

Tears rolled from each of the boy's dark brown eyes as he looked up at Whit. "I know the one it is," he said.

Whit frowned. "You do?"

"Uh-huh. Will he try to make me dead again?"

His mother broke down at that point. Watkins went to her.

Whit reached over and took Tommy's hand. "If you show us which one it is, we're going to go arrest him."

"Put him in jail," Tommy said.

Whit managed to smile at the boy. "You know about jails?"

"That's where they put bad men."

Whit nodded. "That's right—and that's where we'll put this man. Are you not telling us which one because you're afraid?"

"He might make my mommy dead, too."

On hearing that, Whit's eyes flooded. The kid was concerned about losing his mother. "Son, I promise you. We'll do everything we can to make both you and your mother safe."

Margaret Fuller had been weeping quietly. At that point she eased away from Watkins and bent down to her son. "The man came to our house because you know what he looks like, Tommy. If the police don't get him, he may come back."

Tommy's small hand snatched up the fourth photo from his right. "This is him."

Whit took the photograph and showed it to Terry Watkins. "Dewey Malcolm Johns."

Watkins sagged with relief. "I'll go see which magistrate's on duty."

"Go ahead and call him," Whit said.

The city officer left the room.

Whit went around to the other side of the table and sat down next to Tommy. "You're a brave young man. We're going to try to arrest this man tonight."

Tommy's mother was still standing behind her son.

"Is that enough? The word of a four-year-old?"

"We have a little more than that, Mrs. Fuller. Your neighbor . . . Mr. Hinkle?"

"Sam?"

"Yes, ma'am. He managed to get the license tag number of the vehicle in which the assailant fled. The car is registered to this man." Whit was holding up the photo.

Margaret Fuller reached out for it, and Whit let her take it. "So he's the one that did it." She shivered and handed the photo back to Whit. "Does he have a history of that sort of thing? Kidnapping kids, and killing 'em?"

Whit shook his head. "No, that's still a mystery. He's had some trouble before, but nothing like this."

The woman took a deep breath. "Can we go now?"

Whit patted Tommy on the head and stood. "I'll have one of the city officers take you—" He stopped. "Where are you going to be staying tonight?"

"With my sister, Mr. Pynchon."

Tommy was getting out of his chair. His mother bent down. "You go on out into the hall. I want to talk to Mr. Pynchon for a minute."

"I wanna stay with you," the boy said.

"Just for a minute?" she said. "I won't be long."

The boy's eyes teared up again, but he shuffled on out to the hallway.

"He's a fine kid," Whit said.

"I can't imagine raising him alone," she said.

"If there's ever anything I can do," Whit said, "please give me a call. Believe me, I don't make that offer lightly. I'm very taken by your son."

She managed a smile, but more tears quickly enveloped it. "This wouldn't have happened if Jerry hadn't tried to keep the kidnapping from me. I don't think I'll ever be able to forgive him for that."

"I'm sure he thought he was doing what was best."

She lowered herself back into the chair. "It was all because of money, Mr. Pynchon." She told him about the dispute over Tommy's day care. "Silly, isn't it? I mean it seems silly now."

Whit had things to do, but the woman needed to talk. He settled down beside her. "We all make those kinds of mistakes. Usually they don't have such dire consequences."

"If he'd just let you talk to Tommy at the day care, then—"

Whit reached over and took her hand. "Mrs. Fuller, what's done is done. Whatever faults he may have had, he must have been a very good father. And you're certainly a good mother. Tommy's the proof."

"What will happen to that man?" She nodded toward the photo that Whit had placed back on the desk.

Whit took a deep breath before he answered. "It'll be a long process, and Tommy will be a part of it, but once it's over, Dewey Johns should spend the rest of his life in prison. There aren't any guarantees, though. I hope you know that."

"I've never had much contact with the court system, Mr. Pynchon. Those I know who have don't seem very impressed. Can he get off on a technicality? Is there a chance he won't go to jail?"

Whit took a moment to frame his response. "There's always that chance. One of the reasons I'm here, though, is to see that we do things right, that we don't do something that lets him walk away. I think Dewey Johns will be tried on charges of murder and kidnapping, and I can say with certainty that my employer, the prosecutor, won't wheel and deal with this guy. Once it goes to a jury, then those twelve people will decide if he's guilty. Given what we've got already, I'm confident the verdict will be guilty. At that point, the same jury decides whether he gets life without the chance for parole or a life sentence with the chance for parole after ten years. In my opinion, that will be the only real issue in this case once we can arrest him. Of course, we don't know yet about the fate of the girl he kidnapped.''

"Do you think she's dead?''

"Twelve hours ago I did. Now, I honestly don't know. I think there's more to this case than meets the eye, but I suspect we'll get a lot better sense about it once we nab this guy. Guess I'd better get the wheels rolling to do that.''

Margaret Fuller pushed herself up from the chair. Her tears had dried. "I hope the little girl's all right. As much as I'm hurting, I know her mother is hurting even worse.''

Whit followed her toward the door. "I want to say goodbye to Tommy. We'll probably be seeing a little bit of each other in the days and months ahead. Remember what I said, Mrs. Fuller. If there's anything I can do, please let me know.''

She stopped before exiting the room. "Just be sure that this man gets what he deserves.''

"I'll see that he gets what the law allows, Mrs. Fuller. What he deserves would be considered cruel and unusual punishment.''

TWENTY-ONE

THE GROUP OF SIX MEN took advantage of the last minutes of darkness to assume their positions in the small mobile-home park. Whit and Sheriff Gil Dickerson were going to take the front door. Terry Watkins, although technically out of his jurisdiction, was in the company of one of Gil's deputies and was moving around to the rear of the green-and-white trailer. The fifth and sixth officers, also deputy sheriffs, remained with the two cruisers parked just out of sight of Dewey Johns's residence. One of them was on the radio, maintaining contact with Tony Danton, who was back in the control room of the Raven County Sheriff's Department.

Whit and Gil moved slowly toward the dusty front yard, using a mobile home adjacent to the suspect's for cover. "I don't see the vehicle," Whit said.

Gil, favoring his injured right leg, struggled to keep up. "Maybe he dumped it."

"I bet he's hit the road."

They had reached the end of the long trailer next to Johns's. The assault on the suspect's residence had been carefully discussed. The fact that it was a mobile home surrounded by other mobile homes made it all that much more risky. The walls of mobile homes contained very little to stop a wayward bullet, and no one wanted innocent parties harmed. That was one reason Whit had decided to wait until first light to make the move. It would attract less attention, and fewer people would be moving about at that quiet time of the morning.

"I'll hit the door," Whit said. "You come in after me."

"Are we gonna announce ourselves?" Gil asked.

"No damned way. Not this time. I wanna get the bastard down and cuffed as quick as we can. If he's got the Winters girl in there, I don't want him to have a chance to get his hands on her."

Gil nodded in agreement.

Whit checked his watch. Before entering the trailer park, all six men had synchronized their watches. Whit was to enter the trailer precisely at 5:40 A.M.; it was now 5:38. "Let's go to it."

Whit crouched as he moved from the cover of the neighboring residence and stayed low as he darted to the side of Johns's trailer. Gil did the same. Then both of the men stayed beneath the level of the windows as they worked their way toward the front door.

"What if he isn't alone?" Gil whispered.

"Up till now he has been. It's a calculated risk." Whit eased up on the small metal porch that provided an exit down from the door. Gil hugged his heels. The prosecutor's investigator tested the handle on the battered screen door. It wasn't locked. He gently pulled it open and then, ever so delicately, tried the knob on the inside door. It was locked.

"Hold the screen back," Whit whispered. Once Gil had it away from the investigator's back, Whit pulled out his small .357. "Time?"

Gil checked his watch. "Count down from ten and then go."

Whit nodded his head with each silent count. On three he drew back his booted foot.

He finished the count aloud. "Two . . . one."

The heel of his boot exploded against the door just to the left of the doorknob. Much to his surprise, the door swung inward. He dived inside and yelled: "Police!" At the same moment, a door on the opposite side of the trailer sprung open, and Watkins jumped into the room.

Whit was on his feet, his eyes swiftly scanning the cluttered living room–kitchen combination. Seeing no one, he darted down the narrow hall, quickly peering into each of the two doors before he finally reached the main bedroom at the end.

Watkins was right behind him.

"Son of a bitch," Whit said. "He's not here."

The other officers were piling into the trailer. Whit wheeled on them. "He's not here. You guys stay outside. We wanna treat this place just like a crime scene."

Whit had two warrants in his jacket pocket. One of them charged Dewey Malcolm Johns with the murder of Tommy Fuller's father. The other was a search warrant, authorizing a search of Johns's residence. Few other aspects of criminal law were as troublesome as search-and-seizure. Even with the courts becoming somewhat less protective of defendants' rights, search-and-seizure remained a mine field of technicalities. In this instance, Whit tried to cover his bases.

The search warrant required that some crime be alleged. In this instance, that was easy—Fuller's murder. It also required a specific description of the place to be searched. That had also been easy since they had a specific address. In applying for the warrant, Whit had to provide his probable cause. No problem there, either. A witness had obtained the tag number of a vehicle belonging to Johns, and Tommy had picked Johns out of a lineup. This was where Johns lived, so it was reasonable to search his residence.

The object for which they were searching was the small-caliber weapon that was used to shoot Fuller. Watkins had wanted Whit to include any evidence related to the kidnapping of the Winters girl, but Whit had demurred. His reasoning was simple. An officer just needed grounds to search for one item. Any other evidence of that crime, or other crimes, found during a lawful search was also admissible. The gun was small enough to be hidden in the smallest places of concealment. If he had been searching for a larger item, the body of a child, for example, the authority of the warrant wouldn't have extended to the search, for example, of a drawer too small to contain a body. Besides, he really didn't want to reveal on the affidavit for the warrant that Tommy Fuller could also I.D. Johns as the man at the day-care center.

"Let's take the place apart," Whit said to Watkins.

In a way, he hoped the gun wasn't in the trailer. Technically, once the gun was found, the warrant's authority ended. If it were there, he certainly hoped that Watkins or Gil overlooked it or waited until everything else had been searched before they "found" it. He had gone over the protocol with them before they had left the courthouse.

"Start here?" Watkins asked.

Whit shook his head. "Let's go to the kitchen."

They moved back toward the living room and turned on the lights. The other officers were standing outside in the yard. The cruisers that had been out of view were now in front of the house. Whit stuck his head out the door. "Did you radio back and tell Tony he wasn't here?"

One of the officers indicated that he had.

"Okay, go on and put out an APB for Johns and his vehicle. Hicks, you take Watkins on back to town."

Watkins was examining a beer can that he'd found behind Johns's dresser. "I think I got something here."

"What, an unopened beer?" Whit asked.

Watkins pulled at the top, and it came away from the rest of the can. "Money." He turned the can upside down and a wad of crisp bills bound with a rubber band fell to the floor.

Whit slipped on a pair of rubber gloves and carefully counted the cash as Dickerson and Watkins looked on. He whistled when he finished. Ninety-six hundred. Not a bad little nest egg for a part-time handyman. The sheriff held out a plastic evidence bag, and Whit dropped it in.

"It looks like payoff money to me," Gil said.

Whit grinned. "Yeah. I was thinking the same thing."

Babs wasn't asleep when Dewey Johns shook her. She had tossed and turned throughout the night, kept awake by the throbbing in her jaw and the anger seething inside her. She didn't think Dewey had slept, either. He had stayed in the living room, and she had heard the sound of the television being turned off and on throughout the night. Once it had sounded as if he were watching one of those foreign sex films some of the cable channels played late at night. Another time she heard shooting and the sound of galloping horses.

As he leaned over her, she could smell the beer and cigarettes on his breath. She turned her head away from him, cautiously resting her bruised face on the pillow. "What do you want?" She spoke through clenched teeth to lessen the pain.

"I need to borrow your car. I might not be back till afternoon."

She lifted her head up. "I was gonna go to the hospital this morning. I think you broke my jaw."

He looked at the purple discoloration that ran from her earlobe down to her chin. "Just a bruise, Babs. You know I'm sorry. If you broke it, you couldn't talk."

"You broke it and you ain't gonna hit me no more, Dewey." It wasn't a question. It was a statement of fact.

Dewey, though, didn't read any threat into her words. "I promise, hon. Never again. Your car keys in your purse?"

"Whatsa matter with your car?"

His eyes narrowed. "Dammit, Babs. I told ya I had car trouble. That's where I gotta go . . . see about getting it fixed. You know me. If I got no wheels, I get real nervous."

She knew he was lying about his car—about everything. "I bet there ain't nothin' wrong with your car, Dewey Johns. You're in trouble, and you wanna run off with some other woman. Ah heard you last night."

His face turned red. "Gawdamn it, what're you talkin' about now? I just need your car this morning."

"And I need to go see about my jaw. I think maybe you loosened some of my teeth."

He sat down on her bed. The stench of his breath was bad enough. But this close to him, she also could smell the soured sweat and dirt on his body. She turned away.

"C'mon, Babs. There's no other woman. You didn't hear that right. It's those damn pills, Tell you what . . . Just as soon as I can get my car towed in, I'll come back and take you to the emergency room—but you best tell them you fell or somethin'."

"Take the damned car," she said. "I'll get a ride."

"Thanks, hon." He stood and fished into his pocket. "Here's a five. Call a cab." He placed the bill on the pillow beside her head.

"You gonna pay the doctor bill, too?"

"Me?"

"You're the one that hit me, remember?"

"Right. Sure. I'll pay the bill. I'll give it to you this evening. The keys in your purse?"

"Yeah, but be careful and don't tear it up."

"Okay, Babs." He leaned over and started to kiss her. She covered her head with a pillow.

"I promise, hon. I won't ever hurt you again."

She heard him leave the room. Then she head the jingle of keys, the opening and closing of the door. Seconds later, the engine of her small red Toyota roared to life. She threw back the covers and headed into the small living room. The phone was on a table beside the television. She was heading for it when she saw her purse still open on the kitchen table. She could see that her billfold was open inside. She rushed to it. The thirty dollars—three tens—she had inside were gone.

"Bastard!" she said, heading back to the phone.

"Like I said, You ain't gonna hurt me no more."

She snapped up the receiver and dialed the Raven County Sheriff's Department.

Dewey Johns needed his money. Things had gone sour in a hurry, and he figured it was time to make himself scarce. The Virginia border was just a few miles south. The cops wouldn't be looking for Babs's small red Toyota. All he needed was enough time to stop at his trailer, grab his cash, and get down into Virginia.

He wished Randi was going with him, but when he'd called her, she'd told him that he'd fucked up and that she wouldn't go anywhere with him. Now or ever. She told him to stay away for good. That pissed him off. She'd turned on him. He couldn't trust her. But she'd find out that you can't play games with Dewey Johns and get away with it. Not with Dewey. After he picked up his money, he'd stop by Randi's place for a last good-bye. He'd catch her before she left for work—and say his farewell with a .22 plug right between her eyes. She had it coming.

The sun was just starting to peek above the mountain ridge to the east of Milbrook as Dewey left the town's city limits. Heading toward the east, and the trailer park, he pulled down the battered visor to block the low glare. The car was a little loud. It sounded as if there were a small hole somewhere in the exhaust system, but it only had 42,000 miles on it. It ran well. Not nearly as fast as the Camaro, but it would have to do.

He kept his eye out for cops as he navigated the twisting two-lane road that swung east of Milbrook and then joined the main highway that ascended Tabernacle Mountain. The towering twin peaks of the mountain finally blocked out the early morning glare as he neared his trailer park. He took the last curve before the turn-in to the park and found himself face-to-face with an oncoming police cruiser.

"Jesus." He hunkered down a little in the import's small seat.

He didn't dare look at the cop car as he passed it. He immediately glanced in the rearview mirror and sighed with relief as the cruiser continued on back toward Milbrook. What the hell was a cop doing out here at this time of the morning? Dewey had decided to make his move at dawn, thinking it to be the least likely time he would encounter any trouble.

The cruiser was around the curve and out of sight, and he relaxed again.

* * *

Todd Hammond, the night-shift dispatcher, was just coming out of the jail kitchen with a platter of bacon and eggs and a steaming cup of freshly brewed coffee when the phone rang. There weren't many perks to working the midnight-to-eight shift, but breakfast was one of them. The jail cooks came in to start preparing breakfast every morning at 6:00. It was served to the inmates at 7:00, but Hammond and the corrections staff always got first dibs.

He set the tray on the desk and snatched up the phone. "Sheriff's Department."

"I wanna report a theft," a woman mumbled.

"A theft?" Hammond got calls about B&E's and fights. He didn't get too many calls on the hoot owl about thefts.

"Speak up. I can barely hear you. Now who stole what?"

"My boyfriend took my car and thirty dollars outta my wallet."

Shit. Hammond shook his head. "The magistrate courts open at eight-thirty, ma'am. You can go in then and sign a warrant on the guy."

"But he's getting away with my car and money, mister."

Hammond despised dealing with domestic squabbles. He disliked this complaint even more so because his scrambled eggs, bacon, and toast were getting cold. He hated trying to butter cold toast. "Look, lady; I've told you what you can do."

"You don't understand. The son of a bitch is getting away."

"I'm sure he'll be back."

"He beat me up, too—last night."

Hammond picked up his coffee. "The magistrate can handle that, too. They open at—"

"Listen, mister . . . I think he did something really bad last night."

"Sure, lady." Hammond hadn't been with the Raven County department for very long, but he'd been there long enough to know this song and dance. Some women figured one sure way to get the police riled was to stool pigeon on their hubbies or boyfriends. The worst of those women even would go so far as to say that their estranged lovers had threatened to kill any cop that came after them. The women figured that guaranteed that the police would go after their subject with guns drawn and their blood boiling.

"I really think he did," she was saying. "His name's—"

"Listen, lady. I've done told you—"

". . . Dewey Johns."

Hammond literally jerked at the name. Hot coffee sloshed out on his hand. "Jesus!" he cried, wiping the scalding fluid onto his uniform pants.

"Did you hear me?" the woman asked.

"Did you say Dewey Johns?"

"I sure did. He's got my car, and he's leaving town."

Hammond moved around to the other side of the desk and found a notepad. "Can you describe the car?"

"Of course I can. It's my car. It's a red 1985 Toyota Corolla. It's got a white interior and some rust on the rear fenders."

"Where was he going?"

"Told me had some trouble with his car, but I heard him talking on the phone to this bitch he's been seeing. He thinks I'm dumb or something, I guess. Anyway—"

"Please, ma'am. Don't you know where he's going? Did he say?"

"Jesus, mister. He stole my car. He ain't gonna tell me where he's going."

* * *

Whit was lifting a grimy mattress when he heard the sound of the car engine. It was distant, but still rather loud. They'd been at the empty trailer now for nearly thirty minutes, and so far their search had produced nothing but the cash. The engine noise intensified. It was the first bit of traffic that Whit had heard. He went to the window and peered out just in time to see a small red foreign import roll by the trailer. The sun was up by now, and there was a glare on the windows. Whit watched it roll deeper into the trailer park.

The deputy who was standing beside the cruiser didn't even glance at it as the car drove by. Whit was just about to turn back to the search when he saw the deputy duck into the cruiser, pull out the mike, and speak into it. Whit rubbed his eyes and wished for night again. He wished for another discovery like the cash, he wished—

A horn blared.

Whit looked back out the window and saw the deputy motioning furiously. Gil and another deputy were already out of the trailer, hurrying toward the officer. Whit rushed to catch them.

"That was him!" the deputy was saying as Whit reached the men.

"Who?" Whit asked.

"The guy in that red Toyota."

Gil and Whit traded glances. "Did you recognize him?" Gil asked.

"Hell, no. A call just came in at the courthouse from a woman who says she's Johns's girlfriend. She says he stole her car—a red Toyota."

Gil was already heading around the front of the cruiser. "You drive, Whit. I'll call for assistance."

"You two stay here at the trailer," Whit told the two deputies.

"But that's my car!" one of them said.

Whit shoved him aside and slid under the steering wheel. The keys were in the ignition. "How many ways are there out of this place?"

The offended deputy shrugged. "Just the one, I think."

Whit fired up the engine.

"Then he can't have gotten out yet," Gil said as he buckled his seat belt. "If we can beat him there—"

Whit floored the accelerator. The spinning tires flung gravel in the car's wake. "Christ, we shoulda kept the other guys here."

"Just get to the damned exit."

The tires of the cruiser squealed as Whit made the turn between them and the entrance to the park.

"There he is!" Gil cried.

Fifty yards in front of them the red Toyota was flying toward the exit.

Gil snatched up the radio. "Unit One to County."

Todd Hammond answered. "County here, Unit One. Have you been advised about the Johns subject?"

"We're in pursuit of him," Gil said. "He's just turning onto Route 226 from the trailer park. He's heading back toward Milbrook."

"Hang on," Whit said as he approached the exit.

Gil dropped the mike and braced himself against the dash as Whit fought the steering wheel, trying to make the turn onto the narrow two-lane.

"County to Unit One . . . County to Unit One." There was panicked desperation in the dispatcher's young voice. The cruiser fishtailed several times before Whit brought it under control. Gil fumbled to recapture the mike.

"County to Unit One. Do you read me?"

Gil had the mike in his hand by then. He decided to do

away with the protocol. "Listen, Hammond. Don't panic on me. Call the Milbrook P.D. Advise them that the suspect vehicle will be entering Milbrook on its east side from Route 226. Ask them to intercept. Be sure to advise them that this is a felony pursuit. You copy?"

"Ten-four."

Before Gil could continue, a third voice came on the radio. "Unit Four to Unit One. Sheriff, this is Hicks. Watkins and I passed a red Toyota as we left the park."

"That was him," Gil said into the mike. "Where are you?"

"Near the courthouse."

"Head for Route 226."

"Yes, sir. On our way."

Whit shook his head and slammed the heel of his palm against the steering wheel. "I can't keep up with him. With that little car he's taking the curves a lot faster than I can."

Gil leaned over and flipped the switches on a console mounted over the radio panel. The cruiser's siren and emergency lights came on. "Shouldn't matter if Hicks can get out here before he gets into town. We'll have him."

They raced on in silence as both men concentrated on the road. At least the curves kept him alert, Whit thought. A few minutes on a straightaway, and he'd be seeing double and falling asleep at the wheel. Finally he stomped on the brake pedal as he approached the last tight curve before the city limits. "We should know in a minute."

The car's tires squealed around the curve, and Whit fought to maintain control.

Whit saw Hicks's cruiser blocking the road and skidded to a stop ten feet away. "Dammit to hell!"

There was no sign of the small red Toyota.

TWENTY-TWO

ROUTE 226 CAME to an abrupt end at the Milbrook city limits, where it formed a three-way intersection with Hawkins Avenue. The avenue itself was only ten years old. In decades past, the lowlands on the southeastern sector of the small city flooded every spring. But during the sixties, when federal money was available for the asking, the creek that bisected the Bottom was widened and dredged. In the years since, the area had become the major site for new development in Milbrook.

The new high school was one of the newest projects to join the strip shopping centers and fast-food restaurants that proliferated in what was still known as Milbrook Bottom. Twice-daily traffic jams were common during the week around the time school began and when classes let out. It was still early for school, but several yellow buses were already streaming through as Dewey Johns reached the intersection.

He shot across Hawkins Avenue and swerved onto the access road to the high school just ahead of a school bus. In his rearview mirror he glimpsed a cop car, its lights and sirens going wild as it sped down Hawkins Avenue. Dewey kept just ahead of the bus, using its bulk to shield him. The access road led to a huge parking lot behind the school. Dewey quickly guided the small car into a space between two vans. He took a deep breath and settled back to consider his circumstances.

After a moment's thought, he slammed his fist down on the plastic dashboard of the Toyota. The force of the blow cracked the sun-weakened plastic. He needed his money. How the hell had the cops zeroed in on him so quickly? He'd been double-crossed. That's how. He was sure of it, and Randi was going to pay.

But the first thing he had to do was get away from here. The cops must have recognized him when he drove by the trailer, and he was lucky to get away. Babs's car was now just as hot as his own. No sense driving it another block. He jumped out of the Toyota and headed across the parking lot toward the athletic fields behind it. He'd hoof it across the fields and slip away in the neighborhood, which was just a few blocks from downtown.

"Watkins has been on the horn with his boys," Whit said into the mike in the sheriff's cruiser, which had stopped near the front of the high school. "They're going to block all the roads out of town. Gil's guys will help, but we'll probably need the state police to assist. We don't have the manpower to seal the town and patrol for him at the same time. Over."

A moment's silence followed, then Tony Danton, obviously uncomfortable communicating on the radio, said, "I'll get hold of them. Can you give me a call?"

Whit looked around for a pay phone. He saw a public phone booth a block or so south in the parking lot of a pizza parlor. "Yeah. Are you going to stay at the jail? Over."

"Uh . . . yes. But—" The balance of his transmission was cut off.

Gil smiled and shook his head. "Tony took his hand off the key. Not too swift on the radio, is he?"

Whit tossed the mike back onto the seat. "I'll go give him a call." As he spoke, his eyes scanned the grounds of the high school and the multitude of small burger joints and shops that lined the avenue.

Gil was about to slide down into the seat. With the continued stiffness in his injured leg, he had no problem allowing Whit to drive. He saw the look on his friend's face. "What are you thinking about?"

"Maybe our boy didn't get as far as we thought. Let's check out the parking lots."

Gil hiked his eyebrows. "Good idea."

Donnie Hicks, the deputy driving the other cruiser, was listening. "What about us?"

"You stay here," Gil said. "Check every vehicle heading out on Route 226."

Both of the cruisers still had their emergency lights flashing, and traffic at the intersection was moving at a snail's pace. Many of the cars were heading into the high-school lot.

Whit hit the siren as he wrenched the cruiser into the stream of traffic. Ahead of him, most of the vehicles pulled off to the side.

"Where to first?" Gil asked.

Whit's attention had settled on the sprawling brick structure of the high school. "Let's take a spin around to the school. It's the closest."

The school buses had emptied their first load of students and were heading out on their second runs. Whit eased the cruiser toward the rear of the school. At that time of the morning, still an hour before classes officially started, only about thirty cars were parked in the huge lot. Whit pulled the cruiser into the first lane. He rolled by the cars quickly, and was almost beyond them, when he spotted the red Toyota tucked between two vans.

He slammed on the brakes. "Son of a bitch! There it is!"

Gil was pulling out his weapon as he opened the door. Whit, on the opposite side, scrambled out first, squinting into the interior of the small car. "I don't see him."

The sheriff, his gun in hand, limped toward the car. "He's gotta be on foot."

Whit whirled, scanning the parking area and athletic fields.

"What if he went into the school?" Gil asked.

The thought had entered Whit's mind, too. "It could be a real disaster, but I don't see why he would do that. It'd make more sense for him to try to get away. Let's get some help over here. He can't have gotten too far."

Tressa Pynchon had gotten up at 6:30 to get ready for her first-hour class at 8:00. She'd started the coffee, and at 7:00 she'd slipped into the bedroom Whit and Anna shared to awaken her father. Anna was in the bed alone, still sleeping soundly.

Tressa went back to the kitchen and looked on the side of the refrigerator. That was the agreed location for notes left by one member of the household for another. The collection of magnets held no words of explanation. She was just about to awaken Anna when the phone rang.

"Ms. Tyree, please?"

Tressa frowned. "She's still asleep."

"This is Barney Williams. I'm a reporter for the paper. I need to talk to her. I don't think she'll mind."

Tressa hesitated. She'd spent too many years living with her father's intense hatred for phones. Her dilemma was solved when Anna, rubbing the sleep from her eyes, stumbled into the kitchen. "Where's Whit?"

Tressa shrugged. "I was wondering the same thing. This is for you." She offered Anna the phone and went to pour cups of coffee for both of them.

Anna came awake quickly on the phone.

"I'll be at the office as soon as I can," she said as she hung up.

"Trouble?" Tressa asked, setting Anna's coffee on the table.

Anna shook her head and sat down at the table. "It sounds as if your father's been busy while we slept. That was my ace police reporter, who lives with a police scanner. From what he can tell, Whit and an army of cops are about to apprehend the kidnapper."

"I didn't even hear him leave," Tressa said.

Anna chuckled. "I didn't, either. He probably had it all planned."

"He'd never admit it, but I think he really enjoys playing cat and mouse with you."

"One thing's damned certain," Anna conceded. "He's getting better at it."

The dawn had turned to full daylight, and the officers were scouring the backyards and out buildings located in the residential area of town adjacent to Milbrook Bottom. The plan to block all roads in and out of the city had been temporarily abandoned in favor of a block-by-block foot search. Terry Watkins, assisted by the sheriff, coordinated the search from the police station while city officers and sheriff's deputies formed a circle around the southeastern sector of the city. The mug shot of Dewey Johns had been photocopied and was being distributed to curious residents in the search area.

Whit, accompanied by Donnie Hicks and a city officer, had started the search at the high school. They had moved across the athletic fields and into the quite neighborhood just north of the high-school compound.

A light blanket of dew covered the grass of the yards. Whit checked every porch and crawl space and wasn't bashful about trying the doors to any sheds or buildings on the properties he searched. He looked into every car he found parked on the street or on private property.

Several times residents came out to see what was going on. He gave them photocopies of the mug shot and told them to stay in their homes with the doors locked. If they saw anyone fitting Johns's description, they were to call the Milbrook Police Department or the sheriff's department.

As he searched, Whit was careful to keep both the deputy and city officer in sight. That was part of the plan. Hopefully it meant that Johns wouldn't be able to slip between them. As a result, Whit—along with his search party—moved from side to side as they progressed forward toward the main business district of Milbrook.

As Whit started to cross a street, a state police cruiser eased slowly down the street. The officer inside looked like one of the detachment's new rookies. He stopped in front of Whit, his window down.

"Say, is this guy the one who snatched that kid?" the young state cop asked.

Whit nodded. "Yeah, he's the one."

"Any idea about where the kid is?"

" 'Fraid not."

"I sure would like to find the fucker," the boyish-looking cop said.

Whit suppressed a smile. "Me, too."

"Well, I'll be patrolling the streets. You guys got walkie-talkies?"

Whit glanced to his right. The city officer was checking vehicles parked along the residential street. "One of the guys with me does."

"Give a shout if you need me."

"Will do," Whit said.

Hicks moved over to Whit. "I guess they're gonna ride around in cars."

Whit shrugged. "Be thankful they're here at all. Tony must have pulled some strings."

The state police cruiser came to an abrupt stop half a block away. Both men froze. "Think he sees something?" Hicks asked.

The backup lights of the cruiser blinked on as the vehicle reversed its course. Whit bent down as the rookie leaned his head out the window. "By the way, there's a television crew around the neighborhood, too."

Whit rolled his eyes as he stood erect. "Just what we fuckin' need."

"It's that blond. The one that's been givin' you such a hard time. Thought I'd warn you."

"I appreciate it," Whit said . . . and meant it.

Dewey Johns's anxious stomach rumbled as he peered through the dense pine needles. He was perched several feet off the ground, clinging to the scratchy trunk of the huge pine. One of the cop cars had stopped just a few feet from him, and for a few sickening seconds he thought the cop had spotted him. Then the car had backed up, but he didn't feel much safer. The neighborhood was crawling with cops.

A dog was barking from one of the houses nearby. He felt like a treed cat with dogs all around him snapping at his ankles. Dogs with badges. Did the local cops have dogs? he wondered. The thought suddenly made him even more anxious. Even if the cops couldn't see him, a dog could find him by scent. He had to get out of here, but he couldn't just walk away.

He heard voices and craned his neck. A cop was talking to someone at the house not fifty feet from where he was hiding. He noticed a pickup in the driveway. If he could get inside, it wouldn't take him but a couple of minutes to hot-wire the ignition.

When the voices died away, he slowly descended from his hideout. He dropped flat to the ground and looked up and down the street. There was no sign of any cops. No sign of anyone. He crawled out from under the tree and walked over to the pickup. The door was locked. He peered through the window and saw the same was the case for the passenger door.

"Damn it." He looked around, worried that someone would see him. The trees in the yard blocked the view of the street. He glanced toward the house, but didn't see anyone looking out. Then he saw the gas can in the back of the truck, and it gave him an idea.

Anna peered through the side windows of her VW Passat, which she'd bought a couple of months ago. She cruised along the streets, passing several search parties and keeping an eye out for Whit. She'd find him in time, if he were here. Even more, she wanted to be present when the kidnapper was caught. It would not only be a good story, but it would vindicate Whit of the charges that he was doing nothing to solve the crime. But most of all, she just wanted the perpetrator captured before another child disappeared.

She turned the corner and slowed as she came upon several people and a state police cruiser in the street. For a moment she didn't know what was going on. Then she spotted the TV camera, and a head of blond hair. Myra Martin was filming an interview with someone from the state police division. "Just where I don't want to be," Anna muttered, and put the Passat into reverse.

She backed up and nearly rammed the new car head-on into Barney Williams's clunker, which had just pulled out of an alley. Barney leaned on the horn, then his jaw dropped as he saw that he'd nearly hit his boss. She pulled up next to him and leaned out the window.

"What have you got, Barney?"

"Sorry, Anna. Have you heard?"

"Did they get him?"

"No, but he killed a guy last night. That's what set off this whole thing. One of the cops told me, but I need to get to the station for all the details. Supposedly the guy was trying to grab another kid."

"How do they know who it is?"

"Don't know, but I'll find out. I guess he abandoned his car at the high school. They figure he headed up here."

"Okay. Get the rest of it at the station. I'll see what happens here." She was about to pull away when she caught Barney's attention again. "You haven't seen Whit, have you?"

"No, ma'am," he said, and drove off.

She knew Barney didn't care much for Whit. He not only refused to answer questions most of the time, but Whit had been downright hostile toward Barney at times.

She shoved the Passat into first and drove on. Whit had to be around here somewhere. She'd look around a few minutes longer, then head to the office.

Dewey stepped out from the trees as the car turned the corner and headed his way. He held up the gas can in one hand and his thumb in the other. His .22 was tucked in his belt and he was ready to put it to use.

He smiled as the car slowed to a stop a few feet from him. He trotted over and reached for the passenger door. This was easy. So easy.

TWENTY-THREE

THE BLOODHOUND SNIFFED at the base of the pine tree and whined and pawed at the ground. "He was here all right," said the uniformed state police officer who was in charge of the dog.

Whit looked up into the tree. A lot of good it did now. The dog, who was called Carla, had sniffed one of Dewey Johns's shirts taken from the trailer and headed through the neighborhood as if she was following a visible trail. Two blocks later, she had stopped at the tree. Now Carla's nose was on the ground again and she was moving toward the driveway of the adjacent house, where a pickup truck was parked.

It was nearly 9:30, and Whit was getting more disgruntled by the moment. If they didn't come up with something soon, they'd have to call off the search. He was tired and his nerves were frayed. The dog seemed like their last hope, but Whit couldn't imagine the bloodhound leading them right to Johns. He might have hidden for a while in the tree when they were searching the area, but Whit doubted that he'd stuck around. Somehow the bastard had found a way out of here.

The dog moved down to the edge of the yard and sniffed around some more trees. Carla turned in circles, her nose to the ground, then she stopped and looked up at her master. She made a couple of more tight circles before sitting down.

"What's she doing?" Whit asked.

The officer shook her head, and it wasn't because she didn't know what the dog's actions meant. "She's lost it. The scent ends right here."

"What do you mean it ends here?"

The officer, whose pinned-up hair was starting to come loose beneath her hat, knelt down and patted the dog on the back. "Just what I said. He came across the field and down this street. Then he hid in that tree. He went over by the garage, then came down here. Someone must have picked him up. Or maybe he thumbed a ride."

"I can't believe he'd get away that easy."

Dewey peered out through the drawn blinds. The street outside of Randi's house was as quiet as ever. He'd snuck in through a back window with no problem, and he doubted that anyone had seen him approach the house. Randi lived across town from where he'd abandoned Babs's Toyota. It was a neighborhood of older, well-kept houses with big yards and lots of trees. Randi wasn't rich, but she had more money than he did, and a lot more than Babs.

He let go of the blinds and headed for the bedroom. Her money must be hidden somewhere in the house, and he'd find it before she got home. She'd paid him well for snatching the kid, but he figured she'd made even more off the deal. A lot more. He'd never thought of kids as anything but a pain in the ass. To think that people would pay good money for them. How'd ya figure? He didn't know what kind of people got the girl or what they were going to do with her. Wasn't any of his business.

But now everything was backfiring. He'd lost his Camaro

and his trailer and his cash to the fucking cops, and he was lucky he wasn't locked in a jail cell for killing the kid's father. He needed money, and he needed it right away. The money first, then Randi. He'd wait until she got home. She'd pay for tipping off the cops. Then he'd take her car and head out of town.

Whit stood in the hall of the hospital waiting for Babs Duncan to wake up. She had a fractured jaw and had been given a sedative a few hours earlier. There'd been no new leads on the whereabouts of Johns, and Babs seemed the only hope at the moment. From what the investigation had pieced together so far in the hours since Johns had been identified was that he was a loner with no close friends besides Babs. He worked as a handyman picking up jobs here and there by advertising in the classified section of the *Milbrook Daily Journal*. His neighbors said they weren't close to him or particularly fond of him, and that the only people they ever saw at the trailer with him was an occasional woman, none of whom they could name.

Whit glanced at his watch and saw that it was 12:30 P.M. Anna and Tressa were probably wondering what happened to him, since he hadn't left behind any message before his quick departure. He walked down the hall to a telephone booth and called the house. Tressa answered on the second ring.

"Daddy, what time did you sneak out of here, anyhow?"

"Early. Real early."

"We heard that the kidnapper was cornered. Did you get him?"

"I wish I could say yes. We're still working on it. Is Anna there?"

"You mean you haven't talked to her?"

"Not a word."

"That's strange. After one of the reporters called and told her about what was going on, she went out to look for you."

"I haven't been real easy to find this morning. I'll give her a call at the paper."

After he hung up, he dug in his pocket for another quarter and dropped it into the coin slot. Although Anna usually worked at night, it wasn't surprising for her to show up at the office for a couple of hours during the day. He didn't know what she did, and didn't want to know. He wished that reporters would feel the same way about his job.

"Anna Tyree, please," he said when the paper's receptionist answered after four rings. That usually meant Anna wasn't in her office.

"I'll page her. Can I say who's calling?"

He told her.

"One moment."

The moment extended into thirty seconds, then forty-five. As he stared down the hall waiting, he spotted the doctor he'd spoken with earlier stepping into the hall. He was about to hang up when the secretary's voice rang in his ear.

"Mr. Pynchon? Ms. Tyree is not in the building right now. Can I take a message?"

"No." He slammed the receiver down and intercepted the doctor. "What's the word? Can I talk to her?"

The doctor, who looked about twenty-five and wore a white lab coat over his shirt and tie, frowned at Whit as if he were seeing him for the first time. "Oh, yes. You wanted to question Miss Duncan. Talk to the nurse at the station. Have her take you in to see her. Miss Duncan's awake, but groggy, and her jaw's wired so she's not going to be very communicative."

"Can she talk?"

"She can mumble. But don't push her. No more than five minutes. Got that?"

"Yeah. Thanks." Cocky son of a bitch, he thought as he headed to the nurses' station.

Anna wasn't sure whether to be angry or worried. She'd talked to a couple of the usual sources at the police department and sheriff's office, but no one had seen Barney. She'd also called the dispatcher at the police department who she knew had been tipping Barney on stories ever since he'd done a complimentary story on him. But the dispatcher hadn't talked to Barney, either.

He'd disappeared, and so had Whit. As she drove to the courthouse, she tried to imagine the two of them holed up somewhere with Barney interviewing Whit on the details about the murder and the investigation. She laughed at the image, knowing that the two weren't together. But where the hell were they? It wasn't like Whit not to leave a message or call her, and it wasn't like Barney to vanish in the midst of a story. She eased to a stop at a light. She was getting carried away. Barney probably had sources she didn't know about. His story would probably be filed by the time she got back to the office this evening.

It had better be.

What she didn't like was not knowing what was going on. She'd been so surprised that Barney hadn't talked to his contacts that she hadn't inquired any further about the murder. But she was going to do it now. If Whit wasn't in his office, she'd talk to Tony Danton.

"Ms. Duncan, how are you feeling?" She was probably a fairly good-looking woman, but her face was distorted now from the swollen, purple jaw. There were circles around her eyes and her blond hair was stringy.

The nurse had explained to the woman who he was, but Babs stared at him as if she hadn't expected that sort of question.

"Better. Got my car back?" she mumbled.

That was it. She thought he was here because of the car and money, and was surprised by the visit. A couple of cruisers had shown up at her door, and after taking her statement she'd been transported to the hospital. "We haven't found Dewey, yet. But he's in more trouble than you know about."

"Knew it."

"Go on. What do you know?"

Whit listened closely as she spoke between her teeth. "The last couple of times I seen him, he's been sayin' stuff about makin' it big and blowin' these boondocks. Wha'd he do? Break into a house again?"

"Yes, he did—and he shot a man to death."

She moaned and turned her head to the side.

"That isn't all. He's a suspect in the kidnapping of a little girl. You know anything about that?"

She raised her head off the pillow, looking startled and frightened. "I got nothing to do with his troublemakin' ways."

Her words slurred together, and he barely understood her. "We think he had an accomplice."

Her face was red, and her eyes were wide with fear. "Not me."

"Mr. Pynchon!" The nurse, who had been standing a few feet from the bed, stepped forward.

Whit held up a hand. "Okay."

He turned back to Babs. "We don't believe it was you.

We think this accomplice picked him up after he abandoned your car.''

"My car?''

"It's okay. He didn't wreck it.''

She let her head fall back on the pillow.

"Any idea who his accomplice might be?''

"A woman.''

"You got a name?''

She shook her head.

"How'd you know it was a woman?''

"He called her somethin' on the phone,'' she muttered.

"What did he call her?''

"Sweet ting.''

"Sweet thing?''

She nodded.

"You know where she lives?''

She shook her head.

"Where do you think he met her?''

"Don't ask me.'' Now she sounded irritated.

The nurse moved forward again. "I think that should be all. She needs to rest.''

"Thanks for your help, Miss Duncan.''

"My car? Gotta get home.''

"You better get someone to take you home, then call the police department about the car. They'll help you.''

"Hope someone does.''

Whit knew he should go home and get some sleep, but he was only a few blocks from the courthouse so he decided to stop by Tony's office and see if there were any new developments. To his surprise, he found Anna talking to Tony. "Am I interrupting an interview—or is it something I shouldn't know about?''

Tony didn't laugh. Anna turned toward him, and Whit's

grin faded as he saw the distraught look on her face. "What's wrong?"

"I've got to go to the hospital right away."

"The hospital? I just came from—"

"It's Barney, Whit," Anna said. "He was shot."

"When? Where?"

"Someone found him crawling on the side of Route 226 outside of town," Tony explained. "He was shot at close range by a small-caliber weapon, probably a .22."

From the way Tony looked at him, Whit could tell he suspected that Johns was the perp. "How is he?"

Tony shrugged. "It just came over the radio a couple of minutes ago. We're waiting to hear back from the officer who found him."

"The kidnapper did it," Anna said. "And he took Barney's car."

"We don't know that for sure," Tony said. "We've got a bulletin out on the car, though."

Whit sighed and his shoulders slumped. He raked his fingers through his graying hair. He felt as if he'd been running in circles for more than twelve hours.

"Whit, go home; go to bed," Tony said. "If anything breaks, I'll call you." He smiled. "Like you called me this morning."

"I'm not ready for bed yet if there's another witness to talk to."

The phone rang on Tony's desk. "Danton."

He greeted whoever had called and listened. "Okay, thanks. I appreciate it."

The prosecutor hung up the phone. "It sounds like Barney's going to make it."

"Can he talk?" Whit asked.

"The officer who was first on the scene said the guy

wouldn't shut up. Barney told him it was definitely Johns who shot him."

"I'll go see what else he has to say," Whit said. "Then I'll get some sleep."

"I'm going, too," Anna said.

Dewey opened the refrigerator door and grabbed a can of beer. He popped it open and sat down at the kitchen table. He'd torn the place apart and had only found three hundred and sixty-two dollars. He knew there was more, but where? He gulped down half the beer and looked up at the clock.

It was after 5:00 and no Randi. She got off work at 4:30 and was usually home within ten minutes. Maybe she'd stopped by the grocery store. Maybe she was talking to the cops. But how could she do that? She must know she wouldn't get away. He'd point the finger at her. But what could he prove? Even though he'd been seeing her for a couple of years, she'd always been real careful.

After he'd gotten out of jail, she'd hired him to replace the worn screening on her porch, and a few other odd jobs from time to time. She'd always paid him in cash, and he didn't have any record of it. She'd made him park his car in the rear driveway, which was sheltered by trees and well off the road. That was where the old, rusted Mazda he'd taken from the guy was parked right now. She'd never allowed him to stay overnight, but slowly she'd drawn him into her plan.

Maybe there was more to her plans than she was letting on. What if Randi reported a burglar in the house? The house definitely looked burglarized. He tried to remember something he knew about her that would tie her to the kidnapping. He couldn't think of a thing. Still, the cops would give her hell. They might get to the bottom of it. But what good would it do him if he was in the slammer?

The phone rang.

He took a final swallow of beer and lifted the phone off the wall. He didn't say a word.

"Dewey?" a voice said after a few seconds.

"Yeah."

"I knew you were there."

"I've been waiting for you."

"I figured that. It's on the radio. Have you heard?"

"No. What do they say?"

"Just that they're looking for you and that you killed a man."

"Did you hear anything about anyone else getting shot?"

"Did you kill someone else?" Her voice was tense.

"Never mind, sweet thing. Why don't you come home and we'll get out of here together like we planned it before?"

"I think you'd better go on your own. I'm not ready to leave yet. I can catch up with you."

He was silent a moment. She sounded nervous, not at all as confident as she'd been last night on the phone. He could hear traffic in the background and knew she was at a phone booth. "One problem there, Randi. The cops got my money. And I'm going to be needin' to buy a car. I can't keep stealing 'em."

"Okay. Go in the freezer. Under the icemaker there's a Baggie with twelve thousand dollars wrapped in tinfoil. Take it all, and get out of the house right away."

He opened the freezer door and rummaged through it until he found the plastic bag. He squeezed it. "Okay. I'll call you."

"No, don't. I mean, not for a while—until things cool down."

She was careful. Real careful. "All right."

"Good luck, Dewey." She hung up.

He quickly pulled the tinfoil package from the Baggie and unraveled it. He smiled as he stared at two thick rolls of hundreds. If she so willingly gave up twelve grand, she probably was paid even more. He spent the next few minutes taking everything out of the freezer and refrigerator. But there were no more surprise packages.

He tossed a few things back inside the freezer, but stopped. What was he doing? Fuck Randi. She could straighten it out herself, just like she'd have to do with the rest of the house. He had to get out of here. He could still wait for her, but he had the feeling she wasn't going to show up, and the longer he had the Mazda, the more likely it was that the cops would find out about it. Someone would be wondering what happened to the guy he'd shot, and the cops would be looking out for his car.

He could always come back and take care of Randi later. He'd drive a couple of hundred miles, then take a bus, or maybe Amtrak. Hell, maybe he'd end up down in Myrtle Beach where they'd been looking for the kid's father. He laughed and headed out the back door.

Anna pounded furiously at the keyboard of her computer. She was just trying to get all of the facts and quotes down, then she'd go back and rewrite. It was a wild, complex story. Dewey Johns had tried to cover his tracks by killing the kid who'd pulled the clown mask from his face. But everything had gone wrong for Dewey. He'd killed the kid's father, beaten up his own girlfriend, then stolen her car. After he'd abandoned the car, he'd tricked Barney Williams into giving him a ride by posing as a motorist who'd run out of gas. He'd shot Barney and left him for dead, but the bullet had struck a rib and missed his vital organs.

Barney said he'd thought the guy looked familiar, but didn't realize why until it was too late. He'd told Anna that he wanted to dictate a first-person story on the encounter to her or another reporter, but she'd told him to take it easy. He could write it himself when he was on his feet again.

She knew that her story wouldn't reflect well on Whit, but there was no getting around the fact that Johns had escaped. When she was finished with it, she'd call Tony's office and make a final check before sending the article to the editor on the copy desk.

Dewey fiddled with the radio in the old Mazda as he drove away from Randi's house. It was a complicated-looking thing. He heard static, then a voice, then more static. Then he knew what it was. What the hell was that kid doing with a police scanner? The guy had tried to talk to him, but he'd told him to shut up and drive. He just hoped he wasn't an off-duty cop. Every cop in the state would be looking for him if he'd killed one of their own.

He played with the scanner's dial, trying to find the right band for the local cops. It had probably been set right in the first place, but he'd spun the dial before he'd known what he was doing. Finally he heard a voice amid the crackling and stopped turning. Another voice responded, but he couldn't understand them, except for the ten-four part. It was all the police code stuff. He was within half a mile of Route 226 when he saw a police car turn onto the road. It was two cars back, and he couldn't tell if it was following him. Then he heard a terse remark over the scanner. "Got a blue '82 Mazda heading west on Fifteenth about a quarter mile from 226."

The radio crackled with static. Johns leaned forward, listening. "You got a license number?"

"Can't see it yet."

"Keep on it."

Johns tightened his grip on the steering wheel. "Oh, shit."

They were onto the car already. He stepped on the gas and cursed. Why did the guy have to drive an old beater with no guts? He'd never outrun the cops. He had to ditch it and lose them on foot again. He glanced frantically around for a side street.

The light at 226 had just changed to red. He ran it. But he didn't see the pickup in time. He swerved the wheel to the left, heard a horn. The pickup caught the Mazda by the rear fender. The car spun around; he fought to control it. Then he heard the crush of metal as the car was hit again, this time on the right side.

A red light flashed; the cop had slammed into him. He reached for the .22, which he'd laid on the floorboard, but he couldn't find it. "Shit." He pushed open the door.

"Hold it. Don't move."

Half in, half out of the car, he looked over his shoulder and saw a .38 aimed across the hood of the Mazda. He heard the scream of another cop car coming up fast. "Don't shoot, man. Don't shoot."

"Hands on the hood. Now!"

TWENTY-FOUR

WHIT BALANCED the headset of his phone between his ear and shoulder and punched Sue Winters's number. As the phone rang, he tried to think of what he would say. After arriving at the office and talking briefly with Tony Danton, he'd gone over the reports of the previous day's events. Most of what he read, he'd already known. One report, though, offered a new bit of information. Dewey Johns's Camaro was discovered behind a storage warehouse about half a mile from the trailer park where Babs Duncan lived. After it had been towed to the police garage and a warrant obtained, the vehicle had been searched. A bolt cutter with shavings of steel on the blade was found in the trunk—and wedged underneath the passenger seat had been a child's white sandal.

"Mrs. Winters? This is Whit Pynchon."

"I suppose you're calling to tell me that you've caught this Dewey somebody. So what? Where's my daughter?"

"We don't know, Mrs. Winters, but we'd like your cooperation in our investigation."

"Well, I'd love to get your cooperation for a change, too."

There was no sense arguing with her. "I'd like to come out to your apartment. There's something we need your help with."

A couple of moments passed before she spoke. This time

her voice wavered. "You've . . . found her, haven't you? You want to take me to the morgue to identify her."

"No. We haven't found your daughter. We have a shoe, though, that may belong to your daughter."

Whit heard a soft gasp or maybe a sob. "I'll come down to the courthouse. I'll be there in half an hour."

"Thank you, ma'am."

Whit hung up the phone and picked up a plastic evidence bag that had been returned from the lab half an hour ago. No distinguishable prints had been detected on the sandal, and Whit couldn't help wondering if the city cop who'd discovered it had accidentally smudged away a print or two when he'd pulled it out from under the seat. But if Sue Winters identified the shoe it would be damning evidence that Johns had kidnapped her.

Prosecuting Johns, at this point, was not the problem. He would be charged for not only the kidnapping of Marcia Winters, but for the murder of Jerry Fuller, the attempted murder of Tommy Fuller, the kidnapping and attempted murder of Barney Williams, and two counts of car theft.

What was missing, though, was a clear motive for the kidnapping of the girl that had set off the string of crimes. But Whit had an idea, and if his idea were right, Marcia Winters might very well still be alive.

The intercom buzzed, interrupting his thoughts. He tapped the answer button and heard Tony's voice.

"You ready to go talk to Johns?"

"What? I thought his lawyer wasn't going to be here until one."

"He's not. But Johns has agreed to talk to us without a lawyer present."

"You're kidding."

"He may just be playing with us, but he does want to talk."

"Well, I'd be happy to talk to the suspect, but Sue Winters is going to be here in a few minutes to I.D. the shoe."

"Christ, Whit. Let me handle that detail. She'll probably think you're torturing her and call the TV station."

Whit laughed. "I do seem to have a hard time getting along with her."

"That's an understatement."

"You can tell her there's a good chance that Marcia's still alive. I don't think she'd believe me."

"You know, Whit, I think it's better not to get into that right now. In some ways, thinking your child's alive and being held by strangers is even worse than finding out the kid's dead. Besides, there's no sense giving her any false hope. We don't know if she's alive or not."

"Yeah, you're right."

Whit dropped off the shoe at Tony's office and continued on to the jail. He found Johns seated at a table in the interview room, smoking a cigarette. There were two butts already in the ashtray. Whit introduced himself and sat down across from Johns. The suspect took a drag on his cigarette, then put it out. He ran a hand through his dark brown hair. Even though he was still in his twenties, his skin looked leathery and weatherbeaten. His blue eyes showed traces of blood vessels, probably from heavy drinking. He was a husky man, the sort who would no doubt gain twenty or thirty pounds in a few years, and, by the time he was forty, he'd look old and paunchy. But if Whit had his way, Johns was going to be spending the rest of his fading youth in prison and growing old there. He might walk free again, but not until well into the next century.

Whit pressed a button on the table, and it switched on a concealed tape recorder. "I understand you want to talk without your lawyer present. Is that correct?"

"That's what I've been saying since seven o'clock this morning. Asshole jailers just act like they don't even hear you."

"They take a lot of crap sometimes. They learn to act like they're not listening. So you want to tell me about the little girl?"

Johns put his hands on the side of the table, leaned forward, and leered at Whit. "You must think I'm some kind of asshole."

Whit's jaw tightened. "I've got better things to do than chitchat with fuck-ups. So you either talk or I walk. Got it?"

"Hey, you don't know nothing about that kid," he shouted across the table. "I hold the cards. That is, if you want to see her alive."

"Is she alive?"

"Last time I saw her she was."

"When was that?"

Johns pulled his pack of Lucky Strikes from the pocket of his T-shirt, knocked out a cigarette, then dropped the pack on the table. He lit up and took a long, deep drag. "I'm not tellin' you that," he said as he exhaled.

"What do you want?"

"Now we're getting somewhere," Johns said. "I'll give you something big, but you've got to deal me a good hand."

"What exactly are you saying?"

"You give me immunity, and I'll finger the one who's behind the kidnapping. I'm just a hired hand."

"My boss doesn't give immunity to guys who pull a trigger. Simple as that."

"Then you tell that girl's mama she ain't never gonna see her baby girl again. You just tell her that, and tell why not."

Whit turned off the recorder. "See you later, Johns. Enjoy your stay."

"Wait a minute," Johns yelled after him. "You just gonna throw away your chance of solving this case?"

"It's already solved," Whit said over his shoulder as he left the room. "You're it."

It was about what he'd expected. When Tony was done with Sue Winters, they'd talk strategy. Johns had so many counts against him, they might be able to drop a couple of them without affecting their case. But he definitely wasn't going to ask the prosecutor to give Johns blanket immunity. No way.

Whit saw someone waiting outside of his office and for a moment thought it was Sue Winters. Then the woman turned and stood up. "Morning, Whit. I heard you arrested the bastard." Norma Wyse extended a hand.

"Not personally," he answered, shaking her hand. "As a matter of fact, I was sound asleep at the time. But don't tell anyone."

She laughed. "Oh, so you don't really work twenty-four hours a day?"

"It all sort of blends together."

There was something dramatic in Norma's appearance. Maybe it was the fact that she was wearing high heels and a stylish purple-and-black suit. Or maybe it was the way her black hair swept back from her face. Or even the scent of her perfume. "So what can I do for you today, Norma?"

"Can we talk in your office? It'll just take a minute."

At that moment, Sue Winters walked down the hall, accompanied by Tony Danton, who held her arm. She was dabbing her eyes with Kleenex, but paused when she spotted Whit and Norma. She looked between them and started to say something. But tears filled her eyes and her shoulders shuddered as she silently wept and hurried off. Whit caught Tony's eye, and they exchanged a quick glance.

"What was that about?" Norma asked.

He motioned toward his office. "C'mon inside." After he closed the door, he told her who had just walked by.

Norma sat down. "Oh, God. I hope that doesn't mean her little girl . . ."

"No, she hasn't been found yet. We don't know anything new at the moment." Whit leaned against his desk, hoping to leave the impression that he was serious about being in a rush. "So . . ."

"I'm here about our case against the Harrisons. I was wondering—"

A rap on the door interrupted them. Whit pushed off from his desk and answered it. Tony looked in and greeted Norma, then gave Whit a questioning look.

"Come on in. We're talking about the case against the Harrisons." Tony didn't look as if he wanted to hear about it, and Whit quickly added that it would take only a moment. "Go ahead, Norma."

"Nice to see you again, Mr. Danton. What I was starting to tell Whit was that I came over to find out if you would object to the welfare department intervening in the case against the Harrisons."

"How so?"

"I would just like to see if we can move things along by using one of our attorneys to help out with the preparation of the case," she explained.

"I don't see any problem with that," Tony said. "I need all the help I can get."

"Great." She stood up, smiled. "That's really all I needed to know right now." She moved toward the door, then turned to Tony. "I want to congratulate both of you on the arrest. I'm glad to see you're making progress."

"Thank you," Tony said. "So are we."

"If there's anything I can do to help Sue Winters, please let me know."

"I appreciate the offer. But right now she's not too happy with anyone who has an official title. She's very upset."

"I don't blame her," Norma said. "I'm sure she's hoping there will be some answers about her daughter real soon."

"So are we," Whit said.

After the door closed, Whit filled Tony in on what had happened at the jail. Tony offered a concise reply. "N.F.D., Whit. No fucking deals with murderers. Period."

"I'm no more comfortable with the idea than you are," Whit said. "But, if we could get the girl back and nab his accomplice at the same time, it might be worth dropping one of the kidnapping counts and maybe the car theft counts."

Tony leaned against the wall, his hand buried in his pockets. "He's not going to buy that. He's interested in results: a short jail term or no time. Personally I don't want to see that guy on the street again." When Whit didn't respond, Tony shrugged. "But you can try it. Who knows, maybe he's dumb enough to bite."

"Let's wait awhile and let him sweat it out," Whit suggested. "If he thinks we're not going to bite, he might take anything we offer."

Reporting events as they occurred was only a small part of what Anna perceived as the duty of a community newspaper. She looked at the relationship of events with issues and how they affected people in Milbrook on a day-to-day basis. That was why she had begun planning a series of articles on the local day-care situation as soon as she and Whit had returned from Myrtle Beach. She'd pulled a file filled with clippings and had been taking notes between carrying out her regular duties as editor. It was perfect timing for the series. Parents all over the county were probably reevaluating their own situations regarding the care of their children while they worked.

Now, a day after the arrest of Dewey Johns, she was meeting in her office with two reporters who would work with her. "The series will look at the quality of care, the cost, and safety . . . particularly the safety in the aftermath of the kidnapping of Marcia Winters."

"Gerry, I want you to start by conducting interviews with the owners of several day-care centers in Milbrook," she said to her regular feature writer. "Don't just talk to them on the phone, either. Get into the centers and observe what's going on. Talk to the teachers. Find out what safety measures are being used, and find out if the people with subsidized day care are less protected than those who can afford more expensive centers."

She turned to the other reporter, a bright, attractive twenty-three-year-old woman who'd just joined the staff two weeks ago after graduating from Wesleyan with a master's degree in journalism and mass communications. She'd probably stay a year or so before moving on to a larger newspaper.

"Marilyn, I want you to interview at least a dozen parents to get their feelings about day care. Get into their personal stories. Some parents are really torn up by the dilemma of working and caring for their kids. It's heart-rendering stuff they'll tell you about, too. You watch."

She sat back in her chair. "Gerry, don't worry about the FunTime Day-Care Center. That's the one I'm going to investigate myself."

"Ah, you're taking the best part," he said.

"Are you kidding? They probably won't let me in the door. I'll be talking to their lawyer and the people who are getting ready to prosecute them."

"How's Barney doing?" Marilyn asked.

"Much better." She'd seen Barney gazing wistfully across the newsroom at Marilyn on several occasions since she'd started. Now she had a surprise for him. "I'm glad you asked. Before you start work on this series, I want you to go down to the hospital and let Barney tell you his story. We'll run it as a first-person piece, but, of course, he's going to need help. Do you mind?"

"Oh, not at all. I was planning on stopping by to see him on my dinner break, anyhow."

"Good." Anna glanced at her watch and saw that it was 2:48. "Well, I'm off. Dewey Johns is scheduled to be arraigned in half an hour. I'm going to sit in on it."

When she arrived at the courthouse, it was ten after three. But she wasn't worried about being late. Over the years she'd acquired a knack for arriving at certain events at the time they began, rather than their scheduled time. Very few meetings and press conferences started on time. If it was a public meeting or a press conference, five minutes after the appointed time was about right. For court cases, ten or even fifteen minutes after the scheduled time was usually early. Of course, she never told her reporters to show up late for anything. That was something they could learn on their own.

As it turned out, she was early. When she entered the courtroom, she was disappointed to find Myra Martin standing with a cameraman on one side of the courtroom. Anna turned her attention to the center of the courtroom where Whit was talking with an attractive woman seated in the first row. She didn't recognize the woman and decided she'd find out who it was. She walked up and slid into the front row next to her.

"Afternoon, Whit."

"Anna, I want you to meet Norma Wyse with the child welfare office."

They shook hands. "Glad to meet you. In fact, I'd like to talk to you later about the Harrison case."

"That would be fine. We can use public support on this case."

"That's a change. Usually it's like pulling teeth to get any answers from Human Services."

"Well, we're normally restricted on what we can say. We like to protect our clients' privacy. But this, of course, is something altogether different."

Just then several handcuffed prisoners were marched into the room and seated on a long bench near the front of the courtroom. "I think that's him right there," Anna whispered.

"Which one?" Norma asked, leaning toward her.

"The second one from this end. The husky one with the wavy brown hair."

Johns turned and peered at them as if he'd heard Anna. "Oh, that's spooky," Anna muttered as she glanced away.

"Look!" Norma nodded toward the prisoners.

Myra Martin was leaning over the railing, saying something to Johns. She stuck a microphone in his face, but instantly a bailiff moved forward and waved her away. Myra backed off, but the instant the bailiff turned away, she shoved the microphone in front of Johns again.

"Get that fucking thing away from me!" Johns yelled.

The bailiff spun around. He pointed to the door and ordered Martin and her cameraman to leave the courtroom.

"You can't do that," the reporter retorted. Her chin jutted defiantly toward the bailiff. "I have a right to—"

"The court officers can remove anyone who is disturbing

the peace,'' the bailiff said. ''Now move before you are arrested.''

Martin's brow furrowed. She turned on her heels, motioned to her cameraman, and left.

''She certainly has gall,'' Norma said.

Anna held her tongue. ''You could say that.''

A couple of minutes later, the judge entered the courtroom and everyone stood up. He introduced himself as Judge David O'Brien and began proceedings. It was another ten minutes before Johns's name was called. He was still in handcuffs as the bailiff led him forward and pulled out a chair at the counsel desk.

The proceedings moved along swiftly, as Anna had expected. She'd come to the hearing to see Dewey Johns for herself and to be present if the defense, the prosecution, or the judge tried anything out of the ordinary. If Tony were dealing with the suspect, dropping charges in exchange for a guilty plea, she was prepared to let him have it on the editorial page. About two dozen curious residents were seated in the courtroom, and she doubted that any of the spectators wanted to see Johns get off easy, if indeed he was the perpetrator of the string of crimes.

She leaned forward and jotted notes in her slender reporter's notebook as the judge read the charges. One count of murder, two counts of attempted murder, two counts of kidnapping, one count of attempted kidnapping, and two counts of car theft. Anna scribbled down the charges. Everything seemed to be accounted for. But she knew she would have to keep close tabs on the case, because charges could be dropped at any number of points.

The judge officially appointed a lawyer to defend Johns. He was a young attorney who worked in the public defender's office. Then O'Brien committed Johns to jail after explaining that the heinous nature of the crimes made Johns an unacceptable candidate for release on a bail bond. Finally he asked the lawyers to step forward to discuss the date for a preliminary hearing.

As Whit, Tony, and Johns's lawyer approached the bench, Anna saw Johns slide open a drawer with his handcuffed hands.

"He's got a gun!" Norma shouted.

"You bitch!" Johns yelled, and spun around. Anna glimpsed the handgun as Johns aimed it at her and Norma. She ducked below the railing, a shot rang out amid screams and shouts, and Norma collapsed on top of her.

She struggled beneath the woman's weight, but then Norma was righting herself. "Are you okay?" She put an arm around Norma.

"I think so."

Anna saw Johns lying on the floor with the bailiff still aiming his .38 at him. Blood oozed from the side of Johns's head and he wasn't moving. Whit dropped down beside him, put a hand to his neck. He shook his head as he stood up. "He's dead."

TWENTY-FIVE

"THERE GOES our only chance to find out what happened to Marcia Winters," Whit said as Johns's body was carried off by ambulance attendants.

Nearby, Tony consoled Norma Wyse. "It's a good thing you were watching him."

"That's for sure," Anna said. "I saw him moving, but I certainly didn't see the gun."

But Whit was less than enthused. "I just wish there had been a chance to take him alive. And where the hell did he come up with that gun?"

"Anybody could've put it in that drawer," Tony said. "With those damned phones in the jail cells, it's easy for an inmate to plan that kind of thing."

Norma gathered up her things. "Well, I'm going home. I'm a nervous wreck."

"And I need a drink," Tony said, "even if it isn't five yet."

As Tony and Norma left, Whit walked over to the counsel table and carefully picked up the automatic weapon with a pen.

"It's so small." Anna squinted at the gun as he dropped it in a paper bag.

"It can still kill."

"It'll make one helluva story. That's for sure. I wonder if I can still catch Norma? She deserves her picture in the paper."

"What are you going to take it with?"

Anna, who was already headed for the door, glanced back. "I've got a camera in the car. Smart ass."

Whit looked over at Donnie Hicks, who was searching for the spot where Johns's bullet had struck. "Reporters."

"She's a feisty one, but I suppose you already know that," the sheriff's deputy answered.

"Yeah," Whit said, not sure whether or not he liked the deputy's casual remark about Anna. "You find that bullet?"

"I don't see it anywhere, sir."

Whit slid the automatic from the bag and onto the counsel table. He carefully snapped open the magazine release catch and pulled out the clip. He took out one of the cartridges and examined it. "Don't think you'll find any bullet, Donnie. The clip's filled with blanks."

"You're kidding! How do you figure it?"

Whit slipped the weapon back in the bag. "Looks like someone was double-crossing him."

"But why bother bringing him a gun at all?"

Whit headed for the door. "Think about it, Donnie."

When Whit reached the prosecutor's office, he found Tony nursing a glass of Scotch and perusing a file. "I found out something interesting," Whit said.

Tony knitted his brow as he stared at a sheet of paper from the file. "You know that welfare fraud case we dismissed against Johns?" he asked, ignoring Whit's comment.

"Yeah. What about it?"

The prosecutor tapped the page. "Look who wrote a letter asking that it be dismissed."

He handed Whit the letter. It was signed by Norma Randi Wyse.

Whit's mind raced. "She didn't say a thing about knowing him."

"And she had the opportunity to put a gun in that drawer," Tony added.

"It was a setup; the gun was filled with blanks. He was supposed to die."

"I'll be damned," Tony said in a soft voice. "You know her address?"

Whit grabbed a telephone book and turned to the rear of it. "Here it is." He read the address. "Oh, my God! I just thought of something." He slammed the book closed. "Anna was going to take her picture. If she didn't catch Wyse before she left, she might've headed to her house."

"Maybe you should be headed there, too. I'll get some county and city boys to back you up."

But Whit was already out the door.

Anna found Norma's house with no problem and parked in the driveway next to her van. She scooped up her Nikon and walked to the rear of the house. Only the screen door was closed. She knocked on it. When there was no answer, she peered through the screen into the kitchen. She knocked again. Finally she opened the screen door and stuck her head inside.

"Norma?"

She heard a noise coming from somewhere inside. She crossed the kitchen and looked into the living room. Something was wrong. The pictures on the wall were tilted at odd angles and the cushions were pulled off the couch and sliced open. Books and knickknacks were piled on the floor around a bookcase. It looked as if someone had been searching for something and didn't care about what they did to the furnishings.

She was about to call Norma's name again when she noticed several suitcases at the bottom of the staircase leading to the second floor. Curious, she moved closer and saw an airplane ticket lying on top of a suitcase. She glanced up the stairs, then picked up the ticket. Norma was heading to the Bahamas this evening. Funny she hadn't mentioned anything about it.

"Anna!"

She jumped at the sound of Norma's voice, then quickly set the ticket down. She looked up and saw the tall woman standing at the top of the stairs. In her hand was a gun, and it was pointed at Anna.

Whit parked on the street outside the front of a two-story, wood-frame house. It was on a slight rise in the center of a yard filled with tall pines and elms. He double-checked the address, then stepped out of the car. He hurried along the sidewalk, but decided against knocking on the front door. He walked along the side of the house, then stopped as he spotted Anna's car in the driveway and Wyse's van next to it. "Gawdamn it."

He reached inside his suit coat and unsnapped the strap on the .357 and took it out as he moved to the back door. His gun had been locked in his glove compartment since the day he'd interviewed the clerk at the Dollar Mart, and he was damned glad he'd left it there. To his surprise, the back door was open. He leaned toward the screen; he could hear voices, but he couldn't make out what was being said. He slipped out of his shoes, and, with as much care and patience as he could muster, he slowly opened the screen door.

* * *

"What's going on?" Anna asked.

Norma lowered the gun. "Oh, God. You startled me. I heard something downstairs and grabbed the gun. Usually people knock before they walk into my house."

"I did knock, and I called out your name." Anna's gaze turned to the suitcases. "Are you taking a trip somewhere?"

Norma smiled as she descended the stairs. "I've got a few days' vacation coming, and I could sure use it after what happened today."

But Anna was confused. "You're not going because of what happened today. I mean, you must've already had the ticket."

Norma shrugged. "Well, I'd been planning it for a while, of course. But it couldn't be better timing as far as I'm concerned."

"I bet."

"So why did you come over?"

Something still wasn't right about this, but Anna couldn't quite put her finger on it. "Oh, I want to take your picture . . . for the newspaper."

"Why?"

"Because of what you did in the courtroom."

Norma stopped on the third step. "Oh, that was nothing special."

"I think people will—will see you as sort of a hero." The words were forced, and Anna was shaking—and at the same time trying not to appear nervous. She sensed something was wrong; she couldn't quite grasp it. "I mean you could've saved a life or two. Who knows."

"That's okay," Norma said coldly. "I don't want my picture in the paper. I hate to rush you, but I've got a lot to do before I leave."

"I understand." Anna took a step back and looked around.

"Why is this room all torn up like this, Norma?" The words rushed out of her mouth, and immediately she wished she'd just left.

"I was looking for something." She walked past Anna, picked up one of the sliced cushions, and returned it to the couch.

"I see. I better get going."

Norma took two quick steps and pointed the gun at Anna's head. "You're too fucking snoopy for your own good, Anna."

"Norma, what's wrong with you?"

"Don't give me that. You just figured it out, didn't you? Too bad you're so damn smart, Anna. Too bad."

"I don't know what you're talking about." But now it dawned on Anna. Norma must have something to do with the kidnapping of Marcia Winters. She was in on it.

"Bullshit."

"Norma, you're just tense. Relax. Put down the gun. Please. I'm not going to hurt you. I won't take your picture. I'll just leave."

"No you won't. You're not going anywhere. I'm going to give you an interview, Anna. I've got a soft spot for incarcerated men. That's how I met Dewey. Then with my connections on the job, I realized just how valuable children could be. You see, Marcia Winters fetched me a hundred grand. That's a lot of money for a welfare worker. I paid Dewey ten of it. 'Course I didn't tell him how much his sweet thing was keeping for herself."

"Norma, you're talking crazy. I don't understand. I'm leaving now." She took a couple of steps backward. "Go on your trip. You need some rest. You'll feel better when you get back."

"Stop right there." She clicked a cartridge into the chamber. "You're not going anywhere."

Anna froze.

Whit edged across the kitchen in his bare feet. He passed the range and the refrigerator, then eased toward the living room. He could hear the conversation plainly now.

"Lie down," Wyse ordered.

"What are you going to do?"

"Shoot you. What do you think?"

Whit peered around the corner and saw Wyse pressing a gun barrel to the back of Anna's head. If he jumped out now, Wyse might pull the trigger before he could stop her.

"They'll get you," Anna said. "Give up right now—before it gets any worse for you."

"It's going to get worse for you."

"You don't want blood on your rug, Norma; it's evidence. And how are you going to get rid of my body? Think about it."

Norma laughed. "I'm not worried. Norma Wyse is already dead. I'm not going to the Bahamas for a vacation. I'm getting a new identity. Some minor surgery. A new hairstyle. Credit cards. A passport. It's been a part of my plan from the beginning."

"So you double-crossed your boyfriend."

Good. Keep her talking, Whit thought.

"Exactly. But don't call Dewey Johns my boyfriend."

Wyse had turned her gun away from Anna's head. Whit reacted instantly. "Drop it, Norma. Now!"

A shot fired, and Anna's body jerked in reaction. But she felt no pain. She rolled over just in time to see Whit rush into the room and kick Norma's weapon away from her.

Norma dropped to the floor a few feet from her. She slumped into an odd position, half sitting, half lying on her side. One leg was tucked underneath her, and she held her arm. Blood was dripping down it and over her hand.

"Anna, are you all right?"

She gasped for breath. "I think so."

Whit read Norma her rights as he arrested her, then asked her what had happened to Marcia Winters.

She didn't respond.

"She told me she sold the girl," Anna said.

"Get me a doctor. I'm bleeding to death."

"You're going to live, Norma—and you're going to be charged with kidnapping and murder. You got that?"

Whit knew that he didn't have a prayer filing a murder charge against Wyse without any evidence that Marcia Winters was dead, and Wyse wouldn't have to prove the girl was alive. But there was no reason not to try. "And you know what that means. Life in prison."

"I didn't murder anyone. The girl's alive."

"Then you better tell us where she is."

"Find her yourself!" Wyse snapped.

"Those rich people who paid you all that money for that pretty little girl are just as guilty as you," Anna said. "Are you going to let them get away?"

Something in Wyse's expression changed, and Whit held a glimmer of hope that she was going to cooperate.

But then a police bullhorn suddenly distracted them. "Norma Wyse, come out of the house."

"They think she's holding us hostage," Anna said. "I'll go tell them."

"No. Christ, they might shoot you."

Whit helped Wyse to her feet and led her into the kitchen. "Open the door for me."

Anna did as he said. But as soon as he got into the doorway, Wyse started fighting and screaming. "I'm going to kill you all," she shouted.

As Whit struggled with her, he saw a blur of uniforms and guns. "Don't shoot," he yelled.

"That's Pynchon," someone shouted.

"Get an ambulance," Whit said as the officers converged on them. "She's bleeding pretty badly."

He turned, and amid the confusion found Anna and wrapped his arms around her. "It's okay. It's okay."

"God, I was so scared, Whit." She wept as he held her.

"So was I. I thought I was going to lose you. I was shaking so much I almost missed her."

Anna looked up at him, tears streaming down her cheeks. "You mean you weren't trying to wound her?"

"Are you kidding? You never try to wound anyone. That's how you miss. I aimed for the heart. She moved, or my hand did."

She squeezed him tight and pressed her cheek to his chest. "You did great, Whit. Just great."

EPILOGUE

"Do I HAVE TO watch this?" Whit asked.

"Sit down," Anna said.

"Yeah, Daddy. C'mon," Tressa said.

Grudgingly Whit settled into his chair and turned his attention to the television as the commercial ended.

"Our top story tonight is about the reunion of a mother and daughter," the well-groomed young anchorman of WWWA began. "You remember that last night we told you about the courtroom-shooting death of Dewey Johns, a suspect in the kidnapping of a three-year-old Milbrook girl. At that time, it appeared that the last link to the whereabouts of little Marcia Winters had just been lost. But how things can change in a day."

The screen flashed to a film clip of a little blond girl running to her sobbing mother who was on one knee with her arms open. Behind Mrs. Winters a woman placed her hands on Mrs. Winters's shoulders. Whit had been present in the courthouse foyer, so he'd already seen Sue Winters and her daughter reunited and knew that the hands belonged to Ardis Harmon. But now he listened to the voice of Myra Martin. "Most crimes do not have happy endings. They leave behind scars and pain and bitterness for the victims. But Marcia

Winters is back in her mother's arms after being kidnapped six days ago.''

The film cut to a courtroom, and the camera zoomed in on the faces of a man and woman in their late thirties who conferred with their attorney at the counsel table. ''The story is a sad one about the desperation of a childless couple on the brink of middle age. Without thinking about the pain they would inflict on others, George R. Lewis and his wife, Arlene B. Lewis, allegedly paid out a hundred thousand dollars to a Raven County Welfare worker to secure them a beautiful young daughter. The couple were arrested in their home outside of Pittsburgh in a raid at daybreak today, and thankfully Marcia was found unharmed inside the home.''

A picture of an all-too-familiar face flashed on the screen. ''The arrests came hours after Norma Randi Wyse, an employee of the child welfare division of the county human services department, was arrested in her Milbrook home by Whit Pynchon, an investigator for the Raven County Prosecutor's Office.''

''Yay!'' Anna and Tressa yelled. Then Myra Martin's face filled the screen, and they listened closely.

''Norma Wyse was shot in the arm during the arrest in a valiant effort by Mr. Pynchon to save Anna Tyree, the editor of the *Milbrook Daily Journal*, who was being held hostage in the Wyse residence. Ms. Tyree had entered the house with the intent to photograph Norma Wyse, who less than an hour earlier had alerted courtroom authorities that Dewey Johns had a gun. No one knew it at the time, but Johns and Wyse were partners in the kidnapping plot.''

The film cut from Martin's face to a news conference where both Whit and Anna stood in front of a nest of microphones. ''Look at you two!'' Tressa yelled in delight.

''What were you thinking when you entered that house

knowing that Anna Tyree was being held captive?" a reporter asked.

"Only that I loved her," Whit answered, "And that I didn't want her to die."

"That's sweet, Daddy. I can't believe you said that in front of all those people."

"I can't, either," Whit said.

"How do you feel, Anna?" Myra Martin asked.

Anna paused a moment. "I'm glad it's over. I'd like to say that Whit Pynchon has proven that all the reports criticizing his efforts in this investigation were simply wrong. He was on top of the case right from the beginning."

"My God, they didn't even cut it," Anna said under her breath.

"It's definitely been a day of miracles," Whit said.

"I'm surprised no one asked about your plans to get married," Tressa remarked.

Anna winked and touched a finger to her mouth. "Shh," she whispered. "That's still a secret."

ABOUT THE AUTHOR

Dave Pedneau was a reporter, columnist, and magistrate court judge. His novels include *A.P.B.*, *D.O.A.*, *B.O.L.O.*, *A.K.A.*, and *B. & E.*, all published by Ballantine.